I0663498

The Inconvenient Process of Falling
By Katie Neipris

Creators Publishing
Hermosa Beach, CA

The Inconvenient Process of Falling
Copyright © 2015 Creators Publishing

FIRST EDITION

Creators Publishing
737 3rd St
Hermosa Beach, California 90254
1-310-337-7003

ISBN 978-1-94244-822-8
CREATORS PUBLISHING

For Grandpa, who taught me all the important things.
I miss you every day.

~~~

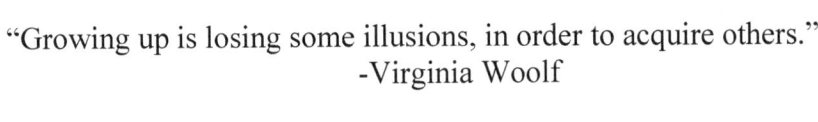

"Growing up is losing some illusions, in order to acquire others."
-Virginia Woolf

Table of Contents

Chapter 1

Friday night

Sally

The night unfurled more quickly here, wrapping the trees in a velvety dark blanket. The darkness was thicker, the shadows less defined; there was so much less contrast than there was at home, with only stark black and no hesitant grays. Sally could barely see Josh's car in front of them as their little caravan climbed higher and higher up the mountain. The trees lined the too-skinny road, impassive silent sentinels whose branches shook uneasily in the wind.

Sam drove slowly. Sally sensed that he was being more cautious than usual; he took the turns carefully, almost too slow and painstakingly deliberate. He fingered his St. Christopher necklace and she wished he would keep both hands on the wheel. Her arms clenched uncomfortably on her lap and she dug her fingernails into her skin. They'd been in the car for three and a half hours and she wanted to get out. She needed to get out.

Finally, Sam pulled onto a fairly horizontal, better-lit road and drove past the small town. Every storefront advertised family-friendly outdoorsy adventures, with bear motifs dominating the décor and titles of small establishments. Wood carvings of grizzlies seemed to be store owners' icon of choice, as many foolish-looking bears sat grinning on sparse lawns. Sally wondered if real bears were embarrassed by such representations and smiled to herself as she pictured irritated grizzlies shaking their heads in disapproval.

She tapped Alex on the shoulder, and he sat up, rubbing his eyes. "Welcome to Bear Lake, dude!" Sam said cheerfully, turning onto Honey Pot Lane, which looked a lot less like the Hundred Acre Wood than Sally would have hoped.

The four of them looked out at the cabins, which were surprisingly like regular houses. There was no escaping suburbia, thought Sally, smiling to herself. The trees were quite a bit thicker than in their neighborhood at home and the road was much steeper, but other than that it was a perfectly average little street. The cabins perched on precarious diagonals, looking like identical wooden owls.

"There it is," Erik said, a bit too late. Sam turned suddenly and bumbled up the steep driveway behind Josh's Jeep. The passengers of the second car leapt out eagerly, stretching their arms and shaking out the ache of sitting in the car too long. Sally looked up at the cabin. It was quite nice-looking from the outside – extremely big, obviously built for the three large generations of large Armstrongs that migrated there every Christmas. She breathed in the air and felt almost light-headed from its coolness. The scents of pine and something smoky lingered pleasantly on her tongue.

The door opened and their friends stood on the porch on top of the long flight of stairs. Sam too-eagerly (why did he always have to have so much energy? it really was quite irritating) leapt to the back of the car and began doling out duffels and sleeping bags. Alex tossed Erik his bag and the two of them made their way up the stairs, leaving her and Sam behind the car together, just them and their bags and his banjo and the silence. He clutched her blue duffel awkwardly in front of him, like he didn't want to hand it over.

Their eyes met briefly and Sally looked away, scowling. She felt the pressure of his stare and looked intently at the Dodgers garden gnome next to the porch. It was almost pathetic how badly he wanted her to look at him. But was she just imagining that? Maybe he didn't care if she looked at him. Maybe it was finally, totally over.

"Sally, please." She stuck her jaw out firmly. "We need to talk about this." He kept sweeping his sun-dyed hair out of his eyes and it was annoyingly adorable and she hated herself for thinking it was adorable. "Sally?"

She didn't say anything, still fixated on the gnome.

"It involves both of us. We need to talk."

The silence was so loud it hurt. It bounced around her brain, the utter lack of noise, until all she could focus on was that he was right there, closer than he'd been in months. There were no roommates or parents or phones, no welcome distractions or ready-made excuses to take her away from what she wanted to be taken away from, only the sound of her quickening heartbeat and his quiet breathing rising and falling together like some strange symphony.

She slackened her jaw stubbornly and felt something inside, the ghost of last summer struggling to crawl out from its cage of happy memories, the little ray of light trying to penetrate the darkness of the past year, and her knees went a bit weak as the ghost began to rise hopefully, enjoying the tingles and that warm feeling inside... but then she remembered, and all the reasons came flying back and everything went dark again.

"No." She said it louder than she meant to and felt the ghost of last summer slipping away back into its cage. She maintained her intent study of the gnome. It looked like a logo-plastered Santa Claus. "No, it doesn't."

He let out a small snort of disbelief. "Of course it does."

The anger rose in her like bile, bitter and forceful and needing to be spit out. "There is no 'both of us' anymore, okay? So just leave me alone." She grabbed her duffel bag out of his hands and stomped up the stairs, grateful for the forty or so steps that gave her the chance to collect herself. She slowed as she neared the door. Inside were her friends, the people that always knew how to have fun. They could always distract her when she needed it, even when her problems were right there. She smiled. This weekend could be just as fun as she hoped. She really needed it to be.

Grace

Grace dumped her sleeping bag on the ground and looked around. The cabin was pleasantly large, not cramped like their tent was last year. Bigger was better and less intimate. She could hear her friends' exclamations of surprise as they explored their new temporary home, their belongings strewn carelessly on the ground.

"Where are we sleeping?" Victoria asked Erik. He looked annoyed to have someone demanding answers from him – but maybe he was just annoyed because it was Victoria, Grace thought wryly.

"Beds are upstairs."

"Can we all sleep in the same room?" she prompted.

"Yeah, I guess." He shrugged and returned his attention to the bag of beef jerky that he'd almost demolished.

She stared at him, waiting for a more satisfactory response, then realized that she probably would not be getting one. "We'll all sleep in the same room."

"Are you sure we'll fit?" asked Josh, surveying the group.

"We'll all sleep in the same room so that we can talk," Victoria said, like it was the most obvious thing in the world (which it was, for the girls). "Everyone needs to bring their crap upstairs to the biggest room."

Grace bent down to pick up her duffel as Alex swooped in. "I'll get it." He saw her glance at his knee and his face darkened for the slightest second. "It's fine." He confidently hefted his, hers, and Victoria's, but she still caught the barely perceptible wince. "Race you!" He swung Victoria's Victoria's Secret bag and slapped Josh in the butt. Josh shoved him back and ran cackling up the stairs with a duffel under each arm as if they weighed nothing. Erik laughed, still occupied with his beef jerky.

Sally quietly let herself in, looking lost. Grace had forgotten that she was still outside. Who else was there? Sally's cheeks were a little red and she was biting her lip like she did when she was thinking hard, when she was in another place. Grace knew where her own dark place was and felt sad that Sally had one too. She watched her friend walk upstairs quickly, like she was avoiding something. The front door opened just as Sally's ponytail whipped out of sight. Oh. Of course. Sam walked in, looking frustrated. He brushed his floppy hair out of his eyes and headed upstairs. Grace wondered if they had fought. As far as she knew, Sally and Sam hadn't talked in months, but she didn't know why. She didn't really know what was going on with anyone during the school year. Of course, after – well, after Christmas she didn't hear much from any of them. This surprised her, though she supposed it shouldn't. She would have reacted the same way. But still.

A drop of sweat trickled down her back – not surprising, considering that it was August and the stuffy cabin hadn't been aired out in months. Did sweat show through red cotton? It was her least itchy Cornell shirt, and she didn't want to get nasty sweat stains. Should she open the windows? Erik's family hadn't been here since spring break, so the windows were probably closed, right? Did the others want her to do that? Should she ask them?

Victoria's voice echoed down the stairs and Grace could picture the entire scene: Victoria trying to arrange sleeping space without lifting a finger, Josh following orders to humor her, Alex trying to help and knocking things over, Erik snorting loudly at Alex's clumsy attempts to be domestic, Sam doing something unrelated and unrequested but hilarious, Sally hanging the clothes and trying to bring order to their happy chaos. Her friends were upstairs being themselves because they knew who they were. At least... they were doing what they would have done last summer. They all had functions and personalities and did what was expected of them. They were upstairs interacting and spending time together and having fun, and Grace... Grace was down here. Alone. Wondering if she should open the windows and not being able to decide.

She sighed. Maybe she shouldn't have come.

Alex

"Don't put all the bags on the floor – we're going to pull the trundle out," Victoria instructed, sprawling on the bed. Josh slid his hand under the mattress of the ancient trundle bed, searching for the bar. He pulled it out and wrinkled his nose at the dust that clung to his fingers.

"Gross, dude," Alex laughed as he slid the duffels to the other side of the room.

"And the pillows!" she commanded, sounding exasperated.

Erik stuck his hand in the bag of beef jerky and frowned when it came up empty. "I'm still hungry." He burped and Victoria looked disgusted.

"Yeah, me too." She scowled. "We should order the pizza now so that we'll be done in time to watch the meteor shower... Sally! You need to order the pizza!" she yelled as she strutted out of the room, leaving the boys to fend for themselves without instruction. Josh watched her leave and grinned when Alex caught his eye.

He looked down at the pillows. They took up quite a lot of room on the floor. "Should I put these on the beds?"

"I guess." Josh grunted as he pulled out the bed, hinges creaking. "Erik, come sit on this and make sure it won't fall."

"You calling me fat?" Erik grinned and plopped down on the trundle, which sank several inches.

Alex laughed. "Dude, how much protein powder did you have this morning?"

Erik smirked. "Enough." He laid down and pulled out his phone. "I never have any reception here. It's annoying as hell."

"*You're* annoying as hell – you keep scaring the girls away." Josh grinned and followed Victoria downstairs.

Alex's phone buzzed. "What's the score?" Erik asked, eyes still glued to his own phone.

"7-1, we're winning. Bottom of the seventh, Mariners are up, Alan just struck out the first batter in three pitches." Another message popped up as he was reading. "Second batter just 'grinded' out."

"Your mom sucks at texting."

Alex was about to retort when his phone vibrated for a third time. "Pop fly to first base. Another five-pitch inning."

Erik whistled. "I don't give a shit about that guy on the Red Sox, Alan has the Cy Young in the bag. Yankees are gonna win their third Series in a row because of him. I bet your dad's pretty stoked right now."

"Are you kidding? He gave up a run today. I bet my dad's ready to disown him."

"True." Erik laughed.

Sally popped her head in the door. "Hey, I'm ordering pizza. Is one large pepperoni and one large veggie okay?"

"Sounds good," said Alex cheerfully. Actually, it didn't sound good at all. His wires still felt uncomfortably tight from his orthodontist appointment the day before.

He probably couldn't chew very much, but everyone else wanted pizza. Maybe he could cut it up in tiny pieces.

"Well, I want Hawaiian. It's my favorite." Erik threw his pillow on the top bunk. "I'm sleeping there."

Sally looked a little annoyed, which Alex thought was unfair. "Victoria gave up her vegan thing so meat is okay for her now, Grace says she's good with whatever but she always eats vegetarian anyway, and everybody likes veggie. You and Josh are the only ones that like pineapple and Sam doesn't like Canadian bacon. Victoria wants this to be six dollars or less per person, so two larges makes the most fiscal sense. I've already thought this all through and we need to keep it simple, and you eat everything, so is pepperoni okay?" She glanced at Alex. "Can you even eat pizza? Your mouth always hurts the next day."

"Oh, no! Get pizza, everyone wants it."

Sally frowned. "Are you sure? I could order you pasta, if you can eat that."

"I don't want pasta," said Erik, eyes glued his phone.

"Erik wants pizza," said Alex.

He thought Sally looked annoyed and wondered why.

Sam

The doorbell rang. "I'll get it!" Sam yelled from the upstairs bathroom. He ran down the stairs, jumping the last four. Victoria laughed. He stepped through the pile of shoes cartoonishly, exaggerating his unwillingness to tread on someone's shoes.

He made it through the minefield of flip flops and opened the door. A pair of bored eyes stared back at him, wide and vacuous in a face riddled with acne. "Here's your pizzas." He shoved the boxes at Sam, looking like he was just as anxious to be rid of them as he was his unflattering maroon t-shirt.

Sam took them graciously and the kid stuck out his hand. "Uh, money?"

"Right! How much is it?"

"Uh, twenty bucks. Plus tip."

He turned around and yelled back into the house. "Hey, can you guys all bring money?" He turned back to face the pizza boy. "So, how do you like delivering pizza? Do you have any good stories?"

The kid stared at him blankly. "No."

"No you don't like being a pizza boy, or no you don't have any good stories?"

The brow line of acne dipped confusedly. "Um." He appeared to be thinking hard. "Well... neither?"

"Dude! Why don't you like delivering pizza? You get to meet so many people! You must have seen some awesome things!"

He looked surprised, like he wasn't used to someone asking his opinion. Perhaps he had never actually thought about whether he enjoyed his job, much less been asked by a customer about it.

Sam heard footsteps behind him and found himself staring at Sally. She held the bills out to him. "I'll pay for it." She was avoiding his gaze.

"Are you sure?" He wanted her to look at him.

"Yes." She stared determinedly at the bills, willing him to take them. He could almost feel the waves of desperation emanating from her, or was he imagining that? Was that feeling of repulsion real or was it all they had left, the result of months of silence and unreturned phone calls and not knowing why.

She stretched her hand out further towards him, her lovely hand that he'd held so many times. He missed her hand, how soft it was, and how small and warm it was, and if he reached out just a little bit further he would touch it…

The bills were already in his palm but he reached a little further than necessary and his fingers brushed her skin. She twitched uncomfortably, surprised. His hand lingered on hers for a moment before she pulled away. For a moment everything else was forgotten and the mouth-breathing pizza boy melted away and it was just them. They stood frozen, shocked by what had just transpired, electrified by the feeling of touching after not touching for so long. Then she turned around and walked back upstairs, leaving Sam with two pizza boxes and a broken heart.

Josh

"Guys! Come down!" Sally's voice reached them just before the smell of pizza did. The boys dropped their belongings and dashed downstairs. Josh breathed in the tomato-y aroma and smiled; he hadn't eaten in nearly three hours.

"Where do you want us to eat?" he asked Sally.

Victoria screeched behind him. "The meteor shower's about to start! Take them outside." She marched out to the balcony and claimed the biggest deck chair. "It's so freakin' gorgeous out here. Josh. Bring me veggie."

Alex tossed Josh a plate, grinning. "So whipped."

Josh swatted him in response. He opened a drawer, guessed correctly the second time, and took Victoria her slice of veggie. Erik and Alex hovered impatiently behind him, the presence of food erasing any semblance of etiquette.

She sprawled on the deck chair, watching him expectantly. "I wanted a bigger one!"

"That's what she said!"

"You know I go for the bigger ones." She winked and exaggerated taking a very slow bite of pizza. He had missed their banter – it was so hard to find a complementary dirty mind, and even harder to find a girl equal parts hot and smart.

"Satisfied?"

"Hardly. Go get me a water. And a napkin!" She grinned coquettishly and unfolded her legs, bare feet dangling off the edge of the chair.

He clapped Sam on the back. "I'm so whipped. These girls, man, these girls!"

Sam grinned half-heartedly, which was weird for him. Josh wondered if it was hard having Sally around.

"I got the waters!" Sally passed him, arms laden with seven water bottles that dragged the V of her shirt down just a bit.

"Do you need help with those?"

"Nope!" she grinned, all white teeth and dimples. He enjoyed flirting with her too, but it was much different than with Victoria. Victoria went all out, but Sally was a bit too innocent. Besides, he wasn't going to try anything with Sam around.

He opened the box of pepperoni and helped himself to a few slices. "Do you want this one?" he asked Grace.

"Uh, no, I'm having veggie." She stared down into the pizza and he knew she was calculating calories again.

He held the box open for a second longer. Closing it seemed like an admission, somehow. Of what? Defeat? Guilt? It had been, what, nine months? He couldn't imagine how she felt now, but he couldn't help feeling like he should know.

He hated seeing her sad. He hated feeling like it was his fault, even though he knew it wasn't.

Sally passed him again, her arms full of napkins, pepper, and parmesan packets. "Did everyone get pizza?" she called.

Josh smiled at her. "You can sit down, you know."

"I just want to make sure everybody got their food and everything they need." She smiled and handed him a napkin. She reminded him of his mom quite a bit. He didn't want to read too much into that.

He tossed Sam a beer and they clinked cans, the moonlight glinting off the Coors mountains. He perched on the edge of Victoria's chair and she immediately draped her legs over him. "It's so pretty tonight!"

"I know, right?" He took a bite and grinned. "Well done, guys."

Alex lifted his slice in a mock toast. "To adulthood!"

Sally followed suit. "May the next few years be the best of our lives." She paused and Josh watched her carefully consider her words. "Hopefully this decade … turns out how we pictured it." Her eyes automatically darted towards Grace.

"Boo, you downer." Victoria tossed her napkin at Sally and he was relieved to see her giggle. "Let's have fun tonight."

She leaned back against him and he felt the tension leave her back. He'd been looking forward to this for weeks: Victoria snuggled against him, an abundant supply of pizza and alcohol, the lake glittering below them. The trees seemed like they went on forever, an infinite line of linebackers guarding the lake, tucking them into a giant pocket that protected them from the outside world. He glanced around the deck, watching his friends settle into their own quiet contemplation.

Everything here was so different from New York. He slumped contentedly against the deck chair and just breathed, letting the crisp chill of the air waft across his face. It just felt so … intimate, like the people you were with could actually hear what you were saying, like you didn't have to make yourself heard. It was a little intimidating too, like everything counted, like you couldn't depend on the presence of something louder or more interesting to distract you from your faults. Here you focused on your friends and they focused on you because really, what else was there to do?

Victoria leaned her head against his shoulder and draped her skinny leg over him. He poked the goose bumps rising on her thigh. "Aren't you freezing?"

"You're keeping me warm!" She dangled her other leg on top of him. Grace turned away and stared out at the lake.

He repositioned her legs so that she was sitting next to him instead of on him. She feigned a pout and leaned back against him. "Excited for the meteor shower?"

"Yeah, should be pretty awesome. I miss seeing stars."

"But you live in New York! You get to see awesome things all the time. I'm still mad you saw my husband without me."

"And I will always lord it over you that I met Jimmy Fallon and you didn't." She punched his shoulder and he laughed. "But I miss nature, too. I miss being home sometimes."

She snorted. "Cottonwood's the most boring town in the entire world. I mean, the Bay Area's great, but it's got nothing on New York."

"It's just … different," he said languidly. Being out here was such a nice change from the hustle and bustle of the city. Now that he thought about it, this was the first time in a while that he could just... sit. Sit and enjoy being able to breathe and being outside with the people he was with, friends who knew him and didn't expect him to be someone else.

Sally

She finished her sliver of pizza and leaned back, closing her eyes. Maybe it was just the exhaustion of packing and driving and taking care of people, but she was almost too tired to think. It felt wonderful. She wondered if normal people were like this. Did normal people – people whose lives weren't burdened by the stress and need for perfection and the other little demons that darted in her brain –think this much? Did they ever appreciate how wonderful it felt not to think, how rare the opportunity was to get out of your own head for a minute or two? She already felt almost relaxed here – probably more than she had in months, she realized.

Which was odd, really, because Sam was here and Grace was sad and the boys were boys and Josh was pure frat now and Victoria was... Victoria. After months of separation her friends still catalyzed her thoughts and challenged her opinions and wrangled with her emotions, and she was relieved to see that they still slid into the familiar patterns, the comfortable ruts of long-established personalities.

It was nice but it also worried her. Could there be room for growth? How could you change around the people that knew you best, who knew you backwards and forwards and knew you so well that they defined themselves by you and you by them? How could you possibly evolve, like really evolve and become a whole person all on your own, when your own makeup was inextricably intertwined with someone else's perception of themselves?

She knew that they looked at her and still saw the girl with two braids and Mary Janes. She still saw the ghosts of their younger selves when she looked at them, and their new officially-collegiate appearances just made the contrast that much more jarring.

Her friends were a part of her. She was a part of them. It was just The Way It Was. These people saw her through the strange and dangerous process of becoming a person. They'd welcomed her into their circle in fourth grade and she'd steadily become the center of it, the maternal, grounded center that kept them in orbit as gravity and life tried to pull them away from each other. She kept them together. She planned movie nights and surprise birthday parties and tried to keep everything the same as long as she could because she knew childhood was slipping away – had slipped away – and she couldn't bear to see it go. She hated to think they were all basically grown-up already. She had grown up so much this year, in spite of everything. She'd been determined to remain Sally Chandler and she stripped away the part of herself that she thought defined that. And if her friends were to learn of this … what would they think? Would they feel betrayed that she had allowed herself to spiral out of control when she had elected herself the dependable center? She'd promised continuity and she'd provided chaos.

She had changed. Her empty plate shook slightly in her hands and she set it on the table, pulling her knees to her chest. This year… God, this past school year had been a nightmare. When she lit out for the territory she'd never imagined going through with it, with any of it. She couldn't believe she had. Her values, her beliefs, her opinion of herself, all compromised. Never in her most desperate, worst-case scenarios had she even thought she'd experience… all that she'd experienced.

How had she faced her parents? How had she faced her friends? Could she tell them, ever? Would she have to carry this around with her for the rest of her life? No one knew. No one could know, ever.

She couldn't possibly tell them. Or Sam. Especially Sam. The looks on the others' faces would be devastating enough, but his... She'd betrayed them, really. She'd betrayed their idea of her, the confidence that they had in her to be the stable member of the group. They weren't supposed to worry about her. She was supposed to worry about them. She'd upset this balance of maternal power. Her moral compass was gone. Her authority, her position within the group as the central, stable figure, gone.

Not that they knew this, of course – or did they? Were they able to sense the changes, the hardened edges that she was sure were glaringly obvious? She noticed it every time she looked in the mirror. She hated it. She couldn't look her mirrored self in the eye. She stopped pretending she had any moral superiority – she knew Victoria hated it when she acted like she did – because she'd deprived herself of it all on her own.

Josh's laugh dragged her out of her reverie and she reentered her own head. She could be here but she wasn't really here, was she? Part of her was gone. Parts of her were gone forever.

But the parts that still mattered were there, she chided herself, trying to channel the same mantra that got her through the past year. Her friends would preserve the parts that mattered. Being reunited with them was her best shot at remembering her old self. She just had to give them the chance, open up, stop shielding herself like she had been all year, but it was so hard. Being reunited with them also reminded her how well they knew her and it was terrifying, like her secrets and sins were spelled out in neon letters on her forehead for all the world to see.

She couldn't even explain it to herself. How could she explain it to her friends, the people who loved her most, when she knew that telling them would make them love her significantly less? How could she justify, in the simplest terms, her transgressions, her crime, her shame? They couldn't possibly understand. She surely didn't. They had a vision of her and they expected her to maintain it and she was failing them miserably.

Josh

Erik, of course, was wearing his USC baseball t-shirt. Typical.

"That could have been you, you know." His dad's voice in his head was unwelcome and he willed it go away.

This was his weekend, his friends' weekend. He didn't know when they'd get this chance again. He needed it to last as long as it could.

He'd missed them so, so much this year – not that he ever articulated it. His new friends were awesome, but it wasn't the same. They didn't inspire the same feelings in him that this group could. No matter where they were, he could always count on them to make him laugh and drag him out of his own mind. As they'd grown, their little adventures expanded geographically, sure, but there was something else, too, some invisible bonus to their gradually increasing freedoms. He just felt like... like he could try anything he felt like and they'd still cheer him on, or climb as high as he dared, and they'd be there to catch him. They offered the sanctuary he wished he could feel at his own house. Childhood friendships held something for him that his frat brothers just couldn't understand. With these friends he enjoyed the sweetness of reckless invincibility because no matter how hard he fell or how badly he screwed up they'd welcome him back.

They always made him feel like he was really home.

Grace

She brushed the needles off the seat and sat down in the itchy chair, watching two squirrels scamper up the tree in front of her. Nature was so ... playful here. So different. A lake and trees and jolly little woodland creatures.

Of course there was nature at Cornell, waterfalls and cliffs, but they made her feel scared, constant reminders of heights and how easy it was to fall. Falling. One letter away from failing. So precarious and so easy and how simple to just capitulate, to admit that you couldn't handle what was going on inside your own head and just... fall. Fail. Surrender. But of course you couldn't – of course you had to keep fighting to stay up, to stay highest, to stay the best and satisfy the voice in your head, because the only way to keep it quiet was to keep climbing higher. Waterfalls were pretty but they weren't very soothing; they were just huge forces of nature that pushed, pushed, kept pushing until you went over the edge. You couldn't resist a waterfall no matter how hard you fought against the current. You would never beat the current of a waterfall and there were rocks at the bottom.

But a lake... a lake was different. You could swim out to the middle, the very middle of a lake like this, and you could look down and never see the bottom, and not have to feel anything. That was a very comforting thought: to not have to react. To not have to be on your game. Like now, in the pale glow of the moonlit balcony, with people who knew you so well that you didn't have to say anything you didn't feel like it. To be lost in your head, knowing that the people around you would keep you anchored to the present, that they wouldn't let you sink too far before pulling you out.

Or would they? When you were five thousand miles apart and you were falling the other person couldn't throw you a rope and save you. And, as it turned out, two hundred-twenty-eight might as well be five thousand too. But here... here they were only feet apart and they would keep her from drowning. They would keep her head above the water. At least, she hoped they would. They would have last summer. She deserved them then.

But now? What do you do when you're no longer worthy of your life preserver? When you're not good enough for the thing, for the person, for the people who kept your head above water, how do you keep swimming? They were here, they were all here. They cared about her. She'd ignored their calls, texts, emails, Facebook messages, Skype dates... and then the stream of contact trickled down into the occasional "what's up" text or Josh's drunk phone calls, and as soon as the multitude of attempts stopped she wanted them to start again, intrusive as they were.

Maybe she deserved it, she thought bitterly. She'd moved to New York. She traded her friends for icy mornings and waterfalls that threatened to drown her. What was it that made her so willing to forget everything? She looked down at her red shirt, at the proud C, the emblem that her family proudly vaunted because it was the family school, the family shirt, and wearing it meant that maybe at last they would acknowledge her part in it, that she could finally be good enough for them. Or was this her family? Because family meant the people that loved you no matter what, that were there for you, that kept you going with their unconditional love, no matter how screwed up you were. In that case, this was her family. Right? But they hadn't really been there the past few months – but that was her fault, all her fault, so how could she blame them?

She loved her friends. She loved them so much.

But what were they talking about now? Sally was moving away from her so that she couldn't hear what she was saying. Oh. Of course. She wanted to talk to Victoria. Her real best friend now, probably. Stanford and Berkeley were close enough for them to hang out, right? They probably knew each other's new friends and had sunny California adventures together. Victoria pulled her phone out of her pocket and showed it to the group. Why? To see what time it was? Oh. They were doing something. Something without her. Sally and Victoria got up and went inside. Grace was the only girl now and the seat next to her felt cold and empty without Sally and now she was sitting by herself, not knowing what to do, feeling awkward and cut off, like the one left without a musical chair. Just like she did for all those months. Was this her fault too? Why were the boys whispering? Oh God. Even the boys ignored her now. Even Sam. She was alone, all alone on the edge by herself, and it was her fault because she was such a bad friend.

"The meteor shower's starting!" Josh yelled inside to the girls, whatever they were doing. Grace had totally forgotten about it. She looked out over the lake, into the empty vast blackness that started where the water ended and went on forever.

"There it is!" yelled Sam. A ball of light darted across the sky, dashing through the darkness like it was being chased.

"Come on, you guys!" Josh yelled to the girls inside. "There's another one!" yelled Alex. Another ball, a bigger one this time, skipped away farther into the sky. Erik whooped.

Grace stared up at the tiny pinpricks of light. Maybe they were just as scared and directionless as her, and they were caught in the celestial currents that dragged them against their will. Maybe she should feel sorry for them because they had no control over their own destiny, and they were going to break into little pieces, smaller and smaller, until they broke through the earth's atmosphere and disintegrated into little chunks that crashed to the ground or on someone's roof or car or head or something.

She felt Sally and Victoria coming through the door behind her, and then the group started singing. For a moment she felt so terribly sad because they were singing without her, then she felt pathetic for feeling left out, then guilty because she probably deserved it. But these thoughts lasted half a second because she realized that Sally and Victoria were carrying a cake, a lovely pink cake with nineteen candles, and that they were all singing "Happy Birthday", and her friends, her family, were doing this because they loved her.

It was so – *nice*. Much nicer than she deserved. And then she started crying, which surprised her, so she cried harder, because they had gone to all this trouble for her. She was crying at the ridiculousness of crying, at sitting there blubbering pathetically when a normal person would smile in self-acknowledgement that this was their moment to be loved and appreciated. She was crying because she had totally forgotten about her birthday, and they had remembered. Because now she was nineteen, and that was light-years away from eighteen, when you were still a kid, really. But nineteen… nineteen could be new. Nineteen could be a fresh start. Nineteen was a year to make your dreams come true, to find some happiness that maybe you didn't deserve before. This year she would find a reason to deserve happiness. This year she wouldn't feel guilty for nice things. This year she would be a whole person. This year she would be happy. And she leaned forward, and a tear dripped onto the cake, and she blew out the candles and wished to deserve the happiness that she felt.

Sam

As they sat quietly on the balcony, Sam glanced over at Sally. She looked so pretty tonight. Unintentionally, of course – she always looked pretty. Pink shirt, denim shorts that she wore on the hottest days, her favorite white sandals, a little silver pin in her blond hair.

Had she known that he would be there? He wanted to believe that she did. She had ignored him for so long that he doubted she would feel fine about spending the weekend with him, especially in such close quarters.

He just needed a minute to tell her about the job.

He hoped it would fix everything – but how do you fix something if you don't know why it's broken? Hopefully this would bring them back to normal and patch up the months of emptiness. He needed to tell her soon, he realized. She needed to know. Their lives could change. They could be together.

He watched her carry the cake through the doorway, dimples illuminated. She stepped carefully through the door onto the deck. All smiles. She probably made it herself.

She started singing, and everyone followed. He sang loudly in his silly way, conducting them with a pine needle.

He looked at Grace. She stared at the cake like she couldn't believe it was there. Tears rolled down her cheeks and he hoped it was because she was happy. Before December, he'd only seen her cry twice in fifteen years (third grade, when she broke her arm on the monkey bars, and seventh grade, when Erik stepped on her science project and ruined her volcano), and now it seemed like she was always crying.

Grace blew out the candles, and he let out an enthusiastic "WOOOO!" The group laughed.

"Grace gets the first piece!" He yelled.

"Well, of course," said Victoria. "And I get the second." Sally laughed and sliced neatly into the cake.

"Grace, do you want the piece with your name on it?"

"No, give her a piece with a flower!" demanded Victoria.

"She doesn't like that much frosting!" said Sally. "Where did I put the forks?" She smiled her lovely smile and leaned down toward them. The V of her shirt dipped down a little bit and Sam saw Josh stare before tactfully looking at something else. Oh.

Sally hugged Grace. "Happy birthday, love! And look! It's God's birthday present to you!"

Grace hung on to her tightly and whispered something to her that Sam couldn't hear. Sally hugged her for a long time and when she stood up he saw tears glistening. She looked up at the sky like she was watching the meteor shower, but she wiped her eye again and he knew her too well to believe that. She dabbed her eye with her sleeve, took a deep breath, and turned back to the cake, all smiles again. "Who wants the flower piece?"

"I want a big one," said Erik.

"Mine first!" Victoria snagged the large piece that Erik was about to grab and snuggled back up to Josh.

Sam grabbed a piece that Sally had already cut and sat next to Erik, who was quickly demolishing his cake. He took a bite. The sweetness lingered in his mouth.

Erik

He tore into his cake. He'd only gotten to eat four pieces of pizza so he was still hungry.

He glanced down at his leg. The bruise bloomed like an ugly purple flower, wrapping itself around his thigh and ducking into his knee pit. Most of his teammates were spending their last week of summer in Cabo, but his dad made him stay home and practice. "I didn't install this batting cage for you to go on vacation," he said dangerously, smiling as he cranked the pitching machine to ninety miles per hour without bothering to check for accuracy.

He moved his leg into the light and realized that he could count still the seams of the ball.

Cabo would be so dope right now, he thought, glaring out at the stupid lake. It was bad enough coming here every Christmas to hear his dad show off to his family. "Erik here hit three-forty last season – not as good as his old man, though!" he'd proclaim to the living room of kiss-ass relatives, clamping down on Erik's shoulder just a little too tight. "What did I hit my freshman year at USC, Erik?"

"Four-fifty, Dad," he'd say through clenched teeth. His stepmom's collagen-enhanced mouth would open in a fake O of sycophantic surprise. The kiss-ass relatives would beam in admiration at their champion uncle/ brother/ cousin / source of free Dodgers tickets.

"Damn straight – four-fifty. A magnificent batting average. I probably would have beaten every offensive record at SC if the Dodgers let me stay for my senior year."

His uncle Pete would pat him on the shoulder, saying something stupid and unhelpful like "You got big footsteps to follow in, son!" Duh. He knew that. Everybody knew that. Everybody who'd ever visited freaking Little Cottonwood, where signs for the Erik Armstrong II Youth Sports Programs covered every fence, knew that. Everybody who stepped foot on USC's campus and worked out in the Erik Armstrong II Sports Complex knew that. Everybody who'd ever watched a Dodgers game since 1980 knew that.

At least this group of friends didn't constantly remind him of it. They never asked for tickets or signed balls or anything. No one here cared that his dad was famous.

It was kind of nice.

Grace

She rested her arms on the balcony and leaned over. It was too dark to see the ground and she wondered if anything was scampering around down there. Bonafide forest dwellers could be scurrying on their merry way right under her feet and she'd have no idea.

They didn't have that back home. Here there were more than just squirrels and seagulls.

They had stars here. She looked up to the sky and smiled, feeling the rush of cool velvety air kiss her face. She definitely hadn't expected a birthday party. Her friends loved her. She was surprised at how happy this made her.

It was such a strange feeling, to be loved, and it made her sad that it was so unfamiliar to her. Usually she felt like… like she was tiny and powerless under the weight of the world. But tonight… tonight she felt like someone that mattered.

She couldn't believe that someone would go to such an effort to do something nice for her. They made a cake and everything. That must have taken some planning. She felt a rush of affection for Sally. Even though she found it terribly embarrassing to be the center of attention, it was nice at the same time. How odd.

There it was – the sound of scurrying paws fluttered under her and she listened to the nocturnal cast take the stage. They just accepted the positions given to them and did what they were supposed to do, and she felt honored to play the audience. There was something tragic and beautiful about a concert that was audible only to those who were listening.

Josh

He helped Sally carry the empty plates to the kitchen and grinned as he watched her unconsciously sweep crumbs off the counter. Always playing mom.

"What is it?"

"What's what?"

"Why are you smilin' like that?" He loved when her accent came out.

"I'm just happy to be back with the gang, Miss Sally."

She swatted him with the roll of paper towels. "I'll let you take the boxes outside, mister. Make sure you close the trash cans so we don't get raccoons."

He saluted her, grinning. "Yes, ma'am." She swung it again, giggling as he jumped away, holding the pizza boxes as a shield.

"I'm awful sorry, Miss Sally, but you'll have to run like the dickens to catch me!"

"Georgians don't say 'run like the dickens,' you goober!" She chased him around the kitchen, swinging the paper towels as he swatted them away, laughing.

"Um, do you want..." Josh halted at the sound of Sam's voice. Sam stood in the doorway, bag of trash in hand. He looked curiously between them. Sally lowered the paper towels.

He realized that he was holding still holding the pizza boxes like a shield. Sally turned bright red and looked at the clock. "Wow, it's eleven-thirty already? We should go to bed soonish if we're leaving early tomorrow." She darted out of the kitchen, avoiding looking either of them in the eye. She was still holding the paper towels.

Sam handed him the plastic bag. He tried to ignore the accusation in his eyes. "Uh, thanks, dude." He added the bag to his trash load and made his exit as smoothly as he could.

Well, that was weird, he thought as he climbed down the mountain of porch steps. He and Sally acted like that all the time, right? And Sam was fine with it, right?

But that was when Sam and Sally were Sam-and-Sally, he told himself as he opened the giant trash can lid and threw in the pizza and cake plates. They weren't anymore. Sam couldn't be mad at him. He'd done nothing wrong.

Sally

Sleeping arrangements were an awkward business, particularly when you couldn't bear to be in close proximity with a certain someone. She could make this work.

Did other people overanalyze these things as much as she did? Sometimes she wondered if she was the only one who could see and sense the connections between people. You could tell so much about people's relationships by only a few moments of interaction, she thought, watching the sibling ease of Josh and Grace. Their gestures, their body language, the way they seemed to anticipate what the other one was going to say before they said it. There was so much to learn by just paying attention. Her friends sometimes paid too much attention.

She kept feeling Victoria's inquisitive gaze darting between her and Sam. The link between them used to be warm and strong. She could feel his presence whenever he entered the room, and she felt slightly anxious until he was restored in his place at her side, with a hand draped around her shoulders or her waist. Now the force between them felt repellant rather than attractive, but due to some horrible law of relationship physics, this only increased the magnitude of her awareness of him. He was everywhere all the time and it was driving her crazy. She dragged her sleeping bag as far away from his as possible.

She hated this feeling, like he had power over her. It was ridiculous. *She* broke up with *him*.

He slipped off his shirt and she tried not to admire the upside-down triangle of his tan back. He'd gotten a little taller since she last saw him, and had obviously spent most of that time at the beach. The hours spent surfing showed in his streaked hair and the little freckles speckling his slightly broader, inconveniently attractive shoulders. He lifted his hand to brush the hair out of his eyes and she watched the lovely chain reaction of golden back muscles.

She didn't deserve to think these things any more. She had surrendered her possession of the tan back and the swimmer shoulders and the light freckles on his nose when she cut herself off from their weirdly in-sync bond.

They just clicked. They had... something. And they would never get it back. She was sure of that.

22

Sam

He crawled into his sleeping bag, trying to ignore the fact that Sally had dragged hers to the other side of the room. How had it come to this?

He turned away from the others and tried to sleep. Erik climbed noisily over him and the bed springs groaned loudly. A large, sweaty foot dangled over his face.

He should be by Sally.

Last year she'd insisted that they tell ghost stories as they were falling asleep, and he remembered loving the feeling of sitting in a circle in the dark, laughing hysterically and pretending to be scared. It looked like that wouldn't be happening tonight. They all seemed so tired. He missed their old energy.

He closed his eyes and thought of better times.

On the first day of fourth grade, Sam sat with his friends in the cafeteria. Erik and Alex wolfed down their sandwiches and ran to claim the kickball field. He opened his Cheetos. Josh handed Grace the PB&J that his mom had made for her. He was about to eat his first Cheeto when the prettiest girl he had ever seen walked up to them.

"'Scuse me?" her voice lilted in a high, unfamiliar accent that reminded him of bells. The three of them looked up and took in this tiny new stranger. She wore a yellow dress that was much more formal than their normal school clothes and her hair was tied in a giant pink ribbon. She smiled at them.

"Mind if I sit with you?" She stood straight and politely with her shiny new lunch pail clasped in front of her, white Mary Janes pointing forward.

"Yeah!" Josh blurted. "Um, I mean, we don't mind!" Grace giggled and Josh elbowed her. He turned back to Sally. "Where are you from?"

She swung a leg neatly over the bench and sat next to Grace. "I'm from Georgia. How 'bout yourself?"

"I'm from here." Josh said brightly.

"So are we," said Grace, fascinated by this nice, pretty stranger. "I'm Grace."

The new girl stuck her hand out. "Pleased to meet you Grace, I'm Sally Chandler. I just moved into my new house on Catalina Drive, just up that hill." She pointed.

Grace's mouth widened with delight. "I live on Catalina Drive too! In the blue house."

Sally's eyes lit up. "Isn't that lovely? I'm so pleased to have already met a kindly neighbor." He loved how she talked, like her words mattered.

"I'm Josh," Josh said, grinning. "I'm at Grace's house all the time. Grace is my best friend. Do you have a dog?"

"Why yes I do! Y'all are welcome to come and play with him. His name's Tiger. He's real friendly. And what's your name?" she asked, turning to Sam.

"Sam." He wanted to say something cool but he couldn't think of anything.

"Are you Samuel or just Sam?"

"Samuel's my real name, but my mom only says it when I'm in trouble."

"Are you in trouble a lot?" she raised her eyebrows.

"No." He felt like he should add "ma'am." "But when I am, they call me Samuel."

"Isn't that funny? I wonder why they'd name you something just to call you something else," said Sally. She smiled at him and opened her lunch box. "My mama baked some cookies to share with my new friends. Would you like some? They're chocolate chip."

Sam gratefully accepted the cookie and as she handed it to him her tiny, warm hand brushed his. She smiled and, at age ten, Sam knew that he had begun the long and inconvenient process of falling in love.

Josh

He yawned and felt the weight of the day. Car trips were fun, but driving for hours was a little wearing. He settled into his sleeping bag and grinned as Victoria slid hers next to his. "Is that really what you sleep in?"

"What, this old thing?" she gestured to her pink t-shirt, which came nowhere near the waistband of her tiny yoga shorts and showed off several inches of flat, tanned stomach. "I always feel obligated to buy my Secrets." Her eyes scanned his bare chest and landed with amusement on his Lakers pajama pants. "Wow, you *would*."

24

He laughed and laid back drowsily, listening to the comforting sounds of electric toothbrushes buzzing in the other room as his friends got ready for bed. Grace filed out of the bathroom, her oversized Cornell sweatshirt and lumpy sweatpants looking comical next to bare Victoria. She'd gained a little weight since he last saw her, not that there was anything wrong with that. It was perfectly natural, and acceptable, considering what she had been through. He yawned again. Poor Grace. She swam across oceans for people who wouldn't cross puddles for her. He just wanted her to be happy.

Platonic friends of the opposite sex were such a rare and extraordinary gift, he thought, closing his eyes. Few people realized it, and even fewer had them. He felt extremely lucky to have one close female friend, let alone three.

He'd known Grace since before he could remember. Their families were linked before they were even born - their dads played baseball together for Little Cottonwood when they were in high school, though he couldn't imagine them being friends. They were cordial on the rare occasions when they were in the same room, but that was once in a blue moon, one filled with annoying antiquated references to a time that his dad clearly mourned. His dad always brought up their high school days whenever Mr. Hastings came to pick up Grace, and Josh loathed the awkwardness of having a father who had hit his prime thirty years ago. Mr. Hastings had clearly moved on.

Her family moved in next door when he and Grace were babies, and stayed there until they were six. By then, a sibling bond had formed between them, and his mom happily shuttled them to each other's houses when the Hastings moved to their finally-renovated house on the slightly nicer side of town. He'd heard Mrs. Hastings tell the story of the seemingly cursed housing project more times than he could count. He could imitate her "Can you *believe* it? Five and a half *years!*" perfectly, always in the same pitch and exasperated tone of someone who was accustomed to having everything her way. No amount of money could prevent or predict the construction problems that would keep the Hastings out of their house: the permit issues (none of the other houses on the street had basements), the defeated contractors who quit when they were unable to meet the needs of their demanding client, the burst pipe that filled the would-be wine cellar with stagnant water that attracted mosquitoes. The construction obstacles to Mrs. Hastings' happiness enabled his most important friendship to come to fruition, and he couldn't imagine life without it.

They grew up in each other's shadows, throwing water balloons, roasting marshmallows on the beach, taking her dog to the park. She taught him to roller-skate; he taught her to climb the trees that lined the Hastings' yard. She lost her first tooth in his driveway and cried until he found it. On hot summer days, his mom helped them concoct Popsicle recipes, and they ate their creations sprawled out on the grass. After the Hastings moved, his mom made sure that he and Grace still got to spend as much time together as possible. Eventually he was old enough to ride his bike to her house by himself, which took twelve and a half minutes if he didn't have to stop for too many cars.

They became more than playmates as they began to understand the full scope of their parents' dramas and convoluted interiorities. They confided in each other, each anticipating an eventual divorce. If one house was simply too tense to handle, the other was always welcome over for dinner. Since both of their houses were usually tense, they often ended up at the park down the street from Grace's, not talking much as they lingered on the swings waiting out whichever fight was worst. The occasional dinners at Sally's were always great, and they obviously loved hanging out in their group of friends, but their situation was unique. None of the others could really understand what it was like living in such a tense home, always one word away from an argument. Sally, with her picture-perfect family, certainly didn't have to worry about that.

Only Grace understood the full extent of his complicated family dynamic, and he was the only one that gained access into the complexities of her equally troubled home.

He knew that it was devastatingly hard to be the plain daughter of a beautiful, successful woman, and he watched this eat away at Grace. He assured her that she was not "fat," "useless," or "stupid," and he propped up her self-esteem when her mom seemed determined to destroy it. She assured him that he was not a "waste of time," and understood his decision to stop playing baseball, even though she'd warned him that he would miss it more than he thought. She was the only person in the world that knew how exhausting it was for him to perform the endless balancing act of defiance and obedience, challenging his dad, worshiping his mom. Grace was the person who held him as he cried the day he quit the high school team.

They sat on the swings for hours, listlessly rocking back and forth, wondering aloud what would become of them when one of their parents finally cracked. They stayed at the park or the beach as long as they possibly could, sometimes dragging either of their younger siblings along, just to keep them out of the danger zone. It was easier once they were both able to drive and could rescue each other at a moment's notice. Very few people had someone like that, and he was so thankful for Grace and all the nights that they spent sitting in his pickup truck in the beach parking lot, watching the waves slap the shore. They could measure their existence in waves. Ripples of fear. Swells of accomplishments. Rogue waves of devastation. But everything evened out eventually, didn't it – every wave subsided, lapsed back into the ocean, returning, giving them time to put themselves back together again. He was her moon. He balanced out her tides.

Some people had a hard time believing that their strong relationship was purely platonic. He supposed that it was hard to see two not-related almost-siblings and not imagine them together, but he knew it would never happen. Grace was his sister, pure and simple, and nothing could change that. Just like nothing would ever happen between him and Victoria. They provided emotional outlets for him that his male friends could not, and he appreciated them dearly. He worried about them. He knew what college guys were like. He was one. The worst breed, apparently, as he'd learned from the expectations laid out by his frat brothers. He prided himself on being slightly less sex-driven than the other guys, but sometimes had to pretend in order to save face. He liked them for the most part – sure, it was nice to feel a part of the brotherhood – but he loathed that each of his interactions with a female was assumed to have an ulterior motive. Sometimes he found himself forcing to remember that the other guys probably didn't have a Grace.

Life without Grace… that was something he did not want to imagine. He opened his eyes a tiny fraction and watched her back rising gently. He wanted her to be okay.

Sally

She waited to use the bathroom until everyone else was done and settled into their sleeping bags. She brushed her teeth and avoided looking at herself in the mirror. The sounds of her friends died down and by the time she was done getting ready for bed, most of them were asleep or about to be.

She turned the lights off and fumbled her way into her sleeping bag, trying to be as quiet as possible. At least two of the boys were already snoring – sounded like Alex and Josh.

It was always so hard to fall asleep in a new place, she thought, struggling to find a comfortable position. Her first night in her dorm was one of the weirdest and most sleepless of her life. She'd spent the night staring at the ceiling (who knew how different ceilings could look, even in the dark? so jarring), missing home, listening to the soft snoring of a stranger sleeping two feet away from her. This is where I live now, she thought. What a weird idea.

Even though she'd just moved to a different part of California instead of across states again, this move was so, so much harder. It made sense. She'd hoped that fourth grade would prepare her for college much more than it did.

She'd stopped defining herself by where she was from when she realized that her southernness was being uprooted by a palm tree – no, a cottonwood tree, she thought wryly. After fifth grade, she was a member of Little Cottonwood, and that was that. She considered herself a native and prided herself on how quickly she blended into California. In high school, geography seemed so unimportant. Everyone was *from here*. No one had to think about it. Everyone defined themselves by it without realizing it.

During the first week of school when people at Stanford asked where she was from, she answered "Little Cottonwood." During the second week of school she answered "Orange County." By the end of that week she'd learned to just say "SoCal." Unless you lived in or next to Little Cottonwood, you were very unlikely to have ever heard of it. Nothing ever happened there. Until this year she hadn't really appreciated how lucky she was to live in such a boring – no, a *safe* town. Sure, they'd bemoaned the lack of activity that characterized Cottonwood. Their little corner of the coast was ideal for lazy Sunday mornings and early dinners that always led to strolling on the pier, but when everything closed by ten it was hard to find things to do at night.

She missed their little beach town when she was at school. The pier was the hub of life and businesses fanned out around it like half of a flower, with Main Street as the longest and most defining petal. She could recite the restaurants in the order they appeared on the street, the same ones that had been there since she moved and became a grateful member of their happy little hamlet. Main Street and its many wonderful establishments became the backdrop of their childhood, the scenery that blessedly stayed the same as they grew. (Only the Erik Armstrong II Community Center had changed over the years, growing from one building to covering three lots. The town initially complained, but after he single-handedly sponsored the Christmas parade and the new park everyone suddenly loved him).

At age ten she'd stood out because of her accent, but she didn't mind. She stubbornly clung to her southernness, covering her new walls with pictures of her friends in Athens, her dad's UGA pennant, a poster from her favorite barbecue place where they always went for her birthday.

But her southernness began to melt away the minute she laid eyes on the Pacific Ocean. Her family had ventured out to Tybee Island once or twice but it was nothing compared to this... masterpiece. She held her dad's hand as their family walked to the end of the pier and she stared out at the horizon, amazed by the sheer *bigness* of it. The sun melted into the water and the black shadows of surfers catching the last waves of the day danced past the pier. The chortling of dolphins echoed under them and she knew that she would like it here.

Perhaps it was in that moment that she became a citizen of the great state of California. Her recalcitrant efforts to maintain her old identity ceased as she began to embrace her new one. The citizens of Cottonwood accepted her as one of their own and her classmates soon abandoned their fascination with her newness. The

Chandler family melded easily into the scenery of beautiful blond families. They were home.

It wasn't so much California as Cottonwood that she adored – she realized that as her family embarked upon excursions to sunny San Diego and (the surprisingly disappointing) Los Angeles. A city was just a city but Cottonwood was special, untouched by time and the worries of the outside world. The tiny police force served primarily to direct traffic during parades and spent most of their time patrolling the beach in the police boat, chatting with the lifeguards.

She found it hard to explain this to her new friends, especially those from big cities. The more people she met, the more she realized how much she loved living in a town that had barely changed since 1950. She fell in love with the old-fashioned beachiness of it, the family-owned surf shops and the hand-churned ice cream and the burritos that tasted like they were made by God himself. She walked down Main Street hand-in-hand with Sam hundreds of times. Thousands of times, probably, she thought as she considered their weekly pancake breakfasts at Pier Point Café and their hundreds of picnics at the beach. She missed their group bonfires, Sam strumming his banjo, singing off-key on purpose, Josh concocting s'mores recipes, Victoria and Grace squealing as they ran into the waves, Alex and Erik competing to see who could eat the most hot dogs. Yes, that summed up their entertainment in high school, she grinned to herself. Food and the beach. And each other. Always each other.

She smiled and fell asleep.

Erik

He crawled into the top bunk, avoiding banging his sore leg on the ladder. Last summer his dad held one of his youth group retreat things here and made him come as an assistant coach (unpaid, of course). He had to sleep on the floor while the bratty little kids took up every bed and couch in the cabin. His dad got pissed at him for not smiling when the *Sports Illustrated* photographer came out to take pictures of them by the lake. His ex-stepmom framed that issue and hung it in the kitchen, so every time he ate at home he had to see his dad fake-smiling as he pretended to enjoy teaching the sucky kids how to kayak.

He took off his Rolex and sat it on the bed post. After his dad's sponsorship deal with them in the mid-nineties, Rolex still sent him their newest models. Usually they just sat in the front room next to all of his other sponsorship freebie crap: cases of Coke, boxes of cereal, gloves, bats, balls, sunglasses, countless pairs of cleats and baseball pants. Those came in handy, of course, but there were even more things that didn't – millions of magazines, mountains of fan mail, and tons of invitations to fundraisers and golf tournaments and every damned event that required a celebrity. His dad usually turned down the invitations to the small ones ("If they don't offer you a driver, they can't afford you," he'd say to Erik as he tossed an invitation to a cancer fundraiser in the trash) but always accepted the high-profile ones ("This is the best thing I got out of my third marriage!" he'd say as he brandished an invitation to an Oscars party).

He stared at the Rolex, suddenly hating it. It was the same model as his dad's new one.

He pushed it off the top of the bed and heard its soft thud on the ground. Hopefully it broke.

Chapter 2

Saturday morning

Sally

Sally's eyes bolted open as her internal alarm clock started blaring. She lay confused for a moment before remembering where she was, taking in her prostrate friends spread out around her in the unfamiliar darkness. They were all dead asleep, as far as she could tell. She glanced at her watch: 6:30. Saturday, August 20 – not that she needed her watch to tell her that. With semi-adulthood came the responsible, banal awareness of Always Knowing the Date. She missed the summer days of not knowing.

The tiniest bit of sunlight peeked through the blinds, casting an angelic glow on Grace's face. She looked so innocent asleep, so worry-free. They all looked like the kids they were instead of the adults they were trying to be.

Sally crawled slowly out of her sleeping bag, careful not to make too much noise. Her friends were probably used to sleeping until at least ten, but she didn't sleep very much anymore. She got up at 6:30 every day of summer, just like she had during the school year, and she ran four miles every morning, just like during school. And she still slept less than five hours every night, just like during school.

She stepped carefully over Josh's arm and Victoria's hair, and nearly cleared the minefield of sprawled bodies before she realized that she left her shoes in her duffel. Sighing, she tiptoed back to her area, concentrating very hard on not glancing in Sam's direction. She started to unzip her duffel and froze as she heard Sam stir. How did she know it was him? She chastised herself for assuming so. She stood awkwardly bent over her bag, not wanting to make any more noise and wake someone up. What if he woke up? He'd probably want to use the opportunity to get her alone and talk. He would notice the running shoes and want to go with her because they always ran together.

He snored lightly and rolled onto his side. She picked up the entire bag and retreated to the bathroom.

Ten minutes later, Sally was out the door and flying down the street. The thin air tasted like pine needles and reminded her of flannel shirts. A thrill of chilly air tickled her knees as she soared downhill easily, and she felt herself relaxing. She'd always loved running. Most people hated it because running was about pushing yourself, and most people didn't like to push themselves, but most people were not Sally. When she was running, it was just her against herself, and the rest of the world seemed at bay, if only for a moment.

The street was empty, just her and her feet treading rhythmically on the concrete. Running was dependable. Running was comfort. When her thoughts were muddled and confused and painful she could just slip on her Nikes and... run. It usually cleared her head and let her return to her work more focused and ready to conquer the world. On the rare occasion that she didn't run before class, she spent the day feeling unbearably lethargic, and all of her pent-up energy would swirl around in her brain, begging to be utilized productively. On the also-rare occasion that it rained, she spent hours in the gym, pounding the treadmill until she was too tired to think. Physical pain and exhaustion were so much easier to deal with than the emotional kind. Victoria would call it denial, but she thought otherwise. It wasn't really denial, was it? Of course not. She was just physically exerting herself to the point of exhaustion so she didn't have to think about what was bothering her. Okay, maybe that was denial. But it had worked all school year, so why stop?

She came to the bottom of the street and began the uphill run up the dirt path that split from the sidewalk and led into the forest. She briefly hesitated, picturing masked men lurking behind the trees, then shrugged it off and kept going. Her odds of getting attacked by a serial killer were probably much more improbable than her risk of, say, twisting her ankle or tripping over a rock – which seemed quite likely, given her affinity for klutziness. Maybe she would run into a bear or some less terrifying woodland creature, or she would stumble across a deserted cabin or a forgotten heart carved into a tree or she would find a secret necklace – or maybe she would stop letting her overactive imagination psyche her out and she would just run like a normal person. The path was well-worn with the footprints of other joggers, and it was probably less of a threat to her own safety than she was. Actually, it was definitely less of a threat to her than herself because she was capable of hurting herself worse than anyone could and oh, time for denial again, just keep running.

Grace

There was a foot above her head... and a door closed somewhere far away... where was she... why was she on the floor? Oh. Oh yes. Cabin for the weekend. Friends. She rubbed her eyes blearily and lifted her head from her pillow. Erik's legs dangled off the edge of the bed and he snored carelessly. Sam faced the wall and Sally was gone... she must have been the one that left. She probably went for a run. Grace reached for her phone and squinted at the digital glare: 6:45. Way too early. Too early for running.

She turned to go back to sleep, but Josh had rolled back onto her hair, uncomfortable but comforting. She gently freed herself and grinned at his open mouth, gently snoring. He looked nice when he slept, like a baby. Not like Erik, whose sleeping face was just as blank and bored as his awake face. Or Alex, whose worry lines etched themselves into his face. Josh didn't look worried or sad, he just looked like... him. Warm and familiar and reassuring. She missed him. She felt guilty for ignoring him.

She'd been awake for a whole minute before remembering everything. That had to be a record; it was usually the first thing that popped into her head. Usually the past year's events never left her, haunting her even more than when she was awake. In the strange twilight space between waking and sleeping, she could not distinguish dreams from reality, which was sometimes a blessing and sometimes a curse. Sometimes opening her eyes shushed them, as if sunlight could silence her inner devils before they came back. They always came back.

But a full minute... that was amazing. She hadn't had a full minute without remembering since... since it happened. Maybe being with her friends really could help her. She laid back and listened to the soft chorus of the boys' snores, rising and falling at different frequencies, like some poorly orchestrated symphony.

Victoria grumbled as Erik belted out a particularly off-key note and Grace felt something almost like laughter well up inside her.

She smiled at Josh's sleeping form and closed her eyes, welcoming a comfortable nap. Today would be a good day.

Sally

The trees were getting thicker. Once upon a time her instinct for self-preservation would have kicked in and she would have backtracked, carefully following her own footprints until she safely reached the street. Now she felt a little braver. Now she wanted to go into the darker parts. She wondered if she should be alarmed by her easy willingness to run into a dark forest alone. You always heard stories about missing joggers, girls just like her who assumed nothing bad could happen to them and ran freely through twisty paths and poorly lit trails. They went on a routine run and one terrible moment made this run horribly different from the thousands of other runs, and in this terrible moment the bodies that they worked so hard to maintain were suddenly, violently violated and they were gone forever. Just like that. There were too many stories like that on the news, too many school portraits splashed across the front page under devastating headlines. The same sorts of words always followed in the paragraph underneath; was it standard journalistic practice to make victims of terrible crimes sound like perfect citizens, or was it that terrible fates beheld only young, pretty girls who also happened to be model students, perfect daughters, and thoughtful friends? Girls that met horrific ends were always described as wonderful and kind, but was that because they were murdered and that was standard protocol for murdered girls? What if a really mean, bitchy girl was murdered – how would the newspapers convey her death? Would there be less of an outpouring of grief because of her personality, or would it be just as sad as if a nice girl died? Were people supposed to pretend to feel just as sad? Were they supposed to lie and say nice things about her?

She picked up her speed as she passed a scary-looking clump of gnarled trees. It would be so easy for someone to kill her right now. She wondered morbidly what their hometown newspaper would say. "Stanford Student Murdered During Camping Trip." "Young Woman Killed While Jogging." What would her friends remember her by? How would her family describe her to the newspapers? God, that was weird to think about. She supposed they would milk the academic stuff, especially Stanford, because that was a really big deal to some people. They'd probably describe her high school accomplishments and extracurriculars. How strange that she would have once been okay with this, back when they were brainwashed to believe that extracurricular activities defined a person, as if Christian Club, all of the honors societies, and her thousands of hours of community service showed who she truly was – though that was good enough for Stanford, she thought wryly.

Maybe some journalist would track down her old AP teachers and interview them as if they were writing a rec letter for college admissions. She remembered that her AP U.S. teacher had used the word "perfect" to describe her in his letter, and she'd felt so flattered and pleased with herself. She still had a copy of that letter hidden in her desk at home and she used to read it when she was feeling down, and it made her feel better (how foolish! she thought now) to think that at least Mr. MacMillan thought of her as "a perfect student, a role model for her peers, and an upstanding citizen all-around." He was the advisor for Christian Club, and she'd spent a lot of time with him over the four years. She'd been on the board of the club for three of those years, so she planned events with him and even went to his house a few times to bake cookies with his wife and participate in their prayer group. What a good little Christian girl she had been. She wondered what the MacMillans would think of her if they knew everything that had transpired in the last year, and she laughed grimly as she contemplated their expressions.

Her new Christian friends at Stanford were wonderful, but she was afraid to tell them The Big Thing. They'd known her for less than a year – learning what happened would definitely override any prior perception of her. On the days when she just couldn't bear to be around people, she ignored the nice calls and texts and invitations, just like Grace had with her.

She hoped that Grace didn't do what she did for the same reasons that she did, but that seemed unlikely. She couldn't imagine Grace doing anything as terrible as what she'd done. Maybe she deserved to get murdered out here.

How many hours would she have to be gone for her friends to know she was missing? It was terrible to consider. She looked at her watch – it was almost eight-thirty right now, which meant that most of them would be asleep for another two or three hours, and they had no idea where she was. She should have left a note. She didn't want to worry them.

Her knees tensed as the trail sloped upward, and she felt sweat accumulating under the edge of her sports bra. Maybe her love for her friends was what got her through it, through the ephemeral highs and the unspeakable lows. Maybe her love for them was enough to make her keep going forward. She didn't care so much about herself as she did about them. Her Stanford friends were great. They were wonderful and brilliant and funny and seemed to understand her as well as they could. Her new friends were great, but her high school friends *knew* her, really knew her. They knew all of her secrets – except the big one – and they were still friends after witnessing all of her embarrassing moments, even her terrible braces stage. They accepted her flaws and they remained friends with her even when she was a stressed-out wreck. Even if they couldn't empathize with her dream of becoming an English teacher, they understood her drive to do so. They let her prattle on about her favorite books. Sometimes they even listened to her recommendations, although it wounded her when they didn't immediately love *Little Women*, one of her all-time favorites. Victoria laughed at her when she used the phrase "castles in the air," but she thought that it perfectly described their group, and she felt an eternal debt of gratitude to Louisa May Alcott for introducing it to her. They did build castles in the air – even more castles than they had built on the beach of Little Cottonwood, she thought, smiling to herself. They all constructed perceptions of the selves they hoped to become, and she loved them for it.

They loved her despite the bad parts (well, the bad parts that they were familiar with) and they kept her afloat.

Her thoughts inevitably returned to Sam. Did he keep her afloat? She supposed that he did more than the others. He had once been her life preserver and kept her head above water in high school, when the process of preparing to leave home seemed so terrifying. He remained her rock while she stressed over her twelve college applications, and his total lack of stress kept her feet on the ground. His humor was infectious; his laughter pushed away her anxiety and kneaded out the wrinkles in her forehead. He was the perfect foil to the equally competitive Victoria, who she was perpetually pitting herself against. She and Victoria shared a brain, but she and Sam shared... a soul. She felt herself blushing furiously at the cheesiness of it, but it was true. He was like a balloon, light and airy and cheerful. He didn't just keep her afloat; he soared in the sky and made sure that she did too. He sailed above the water that their other friends drowned in, as if he could not be touched by worrying about the future.

Sometimes this was terribly annoying, and then it felt like he was drowning her. She liked to plan; he never did. She mapped out her future and dreamed about her career and did everything she could possibly do to ensure a better future for herself. He enjoyed life rather than dominating it. She wanted to win; he wanted to play the game and have fun doing it, and sometimes this easy nonchalance drove her crazy.

Their few fights (or, rather, their few tight-lipped discussions – they never fought because that required a skill for confrontation that she did not possess) arose from her wanting to spend another Saturday night editing her college essay when he thought she needed to go out. He was so good about it, she reflected. He said he understood, and he brought her Starbucks at home, and he always had some anecdote that cheered her up and dragged her out of the myriad of stressful thoughts. Sometimes he was able to convince her to go out, and he chatted with her mom and played games with her little sisters while she got ready. And when she finally emerged from her room he always looked so happy, like she was shiny and new, whether she was in a ponytail and jeans or the nice blue dress that made her cleavage look much bigger than it was. He bounced down the sidewalk and opened the car door for her and sang along with the radio while they drove to dinner or the movies or the beach. Sometimes they just drove around in the dark in comfortable silence, and sometimes they went to random places because he felt like it. He had no shortage of ideas, and she was happy to go along with them. The only thing she had to worry about was being home on time, which he usually made sure she was. He always insisted on one last kiss and that often became more than one last kiss, and she felt her cheeks reddening again at the memories of sitting in his car in front of her house, kissing furiously and hoping that her dad didn't look out the window.

The slope leveled out, and she ran more easily across the flat ground. The sun peeked through the trees and illuminated everything in the soft, nature-y glow that she associated with granola bar commercials. She passed the last little clump of thick trees and stood blinking in the sudden brightness. Somehow the trail had gone in a circle without her realizing it and she was less than twenty feet away from where she'd gone in. Huh. She felt somewhat comforted knowing that the trail could lead her right back to where she was, like she had traveled a great distance without being left behind. A year ago she probably would have considered it a waste of time, not knowing that she could learn so much and end up in exactly the same place. She felt strangely light and cheerful. She looked at her watch 8:10. No wonder she felt cheerful. Two hours' worth of adrenaline pumping into their veins would make anyone perk up.

She wiped her forehead with the bottom of her t-shirt, and the morning breeze felt wonderful on her sweaty stomach. Everything seemed a little clearer now, and not just because of the gratifying hormones. Her mind was at peace; she felt strangely hopeful, with an unfamiliar but welcome conviction that today would be a good day. She would move forward. She would enjoy today and look forward to tomorrow, always tomorrow.

She turned right and jogged back up the street, back towards her friends.

Victoria

She'd been awake for a while. Between the snoring, the uncomfortable floor, and her own relentless mind, sleep was impossible. She hated dreams. It was hard enough maintaining composure when you had full control over your consciousness, but once that was gone all your thoughts and worries and fears emerged in full, enraged color.

She was used to snoring guys, but not Erik's snoring. His snoring was as dull and unimaginative as he was, and tediously echoed around the small room, bouncing off of her eardrums until she wanted to scream. It probably wasn't the snoring that bothered her; really, it was probably him. He just grated on her nerves.

Or maybe she just really, really hated snoring.

In the past year she'd woken up to seven guys' snoring – five times in their beds and twice in hers. Those were seven mornings (no, nine – she saw that one guy three times. What was his name? Todd? Tom? Something like that) of waking up disoriented and naked, then recalling the night before. She always woke up before the guy did (snoring!) and she had no problem with getting up and searching for a bathroom in unfamiliar territory. Three of the guys had been in frats, and she walked freely through the frat house in her underwear and the guy's t-shirt looking for cereal and chatting with bemused hungover bros. She always made a point of brushing her hair and teeth as soon as she got up. It was only a walk of shame if you were ashamed, and if your hair looked good and your breath smelled fine you didn't have to be ashamed. She'd become quite accustomed to the morning-after routine: sneak out of bed, find underwear, light grooming, quick and detached good-bye-I'll-probably-never-see-you-again-thanks-for-the-night. She was in and out quickly, and always made sure to get all of her stuff so as to avoid an awkward pick-up-forsaken-articles-of-clothing situation. Sometimes the guys were chivalrous enough to offer their shirt or sweatshirt to her, which she always accepted. She really wouldn't have minded walking back to her dorm in her bra, but if she could get a free shirt out of it, why not?

Another snore rattled around the room and Victoria cringed. Maybe she now identified snoring with the morning after? Could seven (nine) nights be enough to elicit such a Pavlovian hatred? How interesting. The nerd in her was intrigued. When she heard snoring it triggered unwelcome feelings of demeaning self-loathing. But that couldn't possibly be true because she didn't feel self-loathing or shame, right? That was what she told herself, what differentiated her from the other girls tiptoeing out of frat houses at 7 a.m. carrying last night's heels and whatever dignity they had left. She slept with guys not to feel better about herself, like those girls did, and she certainly didn't justify it by "it's college," like so many people annoyingly did. She considered it a matter of pride, of control; she could spend the night with someone without getting emotionally involved. The physical part could be totally detached; it was just an act, a meaningless act, and there didn't have to be an emotional response. She could hold the power and not feel guilty or bad about herself. When the guys had bothered to get her number and actually called within the next few days, she listened to their invitations for a date, but usually declined. What was the point if she'd already slept with them? It was like reading a book when you already knew how it ended. (She read *Princess Diaries* in sixth grade, and that gave away the ending to *Jane Eyre*, which she now refused to read. Sally, of course, tried to persuade her for months to read it).

She glanced at her watch. Ugh. So early… but another one of Erik's snores ricocheted dully around the room and she knew there was no way she'd fall back asleep. Whatever. She could go eat or something.

She threw the covers of her sleeping bag to the side and got up without bothering to be quiet. If they could sleep through Erik's snores they could sleep through anything. Besides, if she had to be awake right now, it was only fair that they did, too.

Sally's sleeping bag was empty – was she seriously running during their camping trip? That girl did not stop. She avoided Josh's outstretched arm, which was reaching towards Grace, who was curled up in a ball. When she was sleeping she looked… tiny. And vulnerable too, like she wouldn't even try to defend herself against the world and had already given up.

Victoria stepped around her friends and made her way outside to the balcony. The air was too fresh and dry and the annoying kind of crisp that made you freeze in the morning and sweat in the afternoon. She licked her lips and made a mental note to steal Sally's Chapstick later. Her nose itched in the unfamiliar air. A few cake crumbs littered the table, but other than that there was little indication of actual human presence. Thick trees obscured her view of the surrounding houses, and it was easy to imagine that there were no other people around.

Her ears hurt and she twitched. She curled her legs up and wrapped her arms around her knees, wondering why she felt so strange. She sat there a moment with her eyes closed and pulled her face into her knees, and then she realized: it was the silence. It was totally silent here. She wasn't used to silence. She was used to city noises and the ramblings of protestors and the late-night yells of wayward students echoing around the dorm plaza. She was used to trying to shut noises out and focusing on focusing. Tuning out the unpleasant had become second nature to her.

She sat in the sunny still silence.

God, was this what people called peaceful? It wasn't peaceful at all.

What was peaceful about having nothing going on around you? At least at Berkeley, where it was perpetually noisy and lively and boisterous, there was a sense of vitality. There was an energy, a stress-and-caffeine-and-sometimes-alcohol-fueled force that propelled people and made them exciting.

This was... boring.

Because really, what did she have to do besides sit out here and wait for her friends to get up? She could go eat breakfast, but she wanted hot food and didn't feel like cooking. She'd just make Sally do it when she got back from her run. But until she did that, what was there to do? What was she supposed to focus on?

She looked at the cake crumbs on the table and thought of last night: her friends' laughter, the surprise conveying of the cake, sprawling out comfortably over Josh and not having to worry about sleeping with him. It was nice to be around guys with whom she had no interest in being intimate. These friends represented her sole platonic male relationships.

Last night Grace had cried, and this surprised her. Sally had whispered to her that they were happy tears, but were they? No one just cried over a birthday cake. There had to be a reason. But Grace was not Victoria and she did not think like Victoria and she was, in some ways, the complete opposite of Victoria.

Sometimes she envied Grace. Sometimes she pitied her. How could someone with such a brilliant mind have absolutely no idea what to do with it? She was like a dandelion seed floating in the wind, totally directionless. When you tried to do everything you ended up doing nothing. When you didn't know which direction to take you tried to take all of them and got caught in the middle, stuck in a static state of being that you were responsible for. If you just drifted you would never get anywhere – you'd get lost in the current of whatever you considered to be bigger than yourself. You couldn't float. You had to fight against the current, arm over arm, stroke by stroke, pushing against that everything that tried to defy you, including yourself. Most people couldn't do that. Grace could, she knew she could, but she wasn't, and that frustrated her.

For every action there was an equal and opposite reaction. It was her favorite of Newton's laws; even the universe knew that you were supposed to push back. A neat tripartite edict governed the world with a beautiful simplicity that Victoria admired. She doubted the apple story was true – that was for people like Sally who always needed a cute story to give things meaning – but she didn't doubt Newton's brilliance. He was able to see past the petty banal actions of everyone around him and comprehend that there was something greater at work, that everyone was controlled by the same forces whether they realized it or not. And if they could never exceed the magnitude of the forces acting upon them, they would never move independently away from the current. They would never be great.

Once upon a time Victoria had been convinced she would be great. She'd had so many forces acting upon her and she turned out okay. She would be more than a product of her environment, she told herself. She would not remain at rest. Inertia was for the weak. She would be a force to be reckoned with.

She thought of herself two years prior, getting ready for senior year. How naïve she'd been. Of course she hadn't thought that at the time – she'd marveled at how mature she was and how prepared she felt to escape the small pond that she'd already dominated. It was a different hierarchy then, a different system, and she played the system. She beat the system. She had the teachers wrapped around her little finger because she raised their average and made them all look better. She kissed the requisite amount of ass in order to get her glowing recommendation letters, and she'd spent countless lunches in the counseling office making sure that her applications were all in order. She got the highest grades and asked intelligent questions that stumped her classmates and most of the time the teachers realized that it was easier to agree with her than to try and argue.

What a different world high school had been. Back then it was so easy to be the best. It was so much easier when you could conquer your peers without resistance because really, the vast majority of her classmates were no competition at all. She climbed to the top, gracefully ascending each pinnacle of perfection, knocking lesser beings out of the way in order to reach the summit. It was so easy to get to the top when there were very few other climbers at that altitude, and the opposition quickly thinned as people realized how much effort it took to get there. Her friends were the only ones that offered any real competition. Her classmates were children and she was an adult and they would live in that little town forever and she would move on to bigger and better things, to exotic places and an exciting career. She steamrolled her way to the top, plowing a trail that would surely lead to a gleaming undergraduate career, med school, internship, residency, surgical fellowships.

She couldn't wait to see what spectacular fate awaited her. The great thing about medicine was that there was no shortage of brilliant people carving out new channels of self-promotion. There was always a new award to covet and new technology to master. You had to constantly be at the top of your game because you had people's lives in your hands, for God's sakes. A surgeon required more control than any other profession, and she thought this suited her perfectly.

Then there was the pressure, which she had always imagined but didn't fully comprehend. She told herself that she was used to being under pressure, and that was true. She put more pressure on herself than the rest of the school put together. She felt a hot swoop of embarrassment as she remembered how arrogant she'd been, how confident that she'd sail through Berkeley and come out triumphantly at the top, just like she'd always done.

The first semester of college was a shock to her system. At first she reveled in meeting exciting new people, the kind of people she'd always dreamed of competing against. These kids had stories and life experiences and had *done* things. She had to embellish her own tales of antics and misdeeds to make herself sounds cool enough to be on their level. She'd always considered herself something of a badass – at the very least, a genius with the soul of a rebel – but it was quite sobering to hear what her new peers had already accomplished and realize that there was so much more for her to do. During the first two weeks of college she met kids who scuba-dived with sharks, hiked volcanoes, partied at three-day-long raves with musicians whose names she pretended to recognize, built homes for orphans in Africa, modeled in Paris, and interned for Mark Zuckerberg. There were ambassadors' kids who spent their childhoods all over the world and spoke seven languages, executives' kids who spent their Christmases in the Caribbean and looked shocked when you said you'd never been, kids poorer than her who had just moved to the U.S. to go to college and had witnessed drug wars and political coups. A girl on her floor flew to D.C. once a month to present her gender equality campaign at the White House. A guy in her physics class was training for the Olympics.

So the Berkeley kids were even worthier competition that she'd expected. (What *had* she expected? she wondered). She'd entered her classes with the familiar conviction that everyone was beneath her, that she'd soon be at the top, riding the easy A wave that she'd surfed since kindergarten and had no signs of crashing down.

So much had happened in the first few weeks, all the bad stuff in the beginning… but she wouldn't think about that. She wouldn't let it control her. She would move on and be a force of nature and make other people move out of her way.

She pushed her thoughts away from the unpleasantness, but they drifted to the second-worst occurrence of those first few weeks. Ugh. Calculus.

Suppressing unpleasant thoughts was so much easier in a bustling environment. Here it was so easy to succumb to what was going on inside your head because there was nothing to distract you. Some people considered tranquility a gift, but this silence fell on her ears in an unbearable cacophony, beating on her eardrums as if it was trying to call forth the memories with some tribal chant of pounding silence –

And there they were, rising repulsively within her like thought vomit. Math 1A. She thought it was so easy at first. She went to every lecture and paid attention. She studied. She went to office hours. She tried to convince herself that she was directing her life back to normal.

Math had never been her best subject. In high school that meant that she got an A in comparison to Grace's A+. When she got it right, math was beautiful. The derivatives danced and the

45

series sang and the limits presented themselves like eager actors in a well-choreographed performance. The (correctly solved) problems that took up an entire page were like a perfect play and a painting and a song, all at the same time. When she got the answer right everything unfolded gracefully and her pencil was a conductor, gently guiding the orchestra along. And when there was that light bulb moment and she knew exactly what to do, her pencil flew down the page and the angels sang the hallelujah chorus and there was that moment of ecstasy of being right. Really, it was orgasmic.

But when she got it wrong, when some stupid little detail stumped her, the world came crashing down. The derivatives didn't speak to her; they whispered to her about her future as a failure. The series mocked her and the limits remained stubbornly hidden. Her pencil halted and the violinists jerked their bows screechingly across their instruments while the angels cried.

She didn't like to be wrong, so it was a good thing that she rarely was wrong. But as she looked at her first college calculus test, she felt her face getting hot with the sudden realization that she didn't know what to do. The test questions were not at all like those in lecture or discussion. The conductor had brought the wrong sheet music and was unable to perform.

She stumbled through it, recalling bits and pieces of lecture that vaguely resembled the hieroglyphics in front of her. She watched other people finish the test and bring it to the front until she was one of the last ones sitting in the lecture hall. The professor got bored and left. She tried desperately to summon the familiar brilliance, but it remained stubbornly buried under new, unfamiliar self-doubt. The TA looked at his watch and told them they had five minutes left.

She hurried through, filling in the last few blanks with answers that she knew were wrong. Humiliated, she shoved her test on top of the pile and fled the classroom, already dreading the day they'd get their grades. Usually she couldn't wait to find out her grade on an assignment or an exam, and she fiddled around impatiently for a week or so, obsessing over her answers and looking them up in the textbook to make sure she'd done them correctly. When the teacher finally graded the tests, she grabbed hers first and triumphantly scanned her answers, admiring her brilliance on a particularly difficult question and grinning with pride when she got the really tricky things. She loved being right. She loved the "+" next to the A, such simple but powerful validation that she really was as smart as she thought she was.

But this time was different. The knot of anxiety in her stomach grew tighter and tighter every time she remembered the test. She checked online every few hours, but the grades were never updated; evidently, her professor was one of those old-fashioned dudes who didn't appreciate the advantages of the Internet in academia.

When she entered her calc lecture a week after D-Day, the knot in her stomach constricted tautly. A messy pile of papers crowned the podium, looking like an offering to some sadistic god. She ignored it and sat in her usual front-row seat and felt the terrible bubbling of anticipation as she watched people file in and approach the podium. They attacked the pile like animals, ferociously stripping away the tests that weren't theirs, the unclaimed tests drifting to the ground like inedible strips of flesh. The professor watched bemusedly as his little group of undergrads viciously clawed each other, pulling their tests from curious strangers' hands and shielding them from the eyes of nosy people looking to compare scores. Her heart sank as she realized that the entire class could see her grade. Hers was probably one of the papers that was causing smirks and derisive laughter, one that other pre-med kids looked at and felt reassured because someone that was this terrible at calculus surely couldn't become a doctor so there was one less competitor to worry about and they were smarter than she was –

She was standing in front of the podium before she consciously realized that she was approaching the throng. A beautiful blond girl emerged from the pack, grinning triumphantly. Victoria caught a glimpse of the red "A" at the top of her test. "I got an A!" she said to her male Asian friend.

"Of course you did, you're such a genius! I got a fucking B."

Ordinarily Victoria would have laughed at this reversal of stereotypes, but this was not the time. She pushed her way through the thinning circle and scanned the few exams still on the table. She pawed through them – not hers, not hers, not hers. The other tests were slowly snapped up around her and she stood blankly at the front of the class, feeling embarrassed as the queue to the front lessened and disappeared. Hers wasn't there. The only one remaining belonged to someone named Sasha.

Her face felt hot and her brained generated a flurry of possible explanations. The professor had left hers in his briefcase. He'd thrown hers away. Her test had gotten lost somehow and she'd have to retake it. Yes! Then she could study more and-

"Excuse me, are you Victoria Holloway?"

Or someone else could have picked up her test accidentally. She turned towards a girl in adorable lace tights and ridiculously large combat boots. "I think that's my test you're holding," the hipster girl said bitchily. She held out a test facedown towards her, and it took Victoria what felt like forever to realize that this was her test and that this girl was Sasha. She grabbed her test and held Sasha's out to her.

Sasha looked down at her A- and rolled her eyes. She grabbed it. "Oh, and I'm sorry."

"It's fine, you grabbed the wrong test –"

"No, I mean about your grade." Hipster Sasha flounced away in her combat boots and her firm conviction that she would succeed in life.

The professor cleared his throat behind her and she realized that the lecture was about to begin. She walked back quickly to her seat, test still facedown. She got out her notebook and her pencil and shoved the test into her bag, aware that the guy next to her was trying to see what she got. The professor began lecturing and she took notes without absorbing a single word he said.

For the entire lecture she sat tall and proud, like the recipient of an A+, and she ignored the whispers of people comparing tests behind her. She looked attentive and smart, and that was all that mattered for the moment. She wouldn't let the other kids think she'd been defeated.

When the hour was over – God, it seemed like five – she grabbed her bag and walked coolly outside, like she wasn't in a hurry at all. She had an hour before her next class, so she found a nice-looking wall and sat down like a normal, relaxed person. Other kids milled about on the quad, talking and laughing and walking to class with their headphones and their happy thoughts and their confidence in their futures. She could be like them. She still was like them. She casually opened her bag and forced herself to shuffle slowly through her things and not look demented.

The test was now crumpled and she smoothed it out. The back side had a lot of scary red marks. She wasn't used to those. They looked like the bloody claw marks of some vindictive monster's assault on her soul. She slowly turned it over and her eyes stared widely at the giant "C-" at the top of the page.

She closed her bag and stood up, adjusting her short skirt. The sun beat down on her already tan legs and everyone was going about their day like the accomplished people that they were. The clock tower gleamed and the kids in Berkeley shirts gleamed because they went to Berkeley and they belonged here. They were the best and brightest.

She walked over to the trash can and threw her test away like she was doing it a favor.

Victoria cringed at the memory of the midterm, her first (and not her last) C in college. After she got the C she promised herself that this was a fluke, just a one-night stand with failure. She'd gotten it out of her system and now could move on to healthier, more successful relationships.

But then came the physics midterm, and she got a C on that, too. She'd studied. She went to office hours. She knew the material inside and out, but when she sat down to take the test she froze.

She'd planned on going a little crazy for her first college Halloween anyway, and the second C of her life made her very willing to forget. She told herself that if she went out and partied – she hadn't gone out since first week – she'd drink the stress away, dance in her slutty costume, and flirt shamelessly with strangers. It could be a good weekend. It could be a *great* weekend. It all depended on her attitude, and she would not let this one little thing affect her for the rest of the semester. She would move on and learn from her mistakes and all that, but first she needed to blow off some steam.

Getting ready to go out was always one of the best parts about it, and she remembered getting ready with her floormates, all of whom were fellow freshmen and equally excited about their first college Halloween. Midterms stress engendered a lot of pent-up energy that demanded to be spent in as many parties and as little clothing as possible. They darted in and out of each others' rooms, shouting requests down the hallway for a curling iron or eyelash glue.

She of course took the longest to get ready, and could hear the other girls getting antsy in the hallway. Stephanie was anxious to go and kept threatening to leave her, but she knew they wouldn't. They were a relatively innocent little group, and Victoria had stretched the truth about her illicit activities, so she seemed the most experienced and they looked to her for guidance. They stared at her with wide eyes when she talked about getting drunk, and they asked her for advice and took turns calculating how much they thought they could handle.

When she finally emerged from her room, the girls gasped collectively, and she was pleased by their reaction, equal parts admiring, jealous, and intimidated. Her costume looked exactly as she wanted it. The tight red sequined top (well, top was a generous word – it was really closer to a bra) made her cleavage look fantastic, and the short black skirt made her legs look miles long. Unlike most of the girls who tottered up Berkeley hills in five-inch heels, she could actually walk in hers. Her fake eyelashes looked dangerously perfect and the devil horns nestled comfortably in her now-curly hair. She felt unstoppable.

She towered above the other girls and led the way to the frats. Other groups of scantily-clad girls doddered in the same direction, screeching exclamations of excitement and mutual congratulations on their outfits. Clusters of guys in chest-baring costumes darted between the girl groups, staring unabashedly. Those that had obviously pre-gamed struck up conversations with the girls, emboldened by the alcohol that convinced them that they were much more attractive than they were.

A buff guy in a Super Man Speedo and a cape – nothing more – caught her eye and introduced himself. She told him that superheroes were her kryptonite. It was lame, but it worked. When they reached the house he escorted her to the "private party" upstairs. He offered her a cup of jungle juice, which she politely declined (no more red Solo cups for her) and immediately redeemed herself by drinking straight from his friend's handle. His brothers, all of whom wore similarly faux-masculine costumes, responded enthusiastically, and she noted with some satisfaction the discontent of the few other girls in the room who suddenly weren't receiving as much attention. The guys complimented her costume and made lots of unfunny jokes about it, but she laughed anyway and chugged a bit more.

She found herself warming up to them as the night progressed and things grew a little fuzzy, but tried to drown out the little voice in her head by loudly challenging the guys to beer pong. They enthusiastically agreed and she realized that she was the only girl left. It thrilled and terrified her to feel her control slipping, and when she realized that Superman's hand was inching up her thigh faster than she intended she downed the rest of her drink with grim determination.

The next thing she remembered was waking up in Superman's bed, piecing together fragments of the broken night and wondering just where her underwear had gone. It was consensual, but that was really the only good thing about it. The real Superman probably would have been disgraced.

Mr. Clark Kent was the second blast of kryptonite of her fall semester, igniting the process of self-destruction. She told herself that going out would blow off steam so that she could be more productive later. Lying to herself sucked, but if lying meant she could have fun, then she would lie and just deal with it.

Then her grades started slipping. No big deal, they'd pick up again. She was brilliant. In the meantime, she'd enjoy herself. Every night that she went out she looked guiltily at her unopened calc book or TI-89, then she focused on something else, like her makeup or her shoes. Shiny things. Happy things.

A few weeks into it she realized what was going on. She'd lost the control that she'd so carefully cultivated since age six. Now the thing that defined her was threatened; her position at the top was in serious jeopardy, and she'd found a new outlet to feel good about herself. Frat houses were like drugs to girls with terrible self-esteem – they were the last thing they needed and the first thing they wanted. Thursday nights were the one constant in her life and she reveled in the boundless admiration that her gradually more minimal outfits elicited. There would always be free alcohol to make her go all glowy and boys that would say whatever was necessary. She could regulate her flirtation and watch the weak boys bend over backward at her command. She could pit them against each other and make them compete for her. She could control how much attention she received, and enjoyed controlling it even though the attention was often the prelude to a sweaty, half-remembered night that made her want to bathe in Purell.

So she was channeling her weird new feelings of vulnerability into slippery channels of self-destruction. It didn't make her feel any better, but it didn't make her feel that much worse, either. She simply got used to being hungover on Fridays and losing underwear and amassing an impressive collection of t-shirts. She got used to seeing strange bruises of forgotten origin bloom across her skin over the weekend. She got used to her grades – well, she didn't have to think about that right now.

This weekend was about being with her friends and returning to her old, healthier state of mind. Last summer she was whole. Last summer she was innocent, though she would have hated to be called that. Now she wished that she could have that innocence back. She used to be so sure of herself and so confident that she knew everything, and now… now she felt like she knew nothing. Last summer her future seemed so planned out, and she was so proud of her ambition, so brimful of confidence in her destiny. Her potential was the only faith she followed or needed, but she'd lost the right to that special dogma. She no longer deserved to have those convictions.

Maybe this weekend would help her get them back. Maybe if she spent a decent amount of time with her friends, she could reconnect to herself from a year ago. Her friends were basically the same as they were last summer, right? There was no way that they had changed as much as she had. She could rely on their stability and their boring, safer lives. Her friends were here to keep her grounded and remind her who she had been – no, who she was.

She heard someone in the kitchen making welcomed noise. She smiled and went inside.

Josh

He pushed through the throng of sweaty bodies anxiously. Where was it?

52

A scantily-clad Ninja Turtle grabbed his arm and started dancing on him. He pushed her away and continued his search, wading through the crowd of costumes. The strobe light half-blinded him and there was a can in his hand and he drank greedily and looked down and saw that he was only bones and he watched the beer spill between his ribs to where his stomach used to be.

This worried him somewhat, but he kept going. He had to find something, but he couldn't remember what it was. He was so sure that he'd seen something, or someone, that required his immediate attention, or had he imagined it?

Another girl shoved herself on him and he moved away from her impatiently. Wrong girl. So it was a girl he was looking for? That seemed right.

Suddenly he realized that everyone around him was a girl. The house was full of them, and they were closing in on him, locking him in a swaying blockade of colors and feathers and glitter and tutus. He tried to push his way through but the dancing escalated and the circle grew smaller and he was drowning in a sea of girls but none of them were the right one. It was hot, so hot, which seemed silly because he didn't have any skin, did he? He was just bones. Girls closed in on him from every direction and he couldn't see the door and his ribcage glittered in the pulsing light and then he woke up.

He laid there for a moment, totally confused, and then remembered where he was. The hazy dream, already slipping away, confused him even more. What the hell was that about? Usually when he dreamt that he was the only guy in a crowd of half-naked girls he didn't wake up feeling so stressed out.

Who was he looking for? He hated that feeling of looking for something and not finding it. It was so frustrating, like having a word on the tip of your tongue. But when it was a thought at the tip of your brain, the thought disappeared into a complicated nexus of neurons and stuff, and it was dead before it started. Some things retreated and were lost forever, like socks that went into the dryer and never came out. You knew the missing sock had existed – there was a lonely partner sock to prove this – but you never had any idea where the hell it went.

He turned over and saw that Victoria was gone. Sally, too. Maybe he should get up.

Erik snored loudly and that settled his decision. He rolled out of his sleeping bag and stepped carefully over Grace. She looked so tiny and cute when she was asleep.

He went downstairs and opened the fridge. Maybe he could start breakfast for everyone. They all loved his scrambled eggs. He started opening cupboards, looking for frying pans. He pulled a handle, expecting it to slide, but instead it swung open vertically and a few plastic bowls tumbled onto the floor. Oops.

The backdoor closed and Victoria came in from the balcony. "What are you up to?"

"I'm just makin' breakfast. What do you want, bacon and eggs?"

She slid across a bar stool and propped her legs on the one next to it. "Surprise me. But make it delicious."

"Okay, how about..." he looked through the grocery bags. His mom had contributed a loaf of cinnamon bread. "French toast?"

"Sounds yummy." She pulled the container of licorice towards her and pulled out a few Red Vines.

"How does someone eat so much junk food and look like you do?" he asked. It wasn't flirting as much as an honest question. Victoria ate like a frat boy and looked like... she did.

"I have a fantastic metabolism, you know." She grinned and pulled out another Red Vine. He glanced at her long tan legs, which seemed even skinnier than usual. She'd never been fat – she'd always been, well, hot – but she looked really, really skinny. And still hot, but in a slightly tired way. More worn. Not gleaming and vibrant like she used to.

The front door opened and Sally emerged. He couldn't help but notice that she looked skinnier, too. Weren't girls supposed to get the Freshman 15? Sally's tight cross country shirt showed that there was nothing hiding under there that shouldn't be.

"Good morning!" Sally said brightly. She untied her shoes and placed them carefully by the door. "I didn't wake you guys up this morning, did I?" she looked worried, as if causing her friends lack of sleep was a terrible crime.

"Nope! I just woke up," said Josh. She looked relieved and he felt a rush of affection for her.

54

"I woke up because of Erik, not because of you." Victoria sounded annoyed.

"Yeah, he snores to beat the band," Sally grinned. "How long have you guys been up?"

"I just got up, she got up before me. Now she's going to eat a bunch of licorice and then complain that she's too full for breakfast."

"I am not! Fine. I'll stop eating. After this one."

Sally laughed. "I'll help with breakfast. Let me shower real quick, I smell disgusting."

"I'm sure you don't!"

"Yes, you do." Victoria wrinkled her nose comically and Sally giggled. She looked so much happier than yesterday. Josh watched her walk out of the room. Her ponytail bounced in typical cute Sally fashion. She looked awfully good in those shorts.

He felt Victoria watching him. "What?"

"Are you into her?"

"God, no." Hopefully Sally was out of earshot. "We're friends."

"You don't watch her like you're friends."

"Well, I look at her like I look at you."

She laughed. "Touché. So who are you into? I miss hearing about your love life."

He grinned suggestively. "A gentleman doesn't kiss and tell."

"Then I guess it's a good thing you're not a gentleman, for the sake of an entertaining conversation."

"I'm a gentleman!"

"You drunk-dialed me at midnight, which is 3 a.m. your time, to tell me that you just hooked up with two girls at once. You're no gentleman."

He vaguely recalled this from the end of finals week in January. He'd woken up the next morning with a headache and… yep, a congratulatory text from Victoria. He'd almost forgotten that.

"Okay, so maybe I'm not so much a gentleman."

She smiled, then frowned slightly, like something had occurred to her. "You have lots of random hook-ups, right?"

He nodded.

"Do you get the girls' numbers? Do you remember their names?"

He squinted, recalling lots of awkward mornings-after and gathering clothes and possessions that spread haphazardly after wild nights. There were more girls that he left at parties than those that he bothered to take home, and he remembered some of their names. It was a small enough school that you were bound to run into hook-ups at some point, so it was important to know names, but dates with said hook-ups were not mandatory.

"I remember a few of their names, but honestly, I'm pretty drunk most of the time."

"So do they mean anything to you?" She was rarely serious, but she was serious now. If Victoria was serious and not being sarcastic or bossing someone around, then she really meant it. Her eyebrows furrowed in a scary way that he'd only seen a few times, and those were not fun occasions. Very few people in the entire world had witnessed the furrowed eyebrows. The furrowed eyebrows were not a good thing. Most of the time she had this shield around her, but now she seemed a little more… open. Yes, it was openness, he decided. She looked at him earnestly, not joking or flirting. There was no teasing. She wanted a sincere answer and he had no idea why.

"As what? If this is a feminist question, then I respect women and all that and I know that you have a brain and not just a body. I know that. And I acknowledge that the time I spend with these girls is mostly for their bodies and not for their minds, so they don't mean that much." He thought. "Like I spend time with you and Grace for your minds and your personalities, because we're friends and you guys mean a lot to me, but these girls don't because… it's different."

She nodded. "I get it."

They were quiet for a moment. The kitchen appliances gleamed in the sunny silence. She looked out the window, squinting in the brightness. Her fingers tapped the countertop restlessly. Josh felt uncomfortable watching her uneasiness; it was a side of her that he so seldom saw. He was used to the confident girl that walked into every room like she owned it. This girl was just as impatient, but she was quieter. Vulnerable in a way that he wasn't used to seeing.

She turned towards him and smiled without a trace of insecurity. "That was a very nice argument. Way to flatter me."

"Of course. Do you have any other deep life questions for me, or do you want to go wake everyone up so I can make breakfast?"

"Food. Definitely food."

She jumped off the barstool and flounced out of the kitchen. Same as always.

Sam

Sam jumped into the lake, penetrating the smooth sheen of the water. So fresh and clean and warm. Much warmer than he expected. He stroked his way to the bottom and reached out an outstretched arm, skimming the silty ground with his palm. It was surprisingly soft and the dirt sailed smoothly between his fingers. He kicked off and pushed himself to the surface, bursting into the air with a powerful thrust. He seemed to hang there, suspended above the water for an eternal second, before crashing back down with a satisfying splash.

He bobbed to the surface and looked at the shore. Sally stood with her hands on her hips, smiling at him.

"Get in here!" he splashed the water with his hand invitingly.

"Is it cold?"

"No. It's perfect." He splashed the water again, smiling.

"Do you really want me to come in?" Teasing. Smiling. Pretty.

"Yes, I do. I dare you to come in."

"Oh, you dare me, huh?" Smiling. She stood with her hands on her hips for a second longer, long enough to resist, to make it her game, to make him want her to come in even more. She met his eyes and the sweetness turned to something… fiery. Something mischievous and challenging and exciting.

Her eyes stared into his for a second longer and he felt his heart beating, thumping loudly in the water, so loudly that it created ripples that glided away in perfectly synchronized concentricity. He gazed at her, willing her to come closer and wondering if she would. She stared at him again, more seriously, like she was agreeing to something that she had considered for a long time. She slowly kicked off her flip flops next to his. She unbuttoned her shorts and slid them off one leg, then kicked those off too. She fingered the hem of her t-shirt and pulled it slowly over her head. Her underwear was light blue and her bra had polka dots and she looked so lovely, uncovered, that it made him wonder why she ever wore clothes. She slid the hair tie out of her ponytail and the long blond hair cascaded over her shoulders. He loved her hair. Her gorgeous soft hair.

She walked to the water's edge and put a toe in, one little, pink-painted toe. She pulled it out slowly and stepped up on the dock. She walked out and suddenly dove off the side, arcing gracefully and hanging in the air so that he could see everything, her arms stretched out towards the water, her hair falling, her clinging bra, her thin stomach flexed, her toes curled in anticipation. She pierced the surface cleanly, sharply, with a much smaller splash than his, and he paddled over to the large O of bubbles. She tickled his foot as she swam back up, tracing her fingers delicately up his leg. She moved her hand up to his chest and he looked into her eyes, her pretty brown eyes, and they were coming closer to his face, slowly, until they were an inch away. He put out his hand (it moved so differently in the water) and found her, her soft naked hips, and he moved his hand hungrily up and down, feeling how soft and warm she was. Her eyes came closer and her lips met his with a question that his answered, and he pulled her closer to him into shallower water, and his toes clenched the silty ground and her legs wrapped around him and the bra floated away somewhere and her mouth tasted like cake and he pulled her closer, closer into him, and her fingers smoothed his wet hair until they made a fist and smacked him in the back of the head.

"What did you do that for?" he asked, dumbfounded. "That really hurt."

Her eyes glazed over and her voice became Victoria's. "Get up, we're making breakfast!"

He closed his eyes and, in doing so, opened them. Victoria's face was above his. "You've been asleep forever! Get up!" She kicked the side of his sleeping bag and moved on to her next target.

He put his hand over his forehead. He couldn't tell if the sweat was from his hands or his head. His entire body felt hot. Too hot. Of course it had been a dream. A wonderful, graphic, too-vivid-because-it-wasn't-coming-true dream. With a jolt he realized exactly how vivid it was, and felt grateful for the cover of the sleeping bag. He was conscious that Victoria was in the room, very loudly telling everyone to get up. He rolled away from her line of vision and stared at the ceiling and tried to think of something else. Anything else. Something ordinary and... clothed. He focused on the corner of the ceiling. Just an ordinary corner. Wood and a spider and some dust. Regular, real life things. Things that he could explain and control. The wall meets the ceiling and holds it up and makes a corner, a neat corner that you don't think about, and it doesn't drive you crazy and show up everywhere and... damn. Okay. Try harder. He put his hands behind his head and closed his eyes. This was going to be a very long day.

Chapter 3

Alex

He jolted awake as Victoria's voice screeched across the sleeping bags. He stifled a groan and stretched his legs, which were longer than the bed; his feet dangled uncomfortably off the edge of the trundle. One of his socks was missing.

"Get up! We're eating breakfast!" Her voice was too loud for morning, but food sounded good.

He checked his phone and grinned at his brother's first reply, sent at 1 a.m. "Thanks, dude. Miss you too. Don't let the parents get you down." Then a picture sent at 2:30: "check out my new friends - would save one for u if u were here miss uuuuu," before a picture of him with his arms around two pretty girls in tight Yankees tank tops.

He glanced up at Erik's arm dangling off the bed.

His parents were probably mad that he hadn't texted them good morning yet. "Just woke up, about to go swimming," he typed. He stared at it for a moment before changing "swimming" to "hiking." His mom always worried about him in water.

He looked at his phone screen, frowning. He could picture the scene perfectly: his parents perched on the couch, watching the recorded game from last night for the second time, rewinding to watch their oldest son secure yet another Yankees victory, both checking the clock as their youngest failed to assure him that he had made it safely through the night in an unfamiliar setting. Actually, they'd probably be annoyed that he just woke up. They'd been up for three hours.

"Just finished breakfast, about to play catch with Erik. Will go for a hike later." There. That sounded better.

His phone buzzed as he scoured the comforter for his missing sock. "Be careful air is thin up there don't hurt yourself." His dad's came a few seconds later: "We will have party for Alan when he comes home next week & U need to email family & friends with info & make sure U invite Mr. Ulm." Of course.

His knee twinged and he laid back down, biting his lip. It had been... ten months. Ten months of pain. His hands shook as he patted his knee gently, his catcher's knee that had squatted for hours a day since he was five years old, earned him a spot on one of the best college baseball teams in the country, and suddenly collapsed under him during his first college practice. Realizing that he'd been betrayed by his own body hurt more than the torn cartilage.

He would not think about that. He would not be bitter. He would support Erik and be proud of him and not be jealous. He would support Alan and be proud of him and not be jealous. He would help their parents and do what a good son was supposed to do.

He added the party email to his mental to-do list and waited for Erik to wake up.

Erik

Victoria's voice screeched and he groaned. "What?"

"Dude, wake up. We can't do anything if you're sleeping."

He reached for his watch before remembering that it was on the ground. "Alex."

"Yeah?" Alex's voice was groggy but cheerful.

"What time is it?"

"Uh, a little after nine."

"Jesus. I thought we were on vacation."

"She probably just wants to start hiking before it gets too hot."

"Yeah, but I'm the only one that's working out five hours a day. I should get to sleep more." He pulled his pillow over his face.

The hinges squeaked as Alex lifted himself from the trundle. "I'll come and get you when breakfast is ready. You stay here and sleep."

Thank God he had one friend that understood him. None of the others *got* it. It was hard to be Alan Chang's little brother. It was almost as hard as being Erik Armstrong III.

He groaned as he turned onto his side, feeling the soreness of his biceps permeate his entire arm. Yesterday morning his dad insisted that he add fifty pounds to his daily weight routine, and his arms felt like spaghetti. The first few days of new routines always sucked. He didn't doubt that his dad's methods would help him improve – they always did. He just wished that he didn't have to listen.

Most guys would kill to be him, he knew. He supposed it looked like a pretty sweet deal from the outside. Genetic athleticism. Birthday cards from Michael Jordan, Derek Jeter, and Bono. Easy access to the entourage of fawning actresses and models. The guy you call "dad" is a renowned philanthropist who could obviously afford to live anywhere but stays in a modest beach town to coach your baseball team and lead youth camps. What a guy.

If only they knew, he thought grimly. Most people were familiar with his father's public façade, the photogenic humanitarian image he'd so carefully cultivated. Very few had caught a glimpse of the thing that lived under the charitable veneer. His mom, obviously, who had a nervous breakdown when he was eleven and now lived in a "rejuvenation center" (a.k.a. rehab) in Arizona. His two ex-stepmoms, who had both graced the cover of *Vogue*. His newest stepmom, by far his favorite, the only one who treated him like a person instead of furniture. (She could do so much better. He hoped she'd stick around).

And Alex. His teammate from tee-ball to senior year, his fellow sufferer under the dictatorship of Dad the Coach. Alex, who at age five drew the notice of his dad because his nine-year-old brother was already throwing shutouts in Little League.

He remembered standing behind the backstop with his dad, watching young Alan Chang's already signature delivery: the misleadingly slow knee lift, the left hand that seemed to come out of nowhere, the naturally perfect motion that minimized energy output and already allowed him to throw the complete games that would catapult him to Yankees stardom.

His dad looked down at him. "That's Alex's brother?"

"Yep." His hat was too big for him and kept falling down over his eyes. "Are you gonna coach him?"

"Oh, I'll do more than that. I'm going to make him a champion."

And he had, taking Alan under his wing and molding him into one of the greatest pitchers to ever hail from southern California. Though he was coaching Erik's teams, serving as

League president, and leading his summer/winter youth camps, mentoring Alan Chang was always his priority. Alan always came first. Alan got more Christmas presents. Alan got more time with Best Behavior Dad. He skyrocketed through club and high school baseball, signed with the Yankees the day after graduating, and shot through the organization in one summer. In a desperate move that was now considered one of the greatest moments in twenty-first century sports history, the Yankees manager put the nineteen-year-old on the mound with no outs and the bases loaded in the bottom of the ninth, the Yankees one shaky run ahead of the Red Sox. Alan struck out the side and became a legend in one night. He became a household name when the media learned that his beloved coach was none other than the legendary Erik Armstrong, and for the first time, Little Cottonwood made the national news.

He sat up gingerly, feeling his sore ribs groan. The bunk bed creaked as he hauled his considerable weight down the ladder. No one knew how much his dad's workout plans hurt the next day... except maybe Alex, of course.

Josh

"Morning, Erik!"

Erik blinked at the brightness of the kitchen and pulled himself onto a barstool, which looked comically small under him. "What are we having for breakfast?"

"I'm thinking bacon, eggs, and French toast. Sound good?"

"What kind of eggs?"

"Scrambled eggs. I make amazing scrambled eggs."

Erik wrinkled his nose. "I want fried eggs."

"No problem. One fried egg, coming up."

Alex stumbled into the kitchen. His hair looked like he'd slept on one side all night, and his face looked like he barely slept at all.

"Good morning, Alex! How'd ya sleep?"

"Fine!" he said cheerfully. "Do you need help?"

"No, I got it, but thanks. This won't be ready for fifteen minutes, if you want to go take a shower."

"Oh. Okay. Yeah." Alex shuffled down the hallway. Josh heard Victoria's laughter and her shrill "Alex! Why are you so tired?" and Sam's voice making some response. Victoria cackled and burst into the kitchen.

"This guy sleeps so hard! I had to yell at him like ten times before he finally woke up!"

"I was having a crazy dream!" He brushed his hair out of his eyes. They did look unusually tired.

"What was it? You have the funniest dreams," said Victoria.

"I was... at school. I was chasing... a leprechaun." Erik laughed.

"That's it? Your dreams are usually so vivid!"

"Uh... oh yeah, there was a shark and a ... prostitute. A shark prostitute."

Victoria's laugh echoed around the kitchen. "Oh my God. You crack me up."

"Was the shark on land?" asked Josh.

"No, it was in water. I think I was scuba diving or something."

"Then why were you chasing a leprechaun?" Victoria asked insistently.

Sam picked up the box of cereal and imitated a high falsetto. "Because he was after me Lucky Charms!" He looked directly at Josh as he laughed and Josh was relieved that he didn't look mad at all – maybe he'd already forgotten last night's awkward moment.

Sam stretched his arms and yawned widely. "Where should I brush my teeth?"

"In the same place where we brushed our teeth last night!" said Victoria. "God, you're dumb sometimes."

"Hey! That's – yeah, you're right." He grinned sheepishly.

"I think Alex is getting in the shower now, but you can still brush your teeth in there," said Josh. He remembered seeing a shower curtain, not a glass door. If he was the one in the shower, he wouldn't care if Sam came in and brushed his teeth. Or anyone, really. Especially the girls.

Sally

The door didn't lock. The cabin was old enough to have hosted several family vacations with the tribe of cousins slamming

64

doors and locking each other in rooms and cupboards. She tried turning it but it slid back each time, too loose to stick in the door frame. Hmm. Well, a closed door was obvious enough, right? She wouldn't just open a closed door in someone else's house. That was just common courtesy.

She slipped off her shoes and peeled off her sweaty clothes. Ew. That was definitely the worst part about running. Sometimes you really, really smelled. She folded them neatly and set them down out of the splash zone. There. Slightly better.

The curtain was a little stiff, but other than that the shower was fine. She smiled at the array of shampoo and conditioner bottles, so colorful and girly. She almost missed sharing a bathroom with fifty girls, each laden with her own combination of beauty products and matching towels. Living with girls was comforting; they reminded her that she wasn't alone in her insecurities and her neuroses.

She noted that the tub was pretty clean – oh God, there was a spider. An innocent daddy long legs that probably ate mosquitoes, but still, it was a spider. It lingered in the corner of the shower and it didn't look like it would jump onto her head (or worse, her uncovered body) but she really, really didn't want to be in there with a spider. She fumbled with the rusty faucet. The stopper was a little stuck, but after a few moments she heard a satisfying pop and felt the inch of water around her feet disappear down the drain. She pulled the little thing on the top of the faucet (was there a name for it?) and a deluge of freezing water sprayed her in the face. She gasped and jumped into the corner under the spider. Unfamiliar showers could be such tricky things. Unfamiliar showers with spiders lurking in them were downright ghastly.

Her little freak-outs were embarrassing even when she was by herself. Victoria loved making fun of her for that.

The water finally reached a tolerable temperature and she scooted gratefully out of the spider corner. The cone of water felt somehow cleaner than the water at home, almost like it came directly from the lake.

She closed her eyes and let the hot water pour over her, washing away the sweat of a productive workout. It really had been a great run, she thought. Her muscles ached in a good way, the way they did when she really, really pushed herself. Their hometown wasn't too hilly and she'd missed the challenging trails that wrapped around Stanford. Running in college was so much lonelier than in high school. She supposed she could have asked around for a partner, but she didn't think she'd find anyone as willing to get up at 6:30 as Sam had been. The five miles were the most important part of her morning routine; she got to start out the day competing against herself, trying to beat yesterday's time. In the beginning of the year the five miles took her a little less than 34 minutes, but she worked hard and trimmed it down until a triumphant morning in February when she ran it in 29:55, her best time yet. That felt wonderful.

She did miss running on a team, though. Despite the drudgery of high school sports politics, cross country had become an integral part of her life, and she missed competing.

Of course, she'd also loved cross country so much because Sam ran cross country. They spent four years enjoying practices and meets and seven-mile-days together. Some days they ran seriously and raced each other (she won too often and suspected that he let her win); most days they ran hard for the first half and spent the second half jogging and talking. She usually tried to keep a pace to beat her previous time, but he always protested. He was very good at persuading her and she smiled as she remembered his excuses: he had a pulled muscle (he kept her in stitches laughing as he invented names for obscure muscles), his shoes were suddenly too small, he was suddenly overcome by symptoms of a mysterious illness that could only be cured by a kiss. The second half of the run was always her favorite part of practice. Sometimes she let him hold her hand and they just walked together, picking up the pace when they heard a fellow runner approaching. It was always fun to pretend to have been running the whole time, and they often staged exaggerated conversations when the other runner was in earshot. Everyone knew what they were doing, of course, but everyone enjoyed it. Sam just made them laugh, and they loved him for it, so they loved her too.

It took her a moment to realize over the sound of the screeching pipes, but it sounded like the door opened. She stood with the water pouring over her, her thoughts returning hazily back to the present – wait, the door opened?

"Hello?" she whispered. Her voice cracked on the second syllable. She cleared her throat. "Hello?" she asked, more assertively, like someone who should not be interrupted in the shower.

It was silent, and for a moment she was sure that she had imagined it. Of course she did. Her imagination was like a hamster on crack, running in an endless wheel and churning out extraneous possibilities and hypothetical situations that never actually manifested.

She suddenly felt very conscious that she was naked, and that there might possibly be another person in the same room as her while she was naked. There were six other people in the cabin, so technically it was only one-in-six odds, and that came out to – a little more than fifteen, sixteen percent? – chance that it was him. But why would it necessarily be him? He wasn't the type to peep, and he definitely wouldn't want to look at her. None of the guys would. Even Josh, the most concupiscent of all of them, couldn't possibly be desperate enough to want to see her naked. And Victoria was here, so she felt and probably looked very ugly and fat in comparison.

She should know if someone was in there, though. What if a psychotic axe-wielding lumberjack was roaming through the woods, invading cabins and killing everyone inside and he'd already killed all her friends and she was next?

That would suck. They'd wasted their entire lives in school.

She really ought to look. Although if it was a mad axe-murderer, what would be the point of seeing him? It wasn't like she'd have a chance to identify him later. Spider-filled showers weren't exactly the best defense against homicidal maniacs.

Of course it wasn't an axe-murderer. Silly brain. But who was it?

She moved the shower curtain just in time to see the door close.

Well, that answered one question. At least she wasn't crazy.

Sam

He didn't bother to knock because he doubted that Alex would hear it. He just opened the door and went right in like it was his own house.

The mirror was slightly steamed over and he wiped a palm diagonally across it, watching the water bead back into place.

Alex's clothes were piled in the corner. Tennis shoes and – wait. Wait wait wait. Those were not Alex's Nikes. They were way too small and too familiar to be Alex's. They stood neatly next to a folded pile of tiny familiar shorts and a tiny familiar t-shirt and a pink sports bra and pink underwear.

Those were definitely not Alex's.

He'd assumed she was still on her run but she was obviously back. She was obviously in this same little bathroom with him. And, most importantly, she was very close to him, and obviously very naked.

Should he take this opportunity to confront her? She'd been avoiding him so much – not just during this trip, but during the past few months. He deserved to know why. She loved him, he knew. He loved her and she loved him and that was a simple truth of life. And now... she sure didn't act like she loved him.

But she had once, and that was the important thing. She had once and she probably still did, she just needed to be reminded of that.

This might be his only opportunity to demand answers. She was here, and she had no escape. Sally would do whatever she could to avoid confrontation, but she would not be naked in front of him for that. Modest, proper Sally would die before running in front of her friends naked, and probably before being naked in front of him, at least now.

He wondered if she realized that he was there. He should probably do something. Standing there silently was weird, but it was also comforting, in a way. He missed being close to her. He missed the smell of her. He missed holding her.

He missed her. He missed her and he wanted to know why he had to miss her, why he couldn't just have her again. He knew he'd probably messed up in some way, but he deserved to know why. He at least deserved that much. She owed it to him to be honest, to tell him why everything had broken so suddenly.

68

Confronting her wasn't fair. If he confronted her right now she'd think that he… what? Waited for her to get in the shower and followed her in there? That was creepy. That was creepy and weird and seemed really manipulative and douchy. She didn't like being backed into corners; it made her scared. She needed space to think and make decisions.

He'd believed that in the fall, though, hadn't he? He thought he was giving her space. He thought he was being a good boyfriend and respecting her privacy, letting her retreat into her little world. He wanted her to enjoy college and not feel tied down by the boyfriend back home. Had he given her too much space? Had he been too flexible and easy-going? If he had demanded answers in the beginning would he be in this position now, ten months later?

He opened his mouth. He shut his mouth.

He needed to tell her. She would be happy for him, wouldn't she? He'd always felt slight disapproval emanating from her at what she considered to be a lack of ambition. He knew that it sometimes bothered her that he wasn't nearly as driven as she was, and now he'd done something truly, uncharacteristically ambitious, for her. She was all he'd thought of when he submitted his animation sample to Pixar, not daring to believe that he had a chance, and now he did. They offered him a starting salary and everything. He could live less than an hour away from Stanford. She needed to know. He wasn't going to uproot his whole life and move to northern California to be near her if she didn't want to be with him. He didn't care about the job that much. He cared about her so, so much more. She needed to know that. She needed to know that he'd changed.

No. Saying something now would be a mistake, but he would have to say something soon. He owed it to both of them to say something before the weekend was over. He would not drive down this mountain without answers.

He realized that was why he was so interested in this camping trip. If he couldn't get the answers out of her this weekend, when they were isolated and alone, he never would. This was the first time – hell, it might be the last time if he messed this up – that they were together and nearly alone. On top of a mountain was about as far removed from normal society as you could get.

This was his chance. This weekend was his chance. But he would not waste his chance in the bathroom and freak her out. You don't play your ace the minute you were dealt it, right? You hold it in your hand and wait for the right opportunity. He'd get her alone somehow and demand the truth. Or maybe he'd confront her in front of the group? She couldn't ignore five friends at once.

Maybe he could get Victoria to help him out. Victoria was the most demanding, persistent person he knew. Victoria couldn't stand not knowing something. It drove her crazy.

Okay, that might work. Or maybe he should do it himself; that would seem more natural.

There would be an opportunity later, he told himself. He'd make his own opportunity. He made his moments happen.

He glanced at the shower curtain. He couldn't see anything.

She was there and she was naked.

He was suddenly aware of how warm the bathroom was. She always took overly hot showers after running; it relaxed her. She used to take twenty-minute showers that were "better than therapy." She'd never been to therapy, as far as he knew. He hoped she hadn't needed to go.

He loved being at her house when she got out of the shower. She always took her clothes into the bathroom, which he found adorably modest. He'd play with her sisters or chat with her dad while she took her never-ending showers, and she'd come out with damp hair and lean against him and leave a little wet spot on his shoulder.

She might be getting out of the shower soon. He didn't know how long he'd been in there.

He opened the door, feeling the rush of cool air against his face, and closed it quietly behind him.

Victoria

Victoria settled back onto the barstool like it was a throne and sprawled her legs on the counter.

"Josh! When will the eggs be ready?"

"About..." he moved the spatula slowly through the yellow puddle in the pan. "Six, seven minutes? There's a lot of eggs here."

"Okay. Erik, where's the phonebook?"

Erik stopped with his hand halfway in the licorice bucket. "The what?"

"The. Phone. Book."

"Why do you need that?"

She inhaled deeply. He really tried her patience. "We need to call the rental places and find the rates for stuff."

"Oh." She waited for him to respond. He was maddening.

Boys annoyed her. Girls annoyed her. She should have been a cat.

"Do you know where the phone book is?"

"No. But there's a folder with phone numbers of places around the lake."

"Okay. Where's the folder?"

"Um…" he dug his hand deeper into the licorice, his long grubby fingers groping too many strands before finally selecting one. Ugh. She felt sorry for his future girlfriend, if there ever would be such an unfortunate girl. He bit off the tip ferociously. Disgusting. "In the drawer next to the silverware."

"Where's that?" She wanted to scream.

He pointed vaguely. She marched over to the drawer and pulled out a large stack of delivery menus and receipts – aha, a new blue folder, evidently recently replaced. Post-Its at the top separated the paper-clipped stacks into "summer" and "winter."

She pulled out the thick "summer" stack and flipped through the pages. Jet skis would be awesome but that was way out of their budget… zip-lining, ditto…. Here we go, kayaking and pontoon boats. Ooh, paddle boarding! But she'd tried that too many times already, and she wasn't very good.

"Josh! Gimme your phone."

"It's in the bedroom, charging."

"Ugh, you suck. Erik, give me your phone."

"It's off. Why can't you use yours?"

"I don't want to go get it."

Sam walked into the room carrying his toothbrush.

"Sam, give me your phone."

"What?" he looked at her blankly. What was wrong with everyone today?

"Your phone?" she asked. God, boys could be stupid sometimes.

"Oh. Yeah. Here." He handed it to her.

Josh glanced at him. "You okay man?"

"Yep. Just tired."

Wusses. Victoria grabbed the phone and quickly dialed the first number. "Cam's Water Rentals" didn't have a very promising flyer, but why not try it.

After three long rings, she was ready to hang up, but an eager voice answered. "Cam's."

"How much is it to rent a kayak?"

"Well, we've got a whole range of selection to choose from, for different times. We've got the singles, those are real nice, most people take them for an hour--"

"Do you have seven available single kayaks?"

"Seven? No, we've only got five. But we do have some nice doubles, if you're interested."

"How many doubles do you have?"

"Three."

"What's the rate for those?"

"The doubles?"

Stupid people. "Yes."

"Well, let me get out my book here...." She heard pages flipping and wondered how the person that answered the phone and probably had this same exchange a hundred times a day could not remember such a simple detail. "The doubles run for twenty-five dollars an hour."

"And the singles?"

More pages flipping. "Fifteen dollars an hour."

"Can I reserve three double kayaks and a single kayak for this afternoon? Four o'clock?"

"Two doubles and a single?"

No. "No. THREE doubles and a single."

"For what time?"

Dear God. Were all mountain people like this? "Four."

"Let me look at the reservations chart for today...." She drummed her fingers on the countertop. "Yep, that fits in our schedule. You're lucky, we have a big party scheduled to come back in right at four!"

"That's convenient." She rolled her eyes.

"What name should the reservation be under?"

"Victoria."

"Alrighty, Victoria. We'll need one credit card for the deposit, so make sure that someone in your party brings one. The total comes to –"

"Ninety dollars." The line was silent except for the slow thumping of an old accounting-style calculator.

"Yep, ninety dollars." Ta freakin' da. Of course it was ninety dollars. She didn't have to get a 5 on the BC Calc test to calculate the price of kayaks.

"And how much is it to rent a pontoon boat for an hour?"

Pages flipping. Good Lord. "Seventy-five dollars, gas included."

"Okay, we'll take that instead. Four o'clock."

"Thank you, see you at four! Have a nice –" Victoria hung up before she had to listen to a slowly articulated attempt at customer service.

"Is breakfast ready?"

"The eggs and French toast are done, and I'm almost done with the bacon. Can someone set the table?"

"I will!" Sam said brightly. He sprang from his barstool and started opening cabinets.

"The plates are in that one," said Josh, gesturing with his spatula towards the cabinet over the sink. "And the placemats… Erik?" he looked at him expectantly.

Erik pointed at the cabinet next to the stove, making no effort to get up and help. Ugh. Fucking useless.

Alex

He locked the door but didn't bother to turn on the light. The small bathroom had a tiny window that let in just enough light that he could see it was a tiny bathroom. He folded his clean clothes carefully on the counter, avoiding getting his new Yankees shirt wet.

He showered as quickly as possible, not wanting to miss breakfast. Alan's team had a rest day between Seattle and Oakland, so he didn't have to worry about fielding parental texts all day. Alan would probably be hungover and sleep for the entire flight, then wake up in Oakland with his head clear and his golden arm intact. Everything was so easy for him.

Everything had always been easy for him, he thought as he stepped out of the shower. Life was easy for blessed athletes who also happened to be handsome and funny. Since age nine, their parents allowed Alan's entire life to revolve around baseball. He was exempt from doing chores that might hurt his arm. He never had to do dishes. His Asian parents weren't even as strict about Alan's academics, letting him take slightly easier classes to have more time to focus on baseball.

Following in Alan's wake was not easy – not that he ever complained about it. At age five he realized that he would forever be trailing his brother. Comparisons were inevitable. Maybe he wasn't as tall or as naturally talented, but what he lacked in inherent athleticism he could make up for in work ethic. He could be almost as amazing as Alan, just in a different way. He repeated that to himself over and over as they grew, determined to be known as more than just "Alan Chang's brother." Alan was more than happy to have an available catcher that was just as single-minded as he was. Every morning before school they marched to the park, Alex carrying the bucket of balls, Alan dragging the heavy bag with their mitts and the catcher's equipment. In the early days Alan's pitches knocked Alex over and he rolled on his back like a roly-poly. He missed the days of laughing hysterically with his brother when he was imprisoned by his own catcher's gear. Simpler times.

He never went easy on him, which Alex appreciated. Sure, the fastballs hurt his palm and he'd broken a few fingers, but that made him a better catcher and a better athlete. Alan possessed the combination of humble talent and patience that made him a natural coach, and he welcomed his little brother into the secret and subtle world of baseball. During those mornings at the park Alex became acquainted with every kind of pitch that circulated in their Little League. His best friend was the fastball because it was easiest to catch. He was seduced by the curve because it denied logic. Alan introduced him to screwballs and changeups and knuckleballs, each one more exotic than the last. They invented a few of their own, making up names for them: Zigzag, Chang-up, Cowboy. He became a better hitter as he learned to identify pitches as they left the pitcher's hand, and he was grateful for his brother's assistance.

But he was determined to beat his brother in something. Since Alan had little interest in school, Alex decided to apply his baseball work ethic to academics. After their games during the week Alan would usually eat, shower, and fill out his homework as quickly as possible before going to sleep, already thinking of the next game. Alex made sure to do his homework on the weekends so that he could devote more energy to making it perfect. If he was not at the park, he was at the kitchen table, poring over his math book. When their family went to Dodgers games (Mr. Armstrong always gave them tickets) he calculated batting averages and ERAs. He fell in love with the sheer statistics of baseball, which were more extensive than any other sport. When Alan made the varsity baseball team as a freshman (the first player to do so in fifteen years), Alex kept a record of his pitches, categorizing them by type, accuracy, and result. He studied Alan's pitch counts as meticulously as he studied for algebra, and proudly presented Alan with his conclusions.

At first Alan seemed to just be humoring his eleven-year-old brother's obsessive compilations, and the realization that his brother did not take him seriously stung horribly.

During a playoff game against Dos Pueblos, Cottonwood's renowned rival, Alex watched from the bleachers as Alan gave up three runs in a single inning, the first time he had ever done so. Alex carefully observed his release, taking note of which pitches weren't working. He watched the runners signaling to the batter between pitches. His heart sank as he saw his brother's disappointment in his uncharacteristic performance. Their dad, who usually hovered behind the backstop, bragging to everyone within earshot, left the field without saying a word to anyone. Alex watched Alan realizing this and felt a desperate need to help his brother.

Finally, the inning ended and Alan trotted back to the dugout, where Mr. Armstrong said something to him that Alex could not here. For the first time in his entire life Alan looked like he was going to cry during a baseball game.

Alex crept to the side of the dugout opposite the coach. "Hey, can you ask Alan to come over here?" he asked through the fence. The mesh was thick enough to hide the players, shielding them from vicious parents. Mr. Armstrong had a strict no-talking-to-parents-during-games policy.

"Uh, sure," said whoever it was. He waited for what felt like forever, feeling embarrassed and hoping that Mr. Armstrong wouldn't yell at him.

"Dude, you shouldn't be here," Alan whispered through the fence.

"I have to tell you something."

"What?"

"They know what you're throwing. Mix it up a little."

"I'm throwing what my catcher tells me to throw." Alan's voice was torn between loyalty to his team and his realization that it wasn't working.

"*I'm* your catcher," he said emphatically. "Next inning you're facing the two, three, four hitters. Number two hit a single off of your outside curve last time. Three bunted a fastball but only made it because of Jason's error. Four hit that line drive into left, with most of his weight on his front foot."

"Yeah, I remember." At least he sounded like he was listening now.

"You can do this. Slightly more outside, just enough to make Two swing because he thinks he can hit it. If he makes contact it won't go far. Three holds his hands high so throw it low. Four is impatient. Give him the changeup."

"No."

"What?" How could Alan not believe him?

"I'll give him the Chang-up."

Alex grinned and high-fived the mesh. "You got this."

"Thanks, dude." He could hear the smile in Alan's voice and he trotted back to his mom in the bleachers.

Cottonwood went down in six pitches and he leaned forward as he watched his brother run back out to the mound. He tossed a few warm-up pitches. The "4" on the scoreboard under "Cottonwood" didn't look much bigger than the "3" under "Visitors."

The number-two hitter stepped up, looking much more confident than he had in his previous appearance. He moved his front foot closer to the plate and stepped on the chalk as he swung at the first pitch, which just grazed the outside corner. The ball hit the very tip of his bat and dribbled slowly down the first-base line, where Zach the first baseman tagged him.

One out.

Alan glanced towards the bleachers and grinned slightly. Alex watched Three, a tall skinny kid, raise his hands way too high behind his head. Alan fired two fastballs at the bottom of the strike zone. His third pitch was chest-high but the kid's calculating bat dipped just above his knees.

Two outs.

The other side cheered frantically as their best and most imposing hitter stepped to the plate. James Crenshaw, a senior with a full ride to the University of Texas, who would face Alan four years later as a Ranger. Two hundred-fifty pounds of him stepped to the plate, the bat a toothpick in his hands. Alan fired a fastball low and outside, just kissing the corner. Crenshaw let it go, waiting for the home run ball that his team needed. Alan fired one in the same spot. Strike two. Crenshaw spat and took a small step back in the box, preparing for a "surprise" fastball high and inside, one of the famous Alan Chang seventy miles-per-hours that his coach had undoubtedly warned him about.

Alan leaned forward, squinting at his catcher's signals as if not understanding them. He held the ball on the small of his back, seemingly accidentally raising his pointer finger. Alex watched the subtle straightening of Crenshaw's back as he readied himself for the fastball. Alan went into his wind-up, limbs pumping quickly, and delivered the slowest pitch that Alex had ever seen him throw.

Crenshaw's powerful arms ripped through the air and halted as they realized their mistake. The end of his bat swung over the plate even as he restrained the knob in his hands, and Alex watched his eyes widen as the forty-five-miles-an-hour pitch sailed just under his bat and landed with a satisfying pop in Paul's glove.

The team swarmed the mound and for a moment Alex lost his brother in the sea of jerseys. Alan emerged from the milieu and pointed at the bleachers, smiling broadly as his teammates lifted him on their shoulders.

It was the best moment of Alex's entire life.

Grace

Grace perched on the edge of her chair and watched her friends. Josh stood manfully over the stove, towel flung over his shoulder like a chef in a movie. Victoria sat at the counter with her long legs crossed, flipping through papers and trying to control things. So official and pretty and scary and scowl-y. Erik sat next to her, looking bored and useless – although she was equally useless, right? Should she try to help cook something? But the kitchen was so small and she might get in the way. Maybe she should offer? Or was Josh almost done?

"You okay?" Sam's usually bright eyes looked a little darker than usual and she hoped it wasn't because of Sally.

"Yeah, just hungry." She glanced at the realtor paper he was doodling on and he held it out to her. The caricature of Josh wore a cartoon chef's hat, two hands gripping a gigantic pan that waited to catch the eggs he'd just tossed in mid-air. She grinned at the perfect likeness. He'd even captured Josh's same expression of concentration.

"Yeah, hurry up, Josh!"

"Hang on a minute..." Josh checked the bacon and turned off the stove triumphantly. "Done!"

Erik leapt up and began shoveling a huge pile of eggs onto his plate.

"Go ahead, Erik, it's not like there are seven of us or anything," said Victoria under her breath. Josh laughed.

He glanced at Grace. "Do you want to go get the others?"

She avoided looking him in the eye. "Sure."

She made her way down the hall. The bathroom door was closed. Should she knock? Or just say something? She needed to get their attention somehow, so she should knock, right?

She tapped the door lightly. "Um, breakfast is ready."

"Alright, I'll be there in a second." She was surprised to hear Sally's muffled voice instead of Alex's.

The bedroom door was shut as well and she tapped the door again. "Breakfast!"

Alex opened the door looking exhausted. He forced a smile. "Great."

She tried to smile reassuringly at him, to let him know that he wasn't the only one having a hard time. He grinned his sad little

Alex grin and she felt a rush of big-sisterly emotion for him. He'd had a rough year too, between his knee injury and his dog dying (why did dogs and youth sports careers both have an expiration date of fourteen years? terrible timing) and trying to please his unpleasable parents. Poor Alex, always trying to make other people happy, no matter how he felt ... he would always be straddling the rapidly diverging paths of baseball and academia, trying to be the best at both and keep his parents satisfied. At least he knew what he wanted to do with his life; Engineering was a much more respectable major than her Undeclared, right? Alex had his fingers in so many pies, but at least those pies were worthy investments. He could charge down every path of life with the knowledge that he belonged there and would succeed there.

And Grace ... Grace was caught between paths.

She liked too many things and disliked too few things. She lacked the confidence to do anything besides linger indecisively between disciplines, flipping over and over like a log in a storm-tossed river. First it was anthropology, then history, then bio, then psych... she was interested in everything and got good enough grades in everything, but she felt like there was something waiting for her, like when she started the right thing she would feel a blaze of passion and inspiration and know that this was what she wanted to do with her life.

So she took classes in everything and learned a lot of tremendously fascinating things and envisioned a thousand post-baccalaureate degrees and a million careers, but none of them struck the chord of passion that she'd been waiting to feel. She wanted to prove herself extraordinary while she still held the unique position of a college student before surrendering to the cold anonymity of adulthood. Her friends, she knew, were already on their way to conquering the world, leaving a sparkling trail of success, illuminated by their sheer love for what they were doing. Victoria's eyes lit up when she talked about med school and described the surgeries she'd observed during her volunteer work at the hospital. Sally could talk for hours about her favorite books. Grace was just mesmerized by learning and loved the simple act of opening her brain to absorb theories and facts and ideas. She loved traveling the world in a lecture and living vicariously through books. She loved it, but she loved learning about everything, not one specific thing, which was supposedly a good thing, right? But it just slowed her down by pushing her in every direction until she went nowhere. And she really, really wanted to go somewhere. So she waited. And she feared that she would always be waiting.

Sally

She put her sweaty, gross clothes in the plastic laundry bag she'd brought. She hoped they didn't stink up the room – that would be a little embarrassing. She tugged on the rusty window and eventually got it to open.

Her hair was still wet so she threw it in a bun, feeling the weight nestle more comfortably on top of her head. It felt strangely relaxing, today of all days, in this place of all places, where only nature could touch them.

She hung the towel carefully in the bathroom and secretly hoped that no one else would use it. She loved to share things with her friends but towels were not one of them.

The mirror still dripped with the silky beads of condensation so she opened the window in there, too. This one was even trickier to open, but she shoved it firmly and the screen slid open gratefully as the hot air trickled out. Even the bathroom had a nice view. Trees surrounded the house like watchful guard dogs, insulating the cabin with the best protection that nature could provide. There was a lake somewhere behind the trees, a large and lovely lake that she couldn't wait to see up close.

Today might be a very, very good day.

Josh

He put the last plate on the table and felt a little proud of himself. He missed the little slices of domestic happiness that he seldom enjoyed at home. On the rare and happy occasions when his dad was gone, he and his mom cooked together. Sunday breakfasts with her were an almost holy occasion. They carved cantaloupes into stars, dyed pancakes cheerful shades of pink and green, and coaxed eggs to the perfect level of fluffiness until they were so aesthetically pleasing he could probably convince chickens to eat them.

Moving across the country, away from his mom and sister, was the hardest thing he'd ever done. He offered several times to stay home and put himself through LCCC, but his mom was determined to send him to a four-year. Though Fordham wasn't his first choice, they'd given him a generous financial aid package and a work study option. He'd still be in debt for a while, just not as much as if he went to the other schools that accepted him. Sure, Fordham was a little less spirited than the schools he'd envisioned himself attending – he would have rather gone somewhere with a sportier atmosphere, like UCLA or Texas – but he was grateful to be in school at all. At least his frat exposed him to the same testosterone-fueled shenanigans he would have gotten from football culture.

He watched Erik shovel eggs into his mouth. God, Erik was so lucky and he had no idea. His dad may have been a bit of a hard-ass, but he couldn't be worse than his own dad, could he?

Erik was so, so lucky.

Erik

He grabbed the last piece of bacon and swallowed it in two mouthfuls. Since his stepmom went vegan, his house had less and less meat, which was really annoying. Now their fridge was just kale and quinoa and diet green tea crap. Terri did the grocery shopping (well, she made the list and their housekeeper went shopping) so she had control over everything. It never occurred to him to drive to the store himself.

Stepmom #2 (Heidi) was also vegan, but she was also super hot, and his dad's temper hovered just below boiling point in the terrifying months following their divorce. About three months after she left, he and his dad were packing up the high school field after practice. It was early January, not even real pre-season yet, but his dad started them out in a four-hour practice that had gone much more poorly than anticipated. Most of the guys were a little rusty, the Christmas lethargy still weighing them down. His dad kept his comments short but Erik could tell he was pissed. Clearly he was the only one who'd kept up with the weight routine and conditioning, which was pretty easy to do when you lived with the drill sergeant coach.

The field darkened in sections as his dad turned off the lights. The only illumination came from the single bulb of the snack shack, casting a sad glow on the empty dugout. Not a soul was in sight – typical. Everyone else left while he got to clean up. Alex always helped, but he got to leave early for an ortho appointment. He carried the bases into the giant equipment shed, stacking them on top of the last locker. The column wobbled and tipped over, sending the top two back into the pile of stuff. He cursed under his breath. He climbed into the shed, shifting past tees and bags of equipment. The stench of his own jersey blended with the stench of well-used gear and too many pairs of old cleats. It smelled like sweat and dirt and went on forever. Jesus, you could hide a body in here and no one would know.

He grunted as he leaned down to pick up the base. There was one, at least. The light disappeared as his dad appeared at the front of the shed.

"Here." He threw the catcher's gear at him and Erik fell against the Lite Flight.

"Shit, a warning would be nice." He pulled himself up and glared at his dad.

"Watch your mouth. You're just as bad as your lazy-ass teammates."

"At least I've been working out."

"Bullshit, that's expected. You're doing the minimum. You need to apply yourself." He tossed the bag of Wiffle balls and Erik grabbed it. "Oh, and you need to move your weights when we get home. Terri wants to redo the gym."

"Is she moving in now?" Not a surprise.

His dad smirked. "We're getting married."

"Gee, only three months after the last one? Must be a record for you." He regretted it the moment he said it. Sometimes he was able to just think it and not say it.

Dad turned to him. "Excuse me?" He lifted the bat in his hand just an inch, but it was enough.

He looked down. "Sorry. I didn't mean it."

The handle of the bat was tilting slowly upwards. "'I didn't mean it'? You don't mean what you say?"

He didn't say anything.

"Well, this is interesting." His voice was quiet, dangerous, like a lion before it pounces, savoring the anticipation of its prey knowing what's coming because it's happened a thousand times. Erik hadn't realized just how pissed his dad was about the bad practice until now. His arm flexed as the bat lifted and he watched the rippling muscles of an eight-time Gold Glove winner. "You don't mean what you say, so you're a liar. I won't have a fucking liar in my house. Terri's moving in. She's your new mom. You will respect her. You will not lie to her. You will respect me." He brought the bat down slowly and Erik flinched as it hit the Lite Flight machine. His dad backed out of the shed and he breathed a sigh of relief. That was better than he expected.

He turned to find the last base and the shed went completely dark. "Dad?" He waded his way back to the front, hearing – what was that? The padlock? "Dad?" He reached his hand out and banged on the door. "Can you open the door? I get it. I'm sorry."

"You can stay here until you're done lying."

"I'm not a liar, I won't lie anymore, I promise – "

"It's for your own good. I'm going home. And you'd better fucking call Terri 'Mom' next time you see her."

"Dad!" He banged on the door. Silence. "Please!" He banged some more. Nothing.

"Open the door!" He yelled, over and over, until the words didn't even sound like words anymore.

He sank down. Was his dad seriously not coming back? He'd done a lot of shit before, but this really sucked. His phone was in his bag in his dad's car. The field maintenance guys had shown up during their practice, saw that they were still going, and left. He knew the school security guy, but Raymond usually just drove around on his golf cart, headphones keeping him oblivious to anything that would require him to do something. No one else would just happen to walk by the baseball field at the back of the school at 8 p.m., and if they did, they definitely wouldn't have the key to the padlock.

His dad had to come back tonight, right? He was just trying to teach him a lesson. Typical. He'd probably show up in half an hour or something, all smiles. "Did you really think I was leaving you here all night? C'mon, dumbass, let's get out of here. "

His stomach growled horribly. After four hours of practice he would normally go home, eat his post-practice snack of three bananas and an egg sandwich, peel off the layers of his sodden uniform, wash away the grime of sweat and clay, and enjoy his standard dinner of two frozen lasagnas and a loaf of French bread before washing it all down with a thirty-two ounce Gatorade.

God, he was thirsty. Maybe thirstier than hungry, and that was saying something.

There had to be a water bottle or something in here, right? He felt along the floor of the shed, grabbing anything that felt plastic. Not water. Not water. Not water. Something familiar poked him and his fingers scrambled to pick up the sunflower seed. He shoved it in his mouth and ate the whole thing, the sharp edges of the seed sticking uncomfortably in his throat. It tasted like dirt.

He banged on the door again. Nothing. His knocks echoed, empty and unanswered.

His lungs felt weird, like they were weighing him down with water. Too bad he couldn't drink it.

He felt something wet on his face and realized with some surprise that it was dripping from his eye. Oh. A tear. He was crying. When was the last time he cried? He couldn't remember. He stuck his tongue out and licked the saltiness. It didn't make him any less thirsty.

Another one dripped down, and another, and then there was no stopping them. For the first time in years, he was actually crying. For the first time in his life, he didn't have to worry about his dad hearing him. He laid his head on his knees and tried to forget. Fiery anger battled with waves of sadness and finally exhaustion took over and, blessedly, drowned them both.

His head hit the ground, hard, and he gasped as sunlight burned into his pupils. "Wake up, faggot. Go home and shower. Then get your ass back here. First period starts in an hour." The keys jingled as his dad walked past the dugout, whistling.

Sam

Josh's bacon tasted even better than his stepdad's bacon. Dave had made him bacon and eggs at least once a week for as long as he could remember, and it was always delicious, but Josh's just *beasted* it, like so good that the pigs should have been thankful to donate their bodies to such a delicious cause. His mom's efforts to initiate them into her weird world of vegetarianism fell flat as her son and husband continued to champion meat for breakfast.

84

"Mom, if we weren't supposed to eat pigs, they wouldn't taste like this," he often reminded her.

This was Dave's cue. "Yeah, hon. Pigs *want* us to eat them."

She would roll her eyes and brandish her grapefruit at them. "*This* is breakfast food."

"*That* is rabbit food," he said, laughing as he dodged her hand. "Thanks for breakfast, Dave!"

"Always, bud!" He kissed his mom on the cheek and soared out the door, eager to get at least an hour of surfing in before heading to school. His board was already in his VW bus (bright yellow, stubbornly full of sand, always breaking down, his most prized possession) and he drove the six minutes it took to get to the beach, puttering along, singing to Jack Johnson. Twenty minutes after winning the bacon argument he was paddling out for the first waves of the day. He shouted good morning to the other 7 a.m. regulars: Jenna, an accountant during the week and a professional surf photographer on the weekends; Don, whose wife was his and Grace's second-grade teacher; Hazel, the awesome eighty-year-old who was one of the first women to surf Waimea Bay; Gerald, the seasoned veteran who had survived an encounter with a tiger shark and lost his hand but won infinite respect from anyone he told the story to (everyone).

He ducked under the first wall and paddled out. His St. Christopher necklace floated slightly away from his chest, guiding him towards the best waves. A pod of dolphins popped up about thirty feet away from him and he smiled as he watched the small curve of a baby's back breach, shiny black and gleaming against the blue-grey of the early morning water.

He cradled the necklace between his fingers as he sat up on his board, waiting for the next batch. He didn't mind lulls. There was something tremendously comforting about bobbing up and down gently, waiting for the waves the way you waited for a girl to get ready. Sometimes it took forever, but it was always worth it.

He drifted slightly out and felt the adrenaline kick in as the water churned under him. He paddled and lifted himself up as the wave unfurled, carrying him in before surrendering to the shore. He pulled out neatly and grinned, duck-diving under the shore break and popping up in one fluid motion. His necklace broke the surface before he did.

His thoughts turned, as they often did out here, to his dad. Not Dave – his real dad, the one that died when he was a baby. Sunny Whitaker, longboard champion, dead at thirty-two in a plane crash on his way to Maui to judge a contest. The morning of his flight he kissed his wife and left his necklace next to his youngest son's crib.

St. Christopher. Patron saint of surfers, protector of travelers, guardian of fatherless boys. As he turned it over in his hands he couldn't help but wonder – for the millionth time in his life – if his dad would still be alive if he hadn't left his necklace. Most of the time he was able to convince himself that he was just being superstitious, that it was so powerful for him because it connected him to his dad… but sometimes, like now, watching it drift in the water, glinting in the sunlight…now it seemed *real*. Compelling. Magical.

"Thanks, Dad," he whispered. Only the waves heard him.

Victoria

She smiled at Josh as he set her plate in front of her. She loved when guys could cook. She especially loved when they cooked her bacon.

She patted his hand in a friendly gesture but wished she hadn't when she saw Grace looking at her. She didn't know exactly what transpired between them since Christmas, but it couldn't have helped Grace much. The poor girl was already like a lost puppy. And who could blame her? Who could deal with what Grace experienced and come out the other end as a fully functioning, emotionally stable human being?

She hoped Grace didn't think that she was moving in on Josh. She loved him, of course, the way that you love your blissfully platonic male friends. She loved bantering with him and flirting with him, but that was all it was and all it ever would be. They were so similar in the easy ways that made their friendship a good one - they possessed the same quickness in conversation, the same sharpness that made their jokes hard and their jibes harder. They spoke the same dialect of sarcasm that other people rarely understood. She could hang out with him and talk for hours and it was so, so easy, and so, so refreshing to spend time with a male that didn't expect her to sleep with him.

But still, no boy from Cottonwood would ever be worthy of her affections. She wanted to earn an exotic trophy, not settle for a homegrown safety, even if that safety was one of her best friends. Her future boyfriend would be interesting and worldly and smarter than her. She smiled to herself. Smarter than her. What an idea. Too bad Josh wasn't smarter than her – if he were, he'd actually have a shot at being a contender for her affections. He was definitely smart, but his preferred conversation topics were always sports, sports, sports. Not exactly her cup of tea.

Josh was one of the best people she knew, she realized as she watched him serve their friends, grinning and goofy. His treatment of her – like she was as good as he was – was a further testament to how wonderful he was. Or perhaps how stupid he was, she smiled to herself. But Josh had a curious way of seeing past people's defenses and sliding easily under shaky, half-heartedly constructed fences. Their friendship was one that she treasured and feared because it mattered so much to her, yet she was terrified that if he learned the full truth about this past year he would hate her. He wouldn't hate her for what happened to her; he would hate her for not telling him sooner, for not admitting that she needed help, for not opening up to anyone. He would hate that she let herself get hurt even more. He would hate that she acknowledged her hypocrisy and didn't do anything about it –she was always the one to yell at them for being in denial, but her denial beat all. If she were to be completely honest with everyone here, they would be so disappointed in her for not confiding in them. She liked to pretend that she could handle everything, and they usually went along with her act, but she had a sneaking suspicion that even her friends could tell that sometimes she didn't.

She looked around at her friends from her seat at the head of the table and felt strangely affectionate. Erik and Alex ate like starving feral creatures, shoving bacon down their throat to be metabolized into more aesthetically-pleasing-but-obviously-off-limits muscles. Sally and Grace ate like girls, picking at their eggs and trimming off imaginary bits of fat. Sam ate hungrily but politely. Josh was still doing his thing in the kitchen, making sure that everyone else was satisfied before he even thought about feeding himself.

These were her friends. These were her people.

She'd always pictured her future self as a lone wolf traveling around the world, ensnaring romantic conquests and achieving her wildest and most ambitious goals. She didn't think that at nineteen she would be so dependent on other people; she pictured herself as an autonomous and untouchable force that occasionally flitted back home to show off her new feathers before flying away to her life that was much more exciting than theirs.

Berkeley was so much more exciting than Little Cottonwood could ever hope to be. It was on a different scale altogether. Cottonwood was just sand and flowers and mom-and-pop restaurants that closed by ten. Berkeley was alive and vibrant and hills and *excitement*. Berkeley was intellectual conversations and cheap, delicious Thai food and casually seeing the Golden Gate Bridge in the distance. That was definitely one of the most important things she'd learned during this topsy-turvy year, she thought. The higher the hill, the more rewarding the view.

She hadn't really thought about how ridiculous it was for her to expect her friends to remain at home waiting for her. Josh's choice of college on the east coast had seemed like a minor betrayal; she fully expected him to remain at home, obediently awaiting her return, eager to hear all about her own adventures without having very many of his own. She didn't want her friends to change. She wanted her friends to stay exactly the same, as she knew them and loved them, so that she could change as much as she wanted but always have one little familiar thing to return to. Until she'd gone to college she hadn't realized how much she depended on this. Like a wandering child fleeing from her mother in the grocery store, she wanted her friends to remain on the same aisle so that she was free to explore. But when she returned and her mother wasn't in exactly the same place (not that her mother ever took her places), she panicked.

"I'm still hungry," said Erik, wiping his mouth with his sleeve. Alex nodded as he checked his phone.

"Here, have some of mine," said Sally, sliding eggs onto his plate.

"Thank you for breakfast, Josh," said Grace quietly.

"So where are we going today?" asked Sam expectantly, tossing his hair out of his eyes.

Victoria smiled. Perhaps they hadn't changed that much.

Sam

Victoria stood up like she was in charge. Which she was.

"We're taking a boat out on the lake today. I made a reservation for us at four. It's about thirteen dollars each. We have a few hours to kill before then so we should go hiking or swimming. We might have time to go shopping or something, but I doubt we'll find anything here that we don't have at home."

"I don't want to go shopping." Erik was always one to speak for the guys.

"Well, we could go hiking for a few hours, then swim."

"Whatever you want to do is fine with me," Alex said breezily.

"We could always swim after boating," piped up Grace.

"It might be dark by then," pointed out Sally. She was always thinking. "How long is it?"

"Just an hour, so if these mountain people have their shit together and get us going on time, we'll be done around sunset. So we could swim after hiking, or after boating, or both. You're not scared of the dark, are you?" Everything had to be a challenge. Sometimes she was too competitive. She scared him sometimes. She was too hot and too loud. She even seemed taller than she was because she had such a huge, untouchable personality. But he liked that even at her most intimidating, she had a sense of humor, even though most of the time it was at someone else's expense.

"Woooo! It's gonna be awesome!" Sam hated when the group got too serious. He had to shake them up sometimes.

Victoria grinned. "So we have a plan for the day. Let's clean up and get going." And by that she meant other people would clean up while she complained that they were too slow.

Sally got up and started clearing the table. She picked his plate up without looking at him.

"Sally, you're so cute!" said Victoria. "You're going to be an amazing mom."

Victoria carried on talking to Josh but Sam barely noticed. On the word "mom," Sally almost dropped the stack of plates she was carrying. Josh inhaled sharply.

No one else seemed to notice Sally, but Josh looked at Grace concernedly. Victoria looked confused for a moment before her eyes widened in understanding. For the first time that he could remember, she looked embarrassed.

He glanced at Grace, who was staring down at the table. She didn't look like she was crying, at least.

Sally set the plates down and stood hunched over the sink, fists clenched like they did when she was her most stressed. Was she trying not to cry as well? He knew how much she cared about Grace, and he supposed that she'd been devastated. Was she this upset because she loved her friend that much? She was either way too emotional or a truly selfless person. He was still annoyed with her lack of contact, but softened a little at the sight of her pained shoulders. Apparently she was more vulnerable than he thought. And that meant he had to be very, very careful today.

Josh

Sally started clearing the plates. The V of her shirt – today's was blue – dipped down a little, and he tried to not stare, very conscious of Sam at the table. She was so lovely. So lovely and off-limits. She was too much of a friend, and Sam was also too much of a friend. He was content to sit and admire her in her loveliness and motherliness. Domesticity was as comfortable and fitting for Sally as her blue v-neck; it emphasized her femininity and her sweetness. She'd been a pretty girl but she was becoming a beautiful woman, and the fact that she was totally oblivious to this only made her more beautiful. It wasn't just the way that everything clung in the right places or the way her face lit up when she was excited; it was the genuine warmth and love that emanated from her. She was always playing mom to the group, and reigned supreme as the organizer of birthday parties and baker of cakes. Victoria was the planner and Sally made the plans happen, the person who remembered the little details and made sure that everyone was comfortable in her loving, fussy way. She was forever reminding them to bring a sweater, the one who always remembered their respective curfews when hanging out, the one who always printed out directions when they were traveling somewhere new. Parents loved her because they felt that their children were safe with her; a girl like Sally would never get anyone she cared about into trouble. His mom adored her and the two could talk for hours. He realized that she would be a fantastic mother one day.

"Sally, you're so cute!" said Victoria. "You're going to be an amazing mom."

Josh laughed because he was just thinking the same thing, but he immediately wished he hadn't. Victoria's eyes widened and she clapped a hand over her mouth. Sally and Grace froze. Then he remembered. Alex looked sad. Erik noticed nothing. Sam looked at Sally like she was going to break.

It was seven months later, but still. The day stood out vividly in his mind and he wished that he could forget it.

It was the Saturday before Christmas. The semester kids were finally home for winter break. He hadn't come home for Thanksgiving – airfare was so damn expensive, especially around the holidays – and he was looking forward to a long month at home. Four months was a long time to be away from home, and he was so excited to see his mom and his friends.

His plane had gotten in at 11 p.m. the night before, which was 2 a.m. New York time. His mom picked him up at the airport and he got to experience a solid hour of happiness before crashing. (His dad was gone that night, which made his homecoming even better). He eagerly fell into bed, anticipating a solid twelve hours of sleep, marveling at how comfortable his squishy mattress was compared to his dorm bed. His mom had changed his sheets the day before and vacuumed his room. Everything felt soft and warm and utterly wonderful. In the few seconds of consciousness before surrendering to the divine embrace of his bed, he looked around his room and was thankful to be home.

The next morning he awoke to his mom patting him awake. He felt disoriented for a few moments before he saw the look in her eyes. She already carried so many burdens, those of herself and of her children, but she looked even sadder than usual. Something had to be terribly, terribly wrong for her to look like that. He was afraid to ask.

"Is Jamie okay?"

"Your sister's fine, honey." She sat down on his bed, like she did when he was little and afraid of the dark or in need of a bedtime story. "It's Grace's mother."

"Mrs. Hastings? What's wrong? Should we go over?"

She held his hand and looked him in the eyes. He always appreciated how straightforward she was with him. She never kept the truth from him. Maybe it was because he took care of her so often that she felt he was worthy of bearing burdens. He was old enough to carry some of the load. She couldn't always be the grown-up.

The slight wrinkles in her forehead creased and her eyes welled up and her voice almost shook. "Honey, she died in her sleep. Sally just called. Grace is at her house. You should go over there."

He leapt out of bed. "Of course. Yeah. I'll be there in ten minutes."

"Take a shower first. I'll make you some toast."

"Okay. Right. Oh my God."

She kissed him on the forehead. "Grace is going to have a really hard time. She needs friends right now."

He wrapped his arms around her and realized that he was tearing up, too. "I love you, Mom."

"I love you too, honey. I'll make some food and bring it over later. And I'll go grocery shopping for paper plates and things… they won't want to worry about cleaning or things like that."

"Thanks, Mom," he muffled into her shoulder. She squeezed him one more time and gracefully ignored his tears.

That shower was one of the fastest of his life. He washed off the cloying staleness of travel as quickly as he could. Poor Grace. Her relationship with her family was a strained one at best, and this would make things even worse. She did not need this. She didn't deserve for this to happen. How could it? Her mom was only two or three years older than his mom, and she – God, he hated remembering that his mom would die one day. It was the worst knowledge in the world. His mom wasn't old enough to die. Grace's mom wasn't old enough to die. Grace's mom was too healthy to die. She worked out constantly and ate the minimal caloric diet of an Orange County soccer mom who also happened to be a scathingly brilliant attorney. Mrs. Hastings was too… aggressive to die, too quick. She barely ever sat down, much less look tired or sick.

He leapt out of the shower and threw on the summer clothes that his mom washed for him the day before. His toast was waiting in the kitchen and he wolfed it down as he raced to the car. It felt strange to sit in the driver's seat of a car after not driving for so long, but he didn't have time for sentimentality or contemplation. He threw it in gear and drove as fast as he dared to Grace's neighborhood. He noticed a few small changes to the familiar streets and they confused him even more. Later they would discuss how strange and unwelcome these changes were, as small as they seemed to the untrained eye: the new office supply store where the craft store used to be, the Catholic church was painted a different color, the trees had been removed from the planter in the center divider. The tiny shifts in the previously unchanging landscape were as strange and jarring as the reason for his errand, just as unwanted and threatening to the comfortable idea of home. Things weren't supposed to change here. Everything was supposed to be the same when you came home because it was home. Things weren't allowed to change. Parents weren't allowed to die. They were supposed to be there.

He pulled into Sally's blessedly unchanged driveway and ran to the door. Sam's car was already out front. Sally's mom answered immediately. Her eyes were puffy and she grabbed him in a hug.

"Thank you for coming, Josh. The girls will really appreciate it. And just before Christmas, when you guys are seeing each other for the first time… poor Grace. Poor girl."

He felt like he should say something, but his mouth was too dry and he just nodded. She understood.

"They're in Sally's room."

"Thank you, Mrs. Chandler." He entered their spotless foyer. Mr. Chandler was sitting at the kitchen counter, looking distraught. He was in his UGA shirt, nursing a Vitamin Water. Normally he looked young for a dad, but today his eyes looked heavy and tired.

"Hello, son. Good of you to come."

"Thank you." He walked the familiar route to Sally's room through their clean and beautiful house. This was so, so surreal. Sally's home was almost cliché in its picturesque existence and it felt jarringly wrong to feel immeasurable grief here. Bringing tragedy into this house seemed like a violation of some pure and wonderful force that other people aspired to possess. As long as he'd been a regular visitor he'd never heard her parents so much as raise their voices.

Sally's little sisters' softball mitts were lined next to their cleats and he realized how much Sally's house looked like the Cleavers' house in *Leave it to Beaver*. Except in *Leave it to Beaver*, no one's mom died.

Suddenly he realized that he had no idea what to say to Grace. What do you say when something like this happens to your friend? She experienced a loss that for him would be the worst thing in the entire world. She was an eighteen-year-old girl. She needed her mom as much as he needed his. Maybe even more. He hadn't seen her since summer, and their strained absence left things dissatisfying and unfinished. He hadn't even spoken to her. There were so new things to tell her, so many things left unsaid.... And now was not the time to say them. He had no idea what she thought of him. She might even hate him. But he knew, somehow, that he was the person she needed.

He approached Sally's closed door and knocked carefully. Sam opened it looking the most solemn that he had ever seen him. Josh walked in and was surprised by the scene before him.

He didn't know what he had expected. Total devastation? Grace screaming and crying or maybe hitting something? Grace in the throes of an emotional meltdown because life wasn't fair and someone was taken from her that shouldn't be taken from anyone? He was prepared for tears and screams, but not silence. Tears and screams were natural but her silence was terrifying.

She was sitting curled up on Sally's bed, her face a blank mask. She looked terrible. He'd never seen her so... emotionless. Her catatonic body contorted into itself, arms wrapped tightly around legs, fingers clenching around her knees until they went white. Sally perched next to her, ready to be needed. She looked like she'd spent the entire morning crying, but her grief mingled with confusion at her friend's lack of emotions. She looked at Josh desperately and he realized how hard this was for her. Her instincts told her to hug and cuddle and wipe away the tears, but Grace had no tears for her. She was ready to comfort but Grace gave her no opportunity to. So Sally sat on the bed, desperate and confused, waiting for Grace to snap out of it.

Sam returned to Sally's desk chair, watching the girls with concern. This was not his area of expertise and it clearly made him uncomfortable. This was not a time for jokes or silliness. He rarely looked awkward but he looked awkward now. All he could do was be there for Grace (and Sally), but Josh appreciated his presence nonetheless.

Grace did not acknowledge him when he walked in the room. She continued staring blankly ahead. He sat down slowly on the bed next to her. Sally looked at him desperately, wordlessly begging him to do something. Grace sat like a statue between them, silent and rigid.

A thousand words darted through his mind and they all seemed like the wrong thing to say. Nothing seemed appropriate. Everything just felt wrong and he wished that he could find the words to say how sorry he was.

He did the only thing that seemed right. He wrapped his arms around her and hugged her tightly. She felt stiff and cold and for few minutes she ignored his presence, and he could feel the knots of tension tightening in her neck. He just held onto her and she didn't try to push him away.

Suddenly she seemed to deflate in his arms, and the emotions that she'd been holding back erupted. He held her more tightly and rocked her back and forth as she wailed into his chest, sobbing horribly, crying like he had never seen her cry. Watching her break down was heart-wrenching, but in a strange way it was a relief to see her acting like a human instead of an emotionless statue. He rubbed her back the way his mom rubbed his when he cried. She crumbled completely and a flood of tears soaked his shirt, waves of grief crashing into him. Sally hugged her and made her little comforting mom noises.

They held her for a long time. Josh rubbed and rocked and Grace wept and whimpered and Sally held and hummed. They just let her cry. The tears unfurled in great waves and Josh imagined her rapidly emptying tear ducts scurrying to collect more water to spill out. The levees that she guarded herself behind could not stay standing and they deteriorated under the furious deluge of grief.

He had no idea how long they sat like that, the three of them entwined on the bed and Sam waiting patiently in the chair. The line of the sun crept from his edge of the bed onto Grace and it could have easily been an hour.

Finally, her stream of tears trickled out and she deflated again. He let go of her and let her curl up on the bed. She closed her eyes and the terrible silence returned.

Sally spoke first. "Do you want to talk?"

Grace's puffy face went blank again.

"No."

"Do you want some tea? Or water? Or food?" In Sally's world a cup of tea made everything better. Josh usually appreciated her old-fashionedness, but he doubted that her favorite remedy would provide much comfort in this situation. This wasn't a rainy day and Grace didn't have a head cold.

"Water."

"You're probably dehydrated from crying so much." He hadn't meant it as a joke, but Sally and Sam laughed and even Grace smiled a little.

"Good point."

"I'll be right back." Sally, grateful for the chance to play hostess, dashed to the kitchen.

Grace sat up and pulled her legs towards her. Her face was so puffy but she still looked pretty. Pretty and utterly broken.

"Sorry about that."

"I'm sure your mom would be okay with you crying over her." He wasn't quite sure about that. As long as he'd known Grace's mom, she'd rather shown any emotion besides displeasure or competitiveness. He was a little bit afraid of her and she always made him appreciate his mom a little more. God, what a weird thought. He felt even worse for Grace than he already did. Her mom had never taught her how to love properly, and not being able to love the person that deserved all the love in the world... he couldn't imagine what that would be like.

Sally returned with a large glass of water and Grace gulped it down. They waited for her to finish and he wondered which of his million questions he should ask first. Where were her dad and her brother? When did it happen? And the question that seemed most important: How did it happen? Athletic forty-five year-old women did not drop simply dead for no apparent reason. Mrs. Hastings embodied physical perfection. She looked at least ten years younger than she was. She'd completed three marathons. She was tall and confident and energetic and, as he last remembered her, very much alive.

The door opened and Victoria burst in wearing her very tight yoga pants. In any other situation Josh would have paid more attention to them. Her beautiful face registered more confusion than sympathy.

"Grace, what the hell happened? Your mom? How?"

Sally inhaled sharply. Direct demands for difficult answers were not part of the comforting process.

Grace looked down at her hands. It was a very pregnant pause. Josh noticed that Sally and Sam leaned forward curiously and he realized that they too were uninformed. Scenarios dashed through his mind, each one more improbable than the next. Accidental overdose? A fall down the long staircase of the Hastings house? A fire that Grace somehow escaped? Something truly awful and unthinkable - murder?

"She just... didn't wake up."

Victoria looked hungrily inquisitive. She hated not knowing something, especially when the answer was most likely a biological one. "Do you... want to talk about it?"

Sally briefly glared at Victoria and Josh knew she was annoyed that she was pushing Grace. At the same time he was intrigued and wanted to know.

"Last night was... was normal." Grace looked down at her hands. "Max fell asleep early. Dad went to bed. She went to bed. I went to bed. And then I woke up... it was so weird. So quiet. I went downstairs. It was already 8 and her car was still at home, so I went to – to ask her if I should go get the groceries – and I went in her room and she – she was just lying there."

The silence weighed down on them. Sally sniffled and wiped away a tear. Sam shifted uncomfortably. Grace seemed to sink down further into the bed like she hoped it would swallow her. She looked so ... fragile. Without thinking Josh wrapped his arms around her.

They were still for a long time.

Finally Victoria broke the silence. "So you... called 911?"

"Yes." Grace's voice was barely a whisper. "And they came. And they said she was – but I already knew. As soon as I saw her."

"But your mom is – was – so healthy. She's, like, perfect."

Grace gurgled a surprising laugh. "She'd be glad that you said that. That was the only word that she'd ever want to describe her."

"Did they say what happened?"

Josh saw Sally's eyes narrow and he thought she might slap Victoria. She was so, so pushy. Even now.

Grace was very, very quiet and he felt her tense up. "No. They took her to – to figure out why. Why it happened." She was shaking.

Victoria was still standing, hands on hips. Josh felt half exasperated, half amused. She just couldn't stand not knowing the answer. Science was the only thing she believed in and it was letting her down.

She sighed and finally softened. "I'm sorry, babe. This is just... crazy."

"We're here for you." Sally was back in mom mode.

"We all are," Victoria assured her. She looked around the room. "Where the hell are Alex and Erik?"

"They're working his dad's camp today, remember?" She shrugged.

Sally shook her head. "Those boys... baseball is the closest thing they have to religion." Josh chuckled. It felt so weird to laugh. Grace even almost smiled. He tried to put his arm around her but she shifted away from him, a tiny, almost imperceptible inch. He wanted so badly to close the gap, to have her back in his arms, to let her know that her friends cared about her and he cared about her and he'd hold onto her as long as he needed to. But he also knew that Grace needed space, even if it was just an inch.

The guilt of ignoring her had steadily crept up on him and now it seemed like a horrible, horrible crime. They'd never communicated so little as they had the past few months. She had to realize that he was making new friends and having new experiences without her. He knew he'd failed to call her back and reciprocate her efforts to keep her best friend in her life, but he'd assumed that their friendship would remain just as strong anyways. They had years of memories together – surely those counted for something, right? Surely he could return home and they'd bounce back together, back to normal.

Her puffy eyes were still closed but he scooted his hand towards hers and offered his palm. He could give her that much, at least.

He hoped it would be enough.

Grace

"You're going to be an amazing mom!"

Of course Sally would be an amazing mom, Grace thought. She was the mother of the group. She felt more like Grace's mother than Grace's mother ever had. She'd been taking care of Grace since elementary school. She was the one that made Grace feel loved.

She suddenly realized that it was very, very quiet. Everyone was being so awkward. They all seemed to be averting their eyes from her and she didn't know why – oh. Of course. She was the girl whose mom had died and they all thought that they couldn't say "mom" in front of her.

She felt bad for making them feel awkward. It wasn't their fault –

But it was, actually. It totally was. It hadn't even occurred to her to be upset by the word "mom" just now. Maybe seven months ago she would have been sensitive to it but wasn't she supposed to be moving on? Wasn't that what normal people do? Move on from things and not be dragged down all the time?

Friends were supposed to help friends move on. They were supposed to encourage them, not constantly remind them.

Anger welled up inside of her and caustic words swam bitterly in her head. These were her friends. They weren't supposed to make her feel like – like The Girl Whose Mom Died. It was seven months ago, for God's sake. Were they always going to treat her like this? Like she was so freaking delicate that they couldn't use a common word around her? Victoria couldn't give Sally a compliment? Like they had to avoid certain conversation topics because they had moms and she didn't? Was it always going to be like this? She really, really hoped not.

Their reaction was precisely the reason why she hadn't confided in anyone at school. Winter break was a few weeks long, and she'd decided that it was enough time for her to pull herself together. She wouldn't be That Girl at school. Cornell was supposed to be a fresh start for her. It was on the other side of the country. She was supposed to leave all of her insecurities at home and find herself at school. She thought she was doing okay. She made friends and tried to like her classes. She explored Ithaca and felt like Alice exploring Wonderland, unearthing new, fantastical treasures and sights that southern Californians couldn't imagine, like real apple picking and beautiful foliage and actual seasons.

She was doing so well and then December came and everything went crashing down.

So she went back to school and kept her mouth shut. When people asked how her break was she responded "fine" and changed the subject. She tried to keep going. She stopped talking to her home friends less and less because they always wanted to know how she was doing and she didn't want to have to think about that. When she felt like being social, she spent time with her few new friends. In the many more instances where she did not feel like being social, she spent time by herself. She drifted. She often wished that she could be like Sally, who would undoubtedly channel this into academics and working out and making herself better. It was just so hard to push herself when she felt like doing nothing. She didn't want to think or work or go anywhere. She just wanted to curl up on her bed and not have to think about anything. Occasionally she got the beautiful dreamless nap, but her nights were mostly full of restless tossing and half-remembered dreams that she woke from trembling.

Sometimes it was a relief to feel fear. She'd stopped feeling during the day and she worried that her ability to feel emotion was turning in on itself and imploding in a silent bid for self-destruction.

She wandered between classes stuffed in a giant jacket that usually failed to keep her warm. The New York winters were brutal but their numbing quality seemed fitting for what she was (well, wasn't) feeling. While her classmates complained about not being able to feel their noses and fingertips she rejoiced in the stiffening cold. She fantasized about being cryogenically frozen and not having to deal with anything. It seemed so ideal, the notion of staying in one place and time stopping for you so that you could take a nap and not have to answer questions or phone calls or messages. You could just sleep in your little icy palace and let the world pass you by until you were ready to face it.

So she stopped answering Sally's daily phone call. She ignored Victoria's emails (always sent after midnight), Sam's random YouTube links that were clearly an effort to make her laugh. Alex offered Yankees tickets and suggested that she meet up with Josh, an invitation that she always declined. She appreciated their efforts but they just made her remember more and it took so, so much energy to pretend to be happy. She loved her friends so much and she didn't want them to be sad. If they knew how empty and numb she was they would be heartbroken and she just couldn't summon the energy to make more people unhappy when she couldn't articulate everything to herself. She just let the attempts to reach out slide past her like snowflakes and they drifted to the ground, accumulating in a forgotten pile until they melted. She felt bad for letting such lovely things go to waste but it was for their own good, really. If they could even imagine the thoughts that went through her head in the middle of the night… it wasn't fair to burden them. They all had lives, and school, and friends, and more worthy things to occupy their time with than their friend who knew that something was terribly wrong with herself and didn't want to confront it.

It wasn't just her mom dying. That was the most obvious cause of her – whatever she was feeling, or not feeling, but that certainly wasn't all of it. Or maybe it was and it had catalyzed all the other bad things, all the creeping insecurities that lurked in her mind and made her want to forget. Her Alice tale was going backwards and everything was spiraling out of control and she was falling down a hole that would never end.

Her mom would be so ashamed of her, the apathetic blob that was once her daughter and now drowned in her own tears. Of course she'd probably never actually been proud of her; that much Grace knew for sure. But if she could see her now, this listless, exhausted, broken creature, she would disinherit her and say that there was no way they were related. The resemblance that had once been so strong between them withered and diminished in the numbness of it all. Her mom groomed her to be just like her, the flawless little replica embodying productivity and ambition and strength. She had the drive. She could have been anything. She learned at her mother's knee how to deprive herself and hate herself and push herself until she was better. Perpetual dissatisfaction was what made people better. If you were happy with yourself you would never improve, as her mom liked to remind her on her way to work or the gym. Her mom approached everything she did with unshakable, terrifying confidence. Whether she was training for another triathlon or marathon or preparing for a deposition, she was determined to outshine herself.

Grace was weak. Her mom was strong. Her mom could do anything. Or she once might have been. And though Grace was sure of very, very little nowadays, she was completely sure that she was the only one that knew her mom's biggest secret. Did her mom mean for her to find out? Probably not. But if she did…that changed everything. It meant that everything she'd ever taught her was wrong. Everything that Grace blindly accepted and aspired to was a farce. The ambition that she'd so carefully cultivated under her mother's watchful eye meant nothing. The drive that connected her to her similarly driven friends wasn't actually hers. And it was this fear, more than anything, that kept her up at night.

Sam

He had no idea why everyone was so quiet. He noticed Sally before he noticed the awkward silence.

The girls realized these things first – they usually did. Sally looked like she was about to cry and Victoria raised her hand quickly over her mouth.

Grace was his friend and he felt so, so bad for her. It was terrible, what happened to her mom. No one deserved to lose their mom, especially when they were so young. He'd only actually spoken to Grace's mom on a few occasions, and she was as intimidating as hell, but still. She was Grace's *mom*.

He remembered getting the text from Sally. He felt so elated to see her name flash on his phone screen after it hadn't for so many months, and he remembered sitting straight up in bed, ready for whatever she had to say. He expected – what did he expect? An apology, probably. Or an invitation to meet up later so that she could apologize in person and offer some explanation for the months of silence. He didn't know what she could possibly say to explain her avoidance of him, but he wanted to believe that she could. In hindsight, it seemed strange that polite, articulate Sally would deliver an emotionally charged message in a text, but nothing that she did towards him made any sense any more.

He paused for a moment before reading it, relishing the knowledge that Sally was back home and ready to talk. She was communicating again. She wanted him in her life. She would probably come over later, or invite him to her house, and she would tell him she was sorry. She might start crying, because she cried a lot. Admitting she was wrong was so hard for her, but she would feel bad, and he would let her feel bad for a moment before wrapping her up in his arms and telling her that everything was back to normal and they were Sam-and-Sally again. They would kiss. They hadn't kissed since summer. They'd spend the day together doing something she loved. They could walk down to the beach and talk, and then later he would cook her dinner and take her to see the Christmas lights. They'd hold hands and kiss more and in the shadowy comfort of his car they would do more than kiss to make up for the long months of no touching.

His mind raced to delicious dark corners and he smiled, planning for the night ahead. He'd been waiting for this text for a long time and it seemed like she finally stopped being weird and silent.

He pressed "open." He read. He reread.

This was definitely not what he expected. This was not what he wanted.

"Grace's mom died last night. I'm going over right now. She needs us."

This was all wrong. Grace's mom couldn't be dead. That couldn't be right. Sally was… lying? But Sally never lied. She could be silent and heartbreaking and in denial, but not dishonest. And why would she lie?

Grace needs us. Of course Grace needed Sally. Sally was one of her best friends, and so was he. Grace was his closest female just-friend. The three of them hung out all the time and had fun.

Used to hang out. Used to have fun.

Us. It looked so mocking, "us," in the uncaring electronicness of it all. Us. He'd received thousands of texts from her referring to "us" and "we" and "you and I". They were words for couples. They were a couple.

She was going there right now. That sounded like an invitation. Why would she tell him otherwise? She thought he should be there. She thought Grace needed him. Maybe because he was the only other one in their group that had lost a parent. She realized that he was a person with thoughts and feelings. She thought that he could offer emotional support for someone she cared about.

So that was good, at least. Grace needed him and Sally knew that. Why else would she tell him?

He realized that this was the first time seeing Sally since... Thanksgiving. The Thanksgiving disaster. That was three weeks before. It still hurt.

Before Sally left for Stanford, they'd been inseparable. He went shopping with her and her mom for dorm stuff. They planned their Skype sessions around her class schedule. They talked about how long distance would be. It would suck, but they were willing to stick it out. He'd already started at the community college near their house, and it felt like such a waste of time to be in class when she was still here. He wanted to savor the precious moments when they were in the same city. He offered to skip class, but she made him go. "Don't miss class because of me! It's just a few hours a week anyway." It seemed like a huge, unnecessary chunk of time, and as soon as he got out of class each day he sped over to her house. He couldn't believe she was leaving.

On her last night at home, they ate dinner at their favorite Mexican restaurant on Main Street. Afterwards they walked down to the beach, holding hands, not talking much. They made their way to the end of the pier, slowly, just enjoying the sunset and savoring their last moments together.

When they got to the end Sally leaned against the railing. "You realize this is the last time we get to do this until Thanksgiving, right?"

"Yep. So we have to make it memorable." He pulled her closer to him and kissed her.

She leaned her head on his shoulder. "I'm going to miss this."

"Me too."

The sun set lower over the ocean, and they watched as the sky melted from dark pink to orange to purple. The days were getting shorter. September was half over.

"Sam?" She looked up at him, totally serious. She got so serious so easily. He wished she wouldn't, but it also gave him more opportunities to make her laugh.

"Yes?"

"We'll be all right, won't we?" Her eyebrows furrowed together in genuine concern.

"We're gonna make it work."

"Do you promise?"

"Yes."

It was a deal sealed with a kiss just as the sun said good night and slid under the horizon. The sky streaked with navy and they made their way back down the pier, hand in hand.

When he dropped her off she cried and they kissed. He hugged her and she cried some more. They kissed some more. The entire process of goodbyes took an hour.

They walked slowly to the front door and held each other for a long time. He kissed her on the cheek. He strangely thought he might cry.

"I'll call you as soon as I'm settled in, okay?"

He nodded. "Right."

She turned and gave him one last hug. He held onto her longer than necessary. How strange that this would be the last time he would hold her until Thanksgiving.

He kissed her on the forehead and she smiled up at him. She went inside and she was gone.

He couldn't remember the drive home. When he got home he laid on his bed and stared at the ceiling, thinking. He missed her already. They'd laid on this bed so many times, cracking up over cat videos or his own little animations. He wished he didn't have to drive away. He wished she didn't have to go inside. He wished they could stay on her porch forever. Stanford was a world away.

He was so happy for her, and so proud of her, but it was just so far away. At least it was in this state. Selfishly, he'd felt happy when she didn't get into Harvard or Yale. He knew that she was too smart for him and he felt lucky to at least have her in the same state.

But still... Stanford was about four hundred miles away. Judging from the pictures that she spent hours glossing over and making him look at, Stanford was beautiful. He tried to be excited for her. He could tell that she wanted him to be excited for her, and it hurt her when he couldn't summon the same enthusiasm. It was just so hard for him to be excited about her leaving. The brochures and the Internet revealed an amazing campus, beautiful weather, and an unfortunately attractive male population. He disliked the number of hot guys that popped up in all the Stanford pictures, the bro-y types that were also geniuses and probably rich. Why did some guys have all the luck? He couldn't bear the thought of her being surrounded by hot rich geniuses. They were probably funny, too. His humor was the main thing he had going for him, but what if some other guy was just as funny? Or funnier?

He laid in the dark and worried. He never worried about anything.

It would be a very long two months, but they would make it work. They loved each other.

He remained convinced of this for a few weeks. She called him every day and filled him in on her rapidly progressing life. They Skyped and he caught glimpses of her surprisingly nice dorm. He could tell how excited she was, and he tried to replicate this enthusiasm, asking as many silly questions as he could think of and trying to think of fun anecdotes to tell her about his day. She had a much greater wealth of material to fill him in on, and it was like she was growing before his eyes. She lit up with enthusiasm, emanating that addicting energy that made him miss her even more.

Their conversations were always the high point of his day, and he tried to find interesting things to tell her. He drew out the details of his beach days and outings with his friends, trying to make it sound like he was also having fun and enjoying school, but they paled in comparison to her description of parties, new friends, and exciting encounters. She seemed to be making tons of friends every day and she prattled on excitedly about her classes and even sounded excited about the already massive piles of homework. (He never understood why she found homework so fun. Such a nerd). "Listen to this," she told him excitedly over Skype one day. He watched her settle against her bed, a huge book on her lap. She began reading. "Whan that Aprille with his shoures sote – "

"Wait, wait, what?" He pushed his hair aside and tried to make out the cover of the book. "What the hell are you reading?"

She wrinkled her nose at the camera. *"The Canterbury Tales*, silly. They're great."

"Is that even English?"

"It's *Middle* English, Sam. This was written in the fourteenth century." She smiled at her book.

"I don't understand you, Chandler," he said, shaking his head in faux exasperation. "You can keep reading if you want, but I'm taking you outside." He ran down the hallway with his laptop open.

"Hi Sally!" his mom as he ran through the kitchen.

"Hi Mrs. Whitaker!" Sally yelled back. "Ahh, stop running, I'm getting hallway-sick!"

On a dry day in October, he called her at their usual time. The Santa Anas were in full force and he couldn't stop sniffling. The phone rang way past the usual interval. No big deal. He left a goofy message and hung up, expecting her to call back any minute.

But she did not call back. He tried again an hour later. Still no answer. Maybe she'd fallen asleep. He sent her a text asking to call him when she could.

He went out with his friends, expecting a phone call to interrupt their night, but it never came. When he returned to his house at in the early morning, he still had neither call nor text.

The next morning he tried again. Still no response. That was not like her at all.

At 9:00, the time they usually talked, he sat and redialed three times. By the fourth time, he had no expectation and just hit redial out of boredom.

"What?" Her voice caught him off-guard. He really did not expect an answer, but he was happy to get one.

"Hey babe, how are you? What took you so long?"

"Can you just stop calling me?"

Of course he assumed she was joking. Why would she be serious?

"Yeah. Haha. Sorry. How was your day?" Easy, breezy.

"No. Really. Stop calling me." She sounded exhausted and angry.

"What? What's wrong?"

"Just… just leave me alone, okay?"

Silence.

He stared at the phone, dumbfounded. What just happened? In four years of dating, they never had a fight. They definitely never hung up on each other. Sally never hung up on anyone.

There had to be something wrong with her. She sounded like she'd been crying. He hated when she cried.

He paused, then called her again. She picked up after one ring.

"I can't talk to you anymore, okay?"

"What do you mean? You can't talk more right now?"

"No. I mean I can't talk to you ever. We're done."

"This isn't – you can't – no we're not."

"Yes, Sam. We are." He thought he heard a sob before the line went dead.

He laid on his bed. That just happened. She just… broke up with him? Just like that? The girl that he'd been in love with for four years? Christ. Over the phone? How do you undo four amazing years in one phone call?

She seemed so happy just last week. What could have possibly made her do this?

He knew he had a right to be worried about Stanford. Stanford guys, and the school, and everything making her feel so… so free and wild and happy that she could do whatever the hell she wanted, like she didn't have a boyfriend at home.

He loved her. He loved her more than he'd ever loved anyone, except maybe his mom. And his mom loved her too – more than she loved him, he liked to joke. He'd envisioned their life together. A month after they started dating he realized that this was the girl he wanted to marry. Four years later he was just as determined. He'd never told his friends this, because it wasn't a guy thing to do, but he imagined their wedding all the time. It would be at the beach, of course. His sisters and Grace would be the bridesmaids. His mom and Dave would cry out of happiness. He'd be taller. Mr. Chandler would walk her down the aisle and they'd say stuff and kiss and they'd drink champagne and her cheeks would get rosy after one glass… then there was the honeymoon, somewhere warm, like Hawaii or Jamaica, and he'd be the happiest man in the world, and then they'd return home and buy a house near their parents and be together every day and have ten children. He knew she'd make a great mom. He'd wanted her to be the mother of his children since day one.

And now… that was all wasted time.

He wanted to cry. He wanted to die. He wanted to curl up in a ball and fall asleep and wake up and realize that this was just a bad, stupid dream, and he'd call her and she'd laugh at how unrealistic it was.

Then she'd hang up on him.

Anger swirled in his brain and he threw his phone across the room. It hit the wall and fell with a loud thud. He'd never thrown anything out of anger before.

He grabbed his pillow – the same pillow that they'd laid their heads on together – and screamed into it.

He hated Stanford. He hated the fucking school.

He hated her. No he didn't. Yes he did. She thought she could leave him here and go have her own adventures and become an independent college-y girl. Well, he would too. He didn't have to be tied down anymore. He could do whatever the hell he wanted.

He sat up. He could go to a party and get drunk, which she hated and made him promise to not do when they were together. He could go make out with some girl. Hell, he could have sex with some girl. He didn't belong to her anymore.

He leapt out of bed and started fumbling around his room, getting ready to leave. His hands shook slightly. He could go anywhere. He would go – where? Where did people go that had nothing to lose and could do anything they wanted? He glanced at his watch. It was 10:30. And a Thursday. Party night.

After a frantic five minutes of searching, he found his car keys. He dug through his closet and found a clean, nice-ish shirt. He took his other one off quickly and made sure he smelled okay. He was ready.

The door slammed behind him but he didn't notice. He jammed the keys into the ignition and peeled out of the driveway.

He loved to be spontaneous, but he rarely was reckless. This was a new feeling for him. Now he just didn't give a shit what happened to him. He went over the speed limit and turned the volume up on a rap station he hated. The music blared despicably but he didn't care.

Without planning on it, he jammed into an illegal U-turn and started towards the Long Beach frat houses where he knew his CC friends were. Of course there would be a party. It was a frat house. There would be alcohol, enough to get him in whatever state of fuckedupness he wanted. There would be girls. Drunk, half-naked girls. He sped up. For the first time in four years he was a single man.

He just wished he could feel more excited about it.

Grace

She poured herself a bowl of Cheerios and looked out the window at the sprawling driveway. The Christmas lights were still on – her dad had forgotten to turn them off again. They usually had more Christmas decorations, but this year a solitary strand of white lights lined the front of the house.

Her dad's car was gone, but her mom's BMW was still there for some reason. She wondered if they had gone to Max's soccer game together, then remembered that her mom was planning on going into the office today.

Most families were relaxed and sleeping in on Saturday mornings, but most families were not the Hastings. By 8 a.m. her entire family would be gone for the day, off to work and soccer and piano. Grace was going to meet with her college counselor, a client of her mom's who helped organize the lives of privileged seniors with too much money and too many options. Ellen was expecting her at 10, their normal meeting hour.

She opened the fridge. No milk. That was odd. They never ran out of milk. Her mother demanded soy milk in her coffee. There was always milk.

Maybe her mom was sleeping in. She never slept in, but she certainly had seemed more stressed out than usual lately. Maybe she was finally giving herself a break.

Grace felt a twinge of sympathy for her mother. She worked harder than anyone.

She would buy her mom her soy milk. She felt very virtuous as she marched upstairs, anticipating her mom's pride at her proactivity. "Finally, taking some responsibility," she'd say, and do something uncharacteristically maternal, something that Grace felt like she always missed out on. Like ruffling her hair or pinching her cheek. Or even just smiling at her. A real smile from her mother could be the loveliest gift in the world.

She paused outside her parents' bedroom. Her dad hadn't slept there in months. His snoring had become too much of an issue and sleep deprivation was not an option for her mother. Grace usually wasn't allowed in there. Her mom liked her space. When she was little and afraid of the dark or had a bad dream, she stayed in her bed because her mom's reaction would be scarier.

She knocked lightly, in case she was asleep. No answer. She knocked a little harder.

"Mom?" She pushed the door open softly. Her mom was still in bed. Her room was always spotlessly clean, but on this particular morning it held a kind of stillness, like everything was holding its breath, the neatly lined pairs of heels and the waiting Coach bag and the black blazer still draped across the chair....

The clock said 8:30. Her mom was never asleep at 8:30.

"Mom?" she said quietly. "Mom?"

Her mom was turned away from her, back hunched, partially obscured by the comforter. Frozen blond hair lay in white stripes over the black sheets.

"Mom?" She patted the shoulder that should have been softly moving rhythmically with her strong, dependable breaths and was surprised at how rigid it felt.

Her heart pounded and her face grew hot as she stared at her mom's back, stiffly hunched. She reached out her hand to prod her awake, harder this time. Her hand quavered. Her mom was so pale. This could not be her mom. This could not be happening.

"Mom." Her voice cracked and her mouth opened and she might have been screaming and she ran to the other side of the bed and saw that her mom was not going to wake up and then everything went black.

Chapter 4

Erik

Josh took his plate and he watched him put it in the dishwasher. He wondered why Josh liked cooking. That was a girl's job. His mom or his stepmom of the moment (or her housekeeper) did the cooking. At least his dad never made him do that. His dad wanted him to be a man.

Josh was so lucky and didn't even realize it, he thought as he watched him put the dishes away while still looking manly. Josh, who only had to play high school baseball for two years before quitting because he wanted to and could. He could do whatever he wanted because he wasn't the third anything. He didn't have to carry on a legacy. He could be ordinary. He could just quit baseball because he was tired of it.

Erik could never quit.

Sam

They filed out the door and Sam had a strange sense of déjà-vu: same people, same environment, same goal as last year. Even though they hadn't found the waterfall, it was still a fun hike. Maybe it wasn't as fun as surfing, but at least he was outside.

Sally laughed at something that Josh said and he felt an unfamiliar twinge of jealousy. He didn't think that Josh would do anything, but still. He wasn't used to being jealous, but he couldn't help but notice that Josh had really filled out. He looked more... fratty. All bro tanks and big arms. He was still nice, of course. He couldn't imagine Josh not being nice. He just wished that Josh wasn't so funny and muscly. Or maybe he wished that he were more muscly? He looked at his arms. They were just regular surfer arms with regular amounts of muscle. He hadn't really thought about it before. Maybe he should go to the gym more. Maybe Sally now liked guys that went to the gym.

He was so sure that Josh was the only one that knew about That Night... he'd never mentioned it, but he remembered that

Josh was awake when he and Sally returned to the tent…If Josh knew that, and was still moving in on Sally, that was a super douche move.

He watched Sally's ponytail bobbing in front of him down the line as they moved deeper into the woods, and he remembered watching her ponytail bob in front of him on That Night last summer. It was dark, of course, and she giggled as she held out her phone, using the light to guide them to the car. She almost tripped and he caught her, feeling her thin waist curl into his arms. She laughed and they kissed in the darkness, soft and giggly at first, then harder, deepening and intensifying and –

She pulled away when his hand moved up her shirt. "Sam!"

"What?" he asked goofily, hand still cupping her.

"Not out here, I feel like we're going to get eaten by a bear or something." She kissed him on the cheek and he grabbed her hand, continuing towards the car. He remembered her giggling at the covertness of the whole thing, the feeling of fleeing together under the cover of darkness. He loved this feeling, like they were sharing a mischievous secret, unlocking a world that only they could access. Their friends were fast asleep and it seemed like the woods belonged just to them. The tiniest sliver of the moon reflected in his car's mirror and he unlocked it manually, not wanting the alarm to wake their friends. The click of the locks reverberated in the quiet woods and they stifled their laughter. He opened the back door and pulled her onto him, shutting the door quietly and finding her mouth in the darkness.

He picked up where he'd left off outside and felt the familiar weight of her pressing against him. His necklace pushed into her skin and he slipped it off his neck, dropping it on the floor of the car. He pushed her gently onto the seat and leaned into her. It felt wonderful to be out here, totally alone, just the two of them, not having to worry about being interrupted by a parent. They were used to this level of intimacy, but it usually couldn't last very long because privacy was such a rare thing in small houses and small towns. He'd been looking forward to this for weeks and now they were finally, totally alone.

He'd gotten so much better at unhooking bras since they started dating. He was used to this one and it came off with minimal fumbling. Years of this had tuned him into the rhythm of how much leeway she gave him, the few minutes that she allowed him each time. This was usually the farthest she let it go before covering herself up and reminding him that one of their parents was in the other room.

But now there were no parents, and he was curious to see just how far she was willing to go under the cover of darkness. He wasn't going to force her to do anything, of course. He loved her and respected her and didn't want to do anything she was uncomfortable with. He didn't expect anything to happen any time soon, but that didn't mean he didn't want it.

He could feel her unwinding as she too realized the extent of their privacy. She was so used to holding up her defenses, guarding the little corners with modesty and batting his hands away when she felt it was necessary. He knew that she kept herself from getting carried away in the spare moments they usually had, the sweet little seconds they had to themselves in the car or in his room. She always apologized afterwards and he told her that he understood, because he did, and he loved her for it, and he knew that she loved him for being patient. She kept her guard up because there was always the option of getting caught, which would prevent future stolen moments. But now, with the freedom offered by darkness and solitude, he could feel her shedding her defenses instead of building them, loosening the walls that she kept to maintain her image of herself as a Good Girl.

His hand slid further down and she stiffened at first, then let him continue, kissing him harder. Her legs wrapped around him and his hands slid down to the button of her jeans. This could be their only opportunity.

She pulled her mouth away and put her hands on top of his, as if to pull them away. Disappointment coursed through him. He was about to concede when she nodded and pulled his face back to hers. His fingers scrambled to undo the button that had been his enemy for four years, and he smiled as he kissed her.

Alex

"Alex! Are you ready?" Sally asked. She was in another set of workout clothes. Her own running shoes were well-kept but still dirty and obviously often used.

"Yes." His phone felt uncomfortably heavy in his pocket and he held it uncertainly. There wasn't a game today – his parents wouldn't be texting him constant updates. Hopefully that also meant that they wouldn't be texting him constant unnecessary things either. He set his phone on the table. Could he leave it here? It seemed like a minor act of rebellion... but there wouldn't be reception on the trail... what if they needed it?

"Is it okay if I put this in your backpack?" He asked Sally.

She smiled at took it from him. "Of course! No game today?"

"Nope, travel day."

"Wish him luck tomorrow for me." He grinned and stood up, feeling extremely tall next to petite work- and-workoutaholic Sally. He followed her bouncing ponytail downstairs where everyone else was already waiting by the door, wearing their properly used workout shoes.

"Ready?" Victoria glanced around and bounded out the door. Her extremely short shorts looked ridiculous and Alex wondered why anyone would ever wear them to go hiking.

"Erik, it's this way, right?" Victoria pointed up the hill.

"Um, yeah. I think so." Victoria rolled her eyes, which Alex found a little mean.

The hill was much steeper than he thought it was, and he was very conscious of his already heavy breathing. The in-shape people took the lead and he watched Josh's athletic frat boy body calves bobbing the right way in his Nikes. His legs used to be that right kind of muscular, too.

The sidewalk narrowed at the top of the hill and their two rows compressed into a single-file line. Alex fell behind Erik, happy to be last so that hopefully no one could hear him breathing heavily. His knee already hurt and he felt an ache in his chest that had been utterly alien in high school but now was an all-too familiar side effect of physical activity.

They walked parallel to the curtain of green in their single file line. The dirt path had no boundary from the street and cars whizzed past them, a little too close for comfort. He flinched as an SUV barreled past him up the hill.

"Why the fuck aren't there any sidewalks?" Victoria yelled as she trekked in her tiny shorts.

"Wait, you just passed it!" Josh yelled. The obediently came to a halt in front of the barely visible Escondido Trail sign.

"It's hidden, all right," laughed Grace, the one fluent in Spanish. "How are you supposed to see this if you're driving?"

Alex had no idea. The faded sign was obfuscated by draping leaves and he could barely see it from two feet away. The only indication that there was even a trail here was the short hole that stood maybe three feet high.

"Erik, have you gone on this trail before? Is this the entrance?" Josh yelled down the line.

Erik shrugged. "I haven't gone on here before. My cousins did once."

"Well, here goes nothing. If I die, say nice things about me." Victoria and her long, bare legs folded and disappeared within the hole of the forest.

"How is it?" asked Sally.

They waited.

"Victoria, quit goofing off," yelled Josh.

Still silence.

"Are there monsters or something?" Sam yelled into the hedge.

Finally they heard her voice dimly; she sounded much farther away than she could have gone in that span of time.

"It's fine, come on."

Josh looked skeptically at the small hole, shrugged, and entered. "Whoa… it's really dark… okay, it's fine, come on."

Sally, Grace, Sam, and Erik all entered the dark trail, until it was just him standing by himself on the road.

He did not want to go hiking today. He didn't want to be the out-of-breath guy making a fool of himself, and he definitely didn't want to crawl this mysterious portal to physical exertion and embarrassment. They were used to athletic Alex, not broken Alex.

He tried to peer through, but the wall of foliage prevented him from catching a glimpse of anything besides green and darkness.

He looked at the tiny, unwelcoming hole and sighed. He forced a smile and crawled in.

Josh

He'd missed real nature. New York was awesome but this… this was real. He loved Fordham, the buzz of Manhattan, the energy he always felt from living in one of the world's most amazing cities. His classmates were fascinating and brilliant and cool. Some of them were also putting themselves through school, and they bonded over the difficulty of balancing one or two jobs with classes and a social life.

That was maybe the one thing that separated him from this group of friends, he thought, trying not to feel bitter. Sure, they all grew up together and knew everything about each other, but these friends really couldn't understand how hard it was to pay for things yourself – except for Victoria, of course, but her Regents Scholarship covered most of her tuition.

He thought of his dad and this time made no effort to suppress his displeasure. Fucking dad. If it weren't for him he wouldn't have to work two jobs and straddle the widening gorge of tuition that sometimes felt like it would swallow him. None of the others here knew how hard it was to spend sixty-four dollars and know that it took eight hours in the coffee house to save that up.

Hey, he told himself. This is supposed to be your weekend off. Stop worrying.

He bounded up the path behind Victoria and her little shorts, smiling as the breeze tickled his face. This was already such an excellent weekend.

Sam

He watched Sally disappear into the dark hole. Her tan legs plunged in and he wanted to follow them.

Or, better yet, he wanted the tan legs, along with the rest of her, to stay out here, just the two of them, so that he could demand answers. He deserved to get his questions answered.

The confusing months of silence dragged on through fall, but he had hopes for Thanksgiving. It would be her first time back home since she'd left, and he hadn't seen her in person for over two months.

He tried to learn from her Facebook, but she'd deactivated it (he hoped she didn't just block him). After two last invitational texts were ignored- one Monday, one Wednesday – he decided to just drive to her house to talk to her. It would have felt like a surprise three months before, but now felt like he was walking into a trap. He hoped her parents wouldn't be home, even though he was sure they would be.

He drove the speed limit to her house and pulled up just before nine, late enough to not interrupt dinner and early enough that he wouldn't wake the littluns up.

He sat in the car for a minute and took a deep breath. He never felt nervous about coming to this house before, this place of friendliness and warmth and stolen kisses on the porch. Their house looked the same as the last time he'd been here but the circumstances were as different as they could possibly be.

Slowly, he walked up and rang the doorbell. It echoed around the house ominously, like the three ding-dongs were keeping a secret. He saw the front room curtains part and a male face peek out. A few moments later the door opened.

"Hi, Mr. Chandler!"

"Hi, Sam." He looked faintly uncomfortable and Sam recognized the same unsure facial expression that Sally wore when she had to pass on bad news. The pit in his stomach felt heavier.

"How are you?"

"I'm fine, just fine. How about yourself? We haven't heard about you in a while." He crossed his arms concernedly and peered behind him. He stepped onto the porch. Sam was fairly sure that Mr. Chandler liked him, but he also knew that if Mr. Chandler thought he had broken Sally's heart he would lose all credibility and probably be chased off this porch.

"I'm not that great, actually. I was wondering if Sally was home. She hasn't returned any calls or texts...." His uncertainty trailed off into silence, leaving the awkward and obvious: hello, dad of former girlfriend/ soulmate, do you know why she's completely shutting me out of her life? Because she didn't bother to tell me. Or maybe she did and I was just too stupid to understand it.

"Look, son..." Mr. Chandler looked sympathetic, not angry, which was a good sign. Maybe. "She didn't tell us what happened either, she just told us that she wasn't seeing you anymore. We have no idea why and it sounds like you don't either."

Sam shook his head. "Not a clue. I honestly can't think of anything."

"We think she's just adjusting to college. She has a harder course load now and a whole new... well, a whole new life, really. We haven't called her much because we know she's busy and we don't want to smother her. But the few times that she did call us back, she sounded... sad. Stressed and sad."

"But she sounded so happy at first. She loved it."

"That's what we thought, too. She loved it so much the first few weeks, and called us every other day to update us. Then one day she just... stopped."

"I'm worried about her." Sam was mortified to hear his voice crack.

"I know you are." Mr. Chandler smiled at him appreciatively. "We are, too."

"So what do I do?"

Mr. Chandler sighed. "Give her space, I suppose. I really don't know what else to tell you."

"Is she here?"

"Yes, she's sleeping." Sam knew he was not lying. "I'll tell her you stopped by, okay?"

"Alright."

"Sam... as hard as it is for a dad to admit that he likes his daughter's boyfriend, I like you. So does Bonnie. We like you because we know how much you care about our daughter and you've never let anything bad happen to her. We love her more than anything, and you make her happy, so you make us happy."

"Well... thank you."

"And you know as well as I do that Sally is not a hurtful person. She would never hurt someone that she knows cares about her as much as you do."

"But she just stopped talking to me."

"She has to figure things out by herself. You just have to give her space, let her sort herself out."

"Dad? Why is the door open —" Sally stepped onto the porch and frowned. "Oh."

"Hey, sleepy head. You have a visitor," Mr. Chandler said, somewhat unnecessarily. "I'll let you guys talk out here." He smiled sadly at Sam and went inside.

"Um… hi."

"What are you doing here?" He usually thought that Sally was the prettiest girl in the entire world, even when she was tired or just ran ten miles and was drenched in sweat. She was wearing her giant Stanford sweatshirt, the one she usually wore when she was sick, with yoga pants that he recognized as the ones that had once clung in all the right places, but now hung. She looked so much skinnier, and sadder, and paler than the last time he saw her. She looked absolutely miserable. He could have accepted all this and still have found her pretty, but now he realized why she didn't. For the first time that he could remember, Sally looked mean. Her happiness made her beautiful. Her kindness made her shine. But the way her eyes narrowed – not at a test question, or at some injustice in the world, but at home, at him – made her very, very un-pretty.

"Can you just talk to me? You've been completely ignoring me and it's not fair." He vaguely recalled preparing some sort of speech in the car, but now he couldn't remember any of it.

For a moment he thought he saw her soften. Her defenses lowered under the guilt of the crime of rudeness, and her eyebrows unfurrowed and he caught a hollow glimpse of the girl that he loved. He was so ready to hug her, and say it was okay, whatever her reason for silence was didn't matter now. Everything could go back to normal and they would be happy again.

He had no idea how, or why, but something clicked in her mind and the defenses went back up. She was locking him out again, horribly and unfairly, and there was nothing he could do to stop it.

"I told you on the phone, Sam. We're over."

Anger swelled up hot and furiously in his brain and he'd come over here to beg for forgiveness for a crime he wasn't sure he'd committed and he was regretting the words even as they were shooting out of his mouth.

"No, you didn't. You've just been ignoring me and shutting me out, and I'm fucking tired of it." The profanity surprised both of them. They ignored it.

"I can't. I just can't." She opened the door and walked back in the house. She turned and for a foolish instant he thought he saw a flicker of regret.

"Don't come back here, Sam." She closed the door but he could have sworn he heard a sob before it shut.

Josh

He watched appreciatively as Victoria's booty shorts bent down and disappeared into the forest. He followed.

For a few moments he was eclipsed by total darkness, but he could hear Victoria laughing and he followed the sound. A few moments later he was blinking in the sudden brightness.

"What are you laughing at?"

"Nothing." She smirked.

Sally appeared next. "Ooh, that was cool!" She walked gracefully up the path, looking perfectly at home in the forest with her woodland creature goodness. Sally was freaking Bambi.

She joined them on the slope and they watched the rest of their friends file out.

"Ready?" Victoria began the upward descent. "Shit, this part is steep."

He didn't mind it that much. He started a heavy workout regime with some of his frat brothers during spring semester, and though it took up a lot of time, he definitely appreciated the benefits, like ease in physical activity and gratuitous female attention. He bounded easily up the path and grinned at Sally. This felt great, being outside in the sunshine. He missed California weather. In the warm glow of the dappled sunshine it was impossible to not feel relaxed and happy. How could you not, with 75 degrees and friends and a hot girl hiking in front of you?

He forced himself to look away from Sally's perky derriere. Nature. Nature. There was a bird in a tree. There were... bees buzzing in the yellow flowers.

Damn. Different kinds of nature. Not birds and bees.

Grace

Victoria's head disappeared into the shrubbery, and she watched as each of her friends vanished. Sally melted into the darkness and she realized that it was her turn. Okay. She could do this. Why was she even worrying? It was just hiking. She'd done this a million times.

But this time felt different, she couldn't deny it. Maybe because it was the first time since…. But why would that make any difference?

This was just a matter of mind over matter. Mental over physical.

Was she afraid of the dark? No, she didn't think so. She didn't mind the dark so much anymore. After a year of living in upstate New York she was accustomed to far less sunshine than her California-centric friends. Perhaps she was afraid of the physicality of climbing, since she'd been much more lethargic than physical in the recent months. She couldn't remember the last time she'd pushed herself physically. What if she embarrassed herself? She didn't want to be That One Friend, panting and out of breath, as her athletic friends gracefully bounded over rocks and peaks. Oh God, what if they all took their shirts off again? They did that last summer, when they found the river. Sally and Victoria were skinny and could take off their shirts whenever they wanted. Now she had that ugly little pouch of stomach and really, really did not want to take off her shirt.

Sally was already way ahead of her. She'd been counting on just following her, but it was so hard to see in the darkness. She took a deep breath. A leap of faith. Indiana Jones. She stepped onto the trail and into utter blackness. She felt panic rising in her and willed herself to not freak out. Sally was somewhere ahead of her, so there must be a trail with solid ground. Left right left right, one foot in front of the other, just keep moving. She peered around and couldn't even make out a bush or tree. This was so, so freaky. She couldn't even see her hand in front of her face. What if there were animals in here? A bear could be squatting a foot in front of her and she would have no idea.

And there was Sally's voice, her light tinkling voice a beacon alerting her that it was okay, they were alive, there was a way out. She just had to trust her.

The path curved slightly and she felt her direction change. The forest was taking her up and to the right. She lifted her foot uncertainly and stepped onto the incline. This was such a strange feeling, though not an unfamiliar one. The entire school year felt like walking up a hill of darkness. She could never see what was around her or where she was or where she wasn't. Darkness was cruel and lonely.

Yes, that was the word. Lonely. The entire school year could be summed up in one simple, divisive word. That was the word for wandering in the darkness. In this murky corner of the forest she felt the stirrings of all the bad feelings, and they swarmed her with furious vengeance. She'd hoped to leave them at school and start anew this summer, but she secretly suspected that they'd return. She closed her eyes and opened her eyes and closed them again because it looked the same anyways and all she could see was utter blackness.

But her friends were here now. They weren't during the school year. Now she was in the same state as them. (She thought. As long as this path wasn't leading her into Arizona). They would be her light and they would shine for her and their brightness would illuminate her way. She could do it.

Without realizing it, she stepped into light. She blinked and her eyes threw dark circles in the air and she could see again and color was dazzling after so much blindness. It was so... green. Green everywhere, much more Ithaca than Cottonwood, and after two months of sand and concrete it felt odd to be back in real nature.

Victoria, Josh, and Sally weren't as far away as she thought and she happily trailed after them. They looked like a magazine ad for something attractive and healthy, like running shoes or granola bars. She wished she looked attractive and healthy like they did: Victoria, California blond and California tan, Josh, a typical athletic boy whose muscles revealed the hours of practices and yard work, and Sally, so petite and runner-y. They always seemed so above her. Beauty divided. Beauty conquered.

She continued after them, feeling like she was tagging along with her cool older siblings. They climbed easily over boulders and she was still tripping over rocks. For them the forest was just scenery, the trees just props in their daily adventures of being awesome. She saw a different forest. She saw the roots that lay waiting to trip them and the bugs that hummed in the brush and the shuffling of creatures displeased to find strangers in their home. They were intruding on a microcosm they did not belong to and were not welcome in.

She glanced back at the way they'd come and saw Sam emerging from the dark patch, blinking and disoriented. He slowed down before fully regaining his vision, grinned at her, and bounded up the path towards her.

"It's so dark in that part!"

She smiled back. Only he could find that amusing. "Yeah, I know! Kind of freaky."

He looked up at the forest. "Wow, this is... this is really cool."

She supposed, from an outsider's perspective, that it was nice. Sam, born and raised mere blocks away from the beach, rarely exhibited a love for any other kind of landscape. If he could appreciate it, she could try.

So she looked again and tried to see the world through Sam's eyes instead of hers. How *To Kill a Mockingbird* of her. Sally would be proud.

She could be Scout Finch. She could really try.

She put on her mental Sam shoes and looked at the forest and instead of seeing danger she saw opportunity. She could climb rocks. She could jump over roots. She could absolutely jump over them.

Sally

They padded down the trail in an obedient line and Sally stifled a laugh. What did this remind her of? Peter Pan? They certainly did look like small children trumping along enthusiastically and she felt a rush of affection.

"We're following the leader, the leader," she hummed to herself. She smiled. Victoria, of course, led them through the underbrush, closely trailed by Josh and herself. Josh's tank top hung tautly between his shoulder blades and she slipped as she stared. The group's chatter died down as they began a steep ascent. She barely felt the pressure build in her knees and felt grateful for her ritual runs. Working out like a maniac definitely had its benefits.

The hill grew even steeper and she concentrated on her footing. She knew that most people fell when hiking because they tried to walk normally, but that was wrong. Her dad taught her the right way. Once you were in the mountain's territory, the rules of normal movement were gone, and you were subject to the laws of nature. You had to adjust and accept that you were in someone else's home and should abide by their rules. A forest trail had different customs than a flat sidewalk. Her knees bent automatically and she lowered her center of gravity. When she was little and her family went on camping trips she would pretend to be a monkey while she climbed. Life was so easy then.

They stopped talking completely and she realized how the forest wasn't as quiet as they thought. When they were making their rambunctious noises and acting like they were the only people on earth, the outside world ceased to exist. Now, in their silence, the sounds of the forest became audible. They welcomed her into their secret concert and she wondered if it had been playing the entire time and they were just too deaf to hear it.

She wanted to hear it. She wanted the forest to play for her. She opened her ears and listened. She could hear Grace breathing. She could hear Erik mumbling some complaint to Alex. She blocked out her friends and really listened.

Scratching sounds came from the bushes that hugged the trail, and she heard the shuffling of some small rodent scurrying about. A bird cawed. Grace slipped slightly, sending skidding dirt into a brown puff of air. The light breeze tickled the leaves in the tree above. She could hear it all, all the restless mutterings of a world that was not theirs, but allowed them in anyways. There was so much going on in a forest, if only one would pay attention. Whole lives played out before their very eyes in a language that none of them spoke but all of them could understand. All the creepy-crawly things fought the same fight that she and her friends did. At the end of the day, wasn't that what it was really about? Survival? Keeping yourself protected against the elements and battling on? Memorizing the terrain and learning the land and plunging on, recklessly and bravely?

So she was the same as a beetle, or a squirrel, or a bird. Each of them tried to stay alive, despite the other beetles or squirrels or birds that were bigger or smarter or prettier. It all came down to survival. It all came down to pushing yourself above your peers and finding the strength to be better.

How could she not have noticed the scratching before? There were so many noises, so many trappings of this secret and exposed little world. You could learn so much if you just paid attention.

Victoria

"Water break!" Josh called down the line. She was about to protest, but noticed Grace looked kind of crappy. She smiled gratefully at Josh. That was what she envied. Grace and Josh spoke in the beautiful and incomparable shorthand of childhood best friends, a language of gestures and total understanding of the other person that she utterly envied. Even after a year of separation, the other was still firmly engrained in the other's mind, connected by an unconscious thread of awareness. She wanted that. Grace had that and probably didn't appreciate it.

Grace was probably really out of shape, too.

The shade was too cool and she wandered over to the edge of the cliff, loving the warmth. God, she hated cold. She hated being covered up. The wind tickled her scalp and she realized that she was faintly sweaty. Well, nobody's perfect. She whipped off her shirt and laid on the flattest rock she could find. Her tan could use a touch-up.

She stared out at the valley of rocks, hating it. She hated being reminded how small and insignificant she was. The gorge of earth stretched out as far as she could see, patches of green flattened by boulders that had probably been there for centuries. Nature carried on and killed when it needed to and that was that.

She felt suddenly tired. She pushed her shirt into a ball and made a makeshift pillow, feeling the sun warm her stomach. She turned away from her friends, towards the valley of rocks, and tuned out as multiple voices flitted around her. Sally and Josh were talking and Grace and Sam were talking and Erik and Alex were talking and they were all talking about different things and she just wanted to sleep while they talked about boring things...

The strange blurring of unrelated conversations melded nonsensically until they were almost coherent. The ordinary words threaded themselves together, braiding themselves into one long thing that didn't really matter but kept weaving itself together in a soporific chain of nonsense...

"So excited to go to the lake but –"

"I'm still hungry and –"

"Look at this bug, it's so –"

She let herself drift away…

She was seven years old and laying on the hard ground under her bed, hiding from her dad. Her parents were fighting again and she just wanted him to leave. He sometimes left when he smelled and he smelled because he was drinking and when he was drinking he hit…

Something crashed in the kitchen and she wondered who threw it, Mom or Dad, probably Dad if he was drunk but maybe Mom if he was trying to hit her again…

Mom was crying, wailing, and she had to help her… she ran to the kitchen and watched from behind the door as Dad's tall scary friend wrestled Mom to the ground and Dad laughed and yelled "hoar" and slammed the door when he left and the scary guy had a knife and Mom was crying so she ran to save her but the guy shoved her away with the hand with the knife and she fell on her arm and Mom's skirt was pushed up and she yelled at her to run away but she was bleeding….

Victoria gasped as she woke up shaking. God. She hadn't had that dream in … months. Since October.

She held up her arm and looked at the scar. It was so much smaller now, twelve years later. It was hard to imagine how big it had seemed at the time, when it was fresh and gaping, pouring out more blood than she had ever seen. She remembered thinking that it looked like a clown's mouth. She had watched in terrified fascination as her arm bent backwards. The cut gaped open horribly and she was too scared to cry. The guy and her mom were still on the floor and her mom was still crying. The guy's belt was on the floor by the door. She remembered the first aid presentation at school and tied it around her arm as tight as she could with one hand. She bit down on her lip to keep from yelling as the leather touched the inside of her skin, electrifying pain shooting through her. Her blood dripped onto the tiles, mixing with the mud from the man's shoes, and she opened the door quietly and ran outside. More blood oozed out and her white shoes were all red and the lady down the street saw her and started running and the ground came rushing up to meet her.

She woke up and didn't know where she was and wanted to scream when the man reached out to touch her, but her mouth had a thing in it and it was a different man. He explained to her that she was in an ambulance and he held her arm together and promised her that she was going to be okay. And for the first time in her life, she trusted a man. His voice was quiet and nice like a teacher's and he told her they were going to the hospital. Her neighbor was in the ambulance with them and she heard him ask how old her daughter was. The neighbor explained that Victoria wasn't her daughter, no she didn't know where her mom was, or how it happened...

She opened her mouth to tell him that her mom was still at home with the bad man that was hurting her, but she couldn't talk because of the thing, and she started crying because it was so scary and frustrating not to be able to talk or breathe, and her arm really hurt, and she saw the silvery flash of the needle going into her and she was happy when it made her sleep...

When she woke up next she looked down at her arm and saw the thick cast. A nice nurse gave her water and ice cream and showed her how all of the machines in her room worked. She brought her the x-rays of her arm and explained that it was broken in two places but they gave her medicine so that it wouldn't be in-fect-ed, which usually happened with a cut that big. The nurses brought her markers to draw on her cast with and she asked them all to sign it. The nurses were so nice and the doctors were so smart and they all took such good care of her and she wished she could stay in the hospital forever.

Her mom ran in a few hours later and she wanted to ask if she was okay, if the man had hurt her, but then a doctor rushed her mom away and a lady named Karen came in and asked her how she got a cut that big and a broken arm in two places. It felt like school, and she knew the right answer, and she wanted to explain but she couldn't because she kept crying and that was frustrating.

Karen was very nice and hugged her and told her that it was okay to cry, that was normal after something traw-mat-ic happens. Then Karen left to go talk to her mom, so a nurse came in and watched TV with her and didn't make her talk. Then Karen and her mom came in and explained that Victoria and her mom would have to move houses again.

"This time, we're going to a nice area, with nice people and big houses," her mom said, holding her not-broken arm. Victoria nodded.

Two weeks later she had her first day of school at Little Cottonwood Elementary.

Fate could be so strange, she thought. Of course, at the time she didn't fully understand what was going on. She was just happy to go to a clean, pretty school with nice, pretty people. Their new apartment was small but their street was brighter and her mom let her play outside sometimes. There would be no more mean guys, her mom promised, and for a short time Victoria believed her.

She turned towards her group of friends. Her little sheltered, naïve, scar-less group of friends. They knew very little about her parents, and she preferred to keep it that way. All they knew was that her parents were separated and she lived with her mom, whom she never mentioned. She went to their houses and did not invite them to hers. She did not contribute to conversations about parents or background or happy childhood memories, because she had very few, and the few that she did have all belonged to her friends.

She didn't want to think about how life would have turned out if they had stayed at the old house with her dad knowing where they were. She refused to think about it. She refused to think about October. She focused on moving forward.

She took in the view one last time and headed back towards her friends.

Alex

"Are we there yet?" Sam asked.

Josh laughed. "How high do you want to go?"

"Oh, there's a real waterfall this time? You're not just screwing with us?"

"Victoria, I'm sure this time! I looked it up in the travel guide this morning. Escondido is supposed to lead to the waterfall."

"Well, there'd better be an actual waterfall this time, because that was ridiculous last year."

"Hey, we did get to the waterfall," pointed out Sam. "There just wasn't any water in it."

They all laughed, remembering last year's anticlimactic hike. For some reason, Josh had been determined to find the waterfall. He carefully planned out a route that would bypass the steep cliffs that were reserved for the most advanced hikers. Victoria kept making fun of how obsessive he was getting about a waterfall. He loved seeing how bright Josh's eyes got when he was excited about something. He used to light up like that before their baseball games.

"No, I promise, it's going to be awesome," he had said, leading the pack up the trails.

"How do you know?" asked Sally incredulously, arm in arm with Sam behind him. "You've never been here."

"I just have a feeling. It's going to be awesome."

Grace laughed. "Okay, Josh, now we all have seriously high expectations for this waterfall."

Josh smiled at her. "You won't be disappointed."

Alex couldn't remember exactly how long they'd hiked. Later they calculated it and realized that they'd only gone three miles both ways, but it seemed to take forever. Of course, three vertical miles took a lot longer than three horizontal ones, but still. It had been a long and somewhat disappointing trek.

After however many hours they'd spent climbing and clamoring, Josh saw the "waterfall →" sign at the edge of the trail. They left the safety of the trail, crawling over bushes and bug clouds.

He remembered that he had been walking behind Sam and Sally when they suddenly stopped. He halted too and was glad that he was the last one. Josh was standing at the edge of a deep gorge. The smell of sulfur hovered thickly in the air, denitrification ruining an otherwise picturesque experience.

It looked like the perfect place for a waterfall, if there was one. Evidently, there was sometimes a stream of water at the bottom, but the green had since turned brown in the heat of summer. Moss and dead, dry branches stuck out from the long rock wall, which was ingrained with the deep vertical tracks of running water that had long since dried.

"No!" Josh looked genuinely heartbroken. "This was supposed to be the perfect waterfall!"

"Well, this sucks," said Victoria, a little unhelpfully.

"Hey!" Sally shot her a look. "Josh, thank you for finding the way up here. This is lovely. Isn't it?" she asked emphatically.

"Yes, thank you, Josh," said Alex. He really wanted to see the waterfall, but they could also tell that Josh was really disappointed.

"It's okay, guys. I just thought this would be a cool thing for us to experience together."

"It's still an awesome view!" Sam said enthusiastically. Sally beamed and put her head on his shoulder. He put his arm around her and they fit into each other like two puzzle pieces.

Alex felt extremely jealous.

"So what do we do now? We can't go swimming," said Erik. "I carried my towel all the way up here for nothing."

"I brought my camera!" said Sally brightly.

"Let's take pictures!" Alex grinned and slapped Josh playfully on the arm. He hated seeing him look so dejected.

For a solid hour, they took pictures in every pose possible. They alternated photographers and combinations and tried to come up with the silliest poses. A passing hiker kindly offered to help them out so they could all be in one together. They stood facing the camera, arms around each other in a golden chain: Erik, looking the happiest he'd ever seen him, large arm wrapped around his shoulders; himself, grinning widely; Victoria, red mouth open in an immortal laugh; Josh, less bulky, with his braces still on; Grace, throwing bunny ears behind his head; Sally, as in-love as ever; Sam, with one arm around her and the other in the air, reaching for the sky. They sparkled. They were invincible. They looked confident that they'd be this close forever.

Everyone agreed it was a fantastic picture and Victoria, the mastermind of it, dubbed it profile picture worthy.

Before they'd all gone off to school, Sally got nice copies of some of the photos printed out at Costco. All the others were 3x5, but their full-group photo was a glossy 8x10. They signed the back of each other's copies and promised to hang it in their respective dorms. Sally had thoughtfully included his favorite picture, the one of him and Erik standing together at the edge of the cliff in feigned macho poses.

"So are we going to the same waterfall?" Sam jolted Alex out of his reverie.

"Wanna try?" Josh suddenly looked excited.

"Why not?" said Sally. "This summer's not nearly as hot as last summer. There might still be water."

"'Kay, let's do it. I need a good workout." Victoria flicked dirt off her nails and smiled at Josh. "And Josh really wants to see this waterfall." Josh muttered something that made Victoria laugh, but he couldn't hear from the back of the line.

He punched her in the arm playfully and they picked up their pace up the mountain. Alex followed Erik in their little line, and they attempted once more to find the waterfall.

Sam

He followed Grace in line and admired the visual of their group. He loved drawing them and animating his work, presenting it after a group dinner at Sally's house. They would all laugh as they realized that he'd captured their idiosyncrasies perfectly. One of his favorites – he included it in his portfolio that he sent to Pixar – was of them jumping off into a waterfall, the one that they'd never reached last summer. Cartoon Josh jumped first, his cannonball splashing the pink girls. Cartoon Victoria ("Damn, I'm even hot animated," she'd said as she watched her little drawn form) jumped after him, brandishing her fists like Popeye. Sally and Grace used Erik and Alex as paddleboards and sailed down the river after them. ("Where are you?" cried Sally, dismayed that he had forgotten himself. He gestured to the screen as he joined them, incarnated as a beaver with floppy blond hair). Their laughter was music to his ears, especially when it was at something he created. They all needed to laugh more.

His other friends – the ones who, like him, didn't go away to fancy schools and spent their days at the beach – couldn't understand why he was so close to this group of friends. He understood their confusion. From the outside, it didn't make much sense – the geniuses, the athletes, and him.

Unlike the other members of this group, he had not spent his high school career competing in the hardest classes possible; he preferred to float instead of fight against the current. He took average classes and got average grades, covering his notebooks in doodles and his little comics instead of actually taking notes. Everyone loved his comics. The stories were simple, when he felt like telling stories; sometimes he just drew what he felt like drawing. He knew he was good at it, and it made him happy. He drew pictures for Sally and made her happy. Sometimes he'd animate them and send his little creations to her: caricatures of themselves frolicking in the ocean, dancing on the Eiffel Tower, doing cartwheels through the Grand Canyon. They always made her laugh, and this made him happier than the animations did.

He knew his grades weren't spectacular and he had no interest in trying to convince anyone that they were. He applied to one school, the community college where kids from their high school went if they didn't know what they wanted to do with their lives (or just didn't want to move out). Sam was happy to go there and live at home. He usually had class for two or three hours and then spent the rest of the day drawing or surfing. He had plenty of less academic friends that went to LCCC, and he liked hanging out with them just fine. They weren't as driven as this group of overachievers, which was sometimes a relief and sometimes a little boring.

He watched Alex and Erik bound up the path, always competing. Alex's knee wobbled slightly but he kept going. They always kept going.

Josh

Alex and Erik pushed past him. After competing with and against them from tee ball through high school he'd gotten used to the sight of the two of them pushing against each other, making each other better. They'd always been the two best players in their age group and he enjoyed playing on the same team as them, getting an insider's glimpse to their strange telepathic connection both on and off the field.

They'd formed their little triangle in Little League, naturally drawn together because at age six the three of them had already established themselves as the best players in the league, each with their own golden potential and the shadow of genetic ability hanging over their heads. They silently bonded over the shared expectations for each of them: their fathers/ brother were champions, so naturally they would be as well.

Grace was the only one who knew how much he missed it. During junior and senior year he had to remain cool and cavalier and pretend that the absence of baseball from his daily life didn't leave a giant hole in his heart. In spite of his dad's poisoning of the game it had still become a huge part of his life – of his *soul*. If he didn't have to associate every practice and game with his dad brooding behind the backstop he would have played forever. He missed inhaling the leather of his glove, the feel of freshly mowed grass under his feet on the first day of the season, the dugout camaraderie, the pure, unadulterated joy that was flying through the air and hearing the satisfying thump of the ball landing in his glove. He missed the excitement of new uniforms and his favorite sweat-stained hat and taking off his smelly cleats after a double header. He missed the rush of stealing a base and tapping a barely-fair bunt and flicking the ball at an empty base and knowing that Erik would arrive to catch it and seal the double play.

He was good. On some days he was great, but he never tricked himself into thinking that he was on Erik and Alex's level. They could both go pro if they wanted, and they knew it. He was content to have a more relaxed career that ended on a high note. Starting at second on varsity as just as a sophomore was a pretty decent accomplishment and he was proud of himself.

He just wished his dad felt the same way.

Sally

She felt strangely hopeful as they made their way up the path. The forest sparkled and she wondered if this was what it was like to be drunk. She felt light and happy for the first time in a very long time. Even Sam's cheerful comments briefly augmented her own happiness.

There was just so much to see in the forest, so much life. She half-wondered if her enthusiasm was from the adrenaline of the hike, or the company of her friends, or the sheer appreciation of nature.

"There's the trail we took last year!" Victoria pointed at the skinny trail that bisected the one they were on. Sally recognized the familiar scary rocky outcroppings, the ones that kind of looked like they had an imprint of Mickey Mouse.

"Grace! The Mickey Mouse rock!" Grace was the one who noticed it last year. Sally was seized with inspiration.

"Victoria! Take a picture of us!" She fumbled with her backpack and pulled out her camera. "Grace! Get over here!" Sally wrapped an arm around Grace's waist.

It felt so strange to hold her friend after so long. A year ago holding each other was second nature, an almost thoughtless act that required no prior thought or contemplation. They thought little of physical contact. Hugging and holding used to be an automatic act for them, as simple and normal as holding a family member. Physical contact used to be so casual and meaningless and lovely.

Grace was a bit squishier since the last time Sally saw her. Not that there was anything wrong with gaining weight, but it made Sally sad that Grace wasn't taking care of herself, like she'd abandoned her workout routine and fallen victim to freshman dorm food. But she felt smaller at the same time, as if she cowed into herself, sad and lonely and vulnerable. The year's events had taken their toll, and Sally squeezed her friend closer to her, hoping to convey her love through simply touching.

Grace slumped and her stiffness slightly subsided and she led Sally hold her. She turned towards Sally, and for an instant everything felt exactly as it should be. Sally felt truly, utterly happy, and she smiled at her camera, secure in Victoria's hands.

Then the ground came rushing up to meet her and her side pounded and the moment ended, as fleetingly as it had begun.

Grace

She hated pictures. She hated being photographed. Especially now. She didn't want to record her emotions. She didn't want to remember how she felt later. She hadn't posed for a picture for a very long time and she didn't quite remember how.

But Sally was her friend, and this was their rock and she needed to make her friends happy because she was lost in the gloom and she hated knowing that her perpetually lugubrious state caused so much pain for her lovely, empathetic friends.

She felt unequivocally tense as she put her arm awkwardly around Sally. Sally was so, so skinny now. Not in a bad way, necessarily; not in a way that was necessarily concerning. She felt very, very firm, like her strict workout regime still dominated her life. Even her back felt firm and muscular, and her waist was trimmer than ever. Grace was not a jealous person, especially when her friends were involved, because she loved them and they loved her and she did not deserve their kindness. But with her arm around Sally's clearly perfect body she felt a little jealous and she wished she could be her.

Suddenly Sally was on the ground and she didn't know why and then Josh was on top of her and she was on the ground too and she felt herself being dragged and she let herself fall.

She felt like she was watching herself from above. Josh was on top of her and she didn't know why. She was vaguely conscious of Sam and Sally on the ground a few feet away.

Why were they all on the ground? She really ought to have wondered that a few moments before, but the proximity of Josh's face sort of pushed everything else out of her mind. Also, her butt really hurt.

"Are you okay?"

"Yeah." He was still on top of her. She remembered the innocent dog-piles of their childhood, when he was much less heavy.

"Sorry," said Josh.

He climbed off of her, gently, and she stayed on the ground, staring blankly at the sky, panting slightly. Suddenly she was very conscious of the rock under her back. She groaned softly and rolled off of it. Owww. That would definitely leave a bruise.

She sat up gingerly. Sally was just leaping to her feet, looking distressed. Sam had evidently just vacated her and looked like a kicked puppy.

A huge chunk of rock sat on the exact spot where Grace and Sally had just been standing. Mickey was missing a jagged chunk of ear, which nearly crushed them both.

"Holy crap." Even Victoria looked shaken. Sally's face was white. Sam kept looking between the chunk of rock and Sally.

"I'm glad you're okay," Josh said softly. Everyone looked so, so serious and she felt the oddest desire to laugh. Then she looked at the chunk of rock. It wasn't so much a chunk as a boulder the size of a smart car.

"Thank you." She tried to smile at Josh but it felt more like a grimace.

Sam

Wow, their faces were really close. Closer than they'd been in months. He wanted to yell at her for standing under a crumbling rock and kiss her for being alive.

"Are you okay?" she asked him. "Your arm's bleeding."

He looked down and sure enough, blood dripped from a large cut on his elbow. "Um, thanks." He realized that she looked really uncomfortable and he was still on top of her. "Sorry." He climbed off of her, trying not to push her further into the ground.

"Thank you," she said quietly, avoiding eye contact. So that was it, then, he thought. I save your life and you still act like a bitch.

Josh

"Do you want to go back? Do you need anything?" He still felt bad for crushing Grace. He hoped she was okay.

"I'm okay." Grace looked more spacey than usual. Her eyes wandered vaguely around the rock.

"I'm fine." Sally's face was still white but her voice was steady. "Sam's bleeding, though." She looked worried that her almost dying had caused him a small injury.

"You didn't bring any Band-Aids on this hike? God, Sally, you're losing your touch."

Laughing was a relief after what felt like hours of fear, but really lasted less than five seconds. He was happy when she laughed and hoped that she felt a little better.

"Thanks, Victoria." He was glad to see Sally smile.

"I know, right? The one time I'm unprepared, we actually have a casualty and need my bag of stuff."

"You okay, dude? We could totally go back if you want."

He shrugged. "I'm fine, let's keep going." Sam looked thoroughly unconcerned about his bleeding arm.

Victoria inspected it. "You're fine. It's just a scratch. You can put pressure on it to stop the bleeding sooner, but you're probably fine without it."

Sam grinned. "'Probably?' Great. Thanks."

Victoria laughed. "I hereby grant you a clean bill of health. You are allowed to continue hiking." She tapped him on the head with a stick.

"You sound more like a fairy godmother than a doctor," Sally said wryly. Victoria wrinkled her nose and tapped Sally on the head.

"Bibbity boppity boo, you're a slut and I am too!"

Sally frowned and turned bright red. Really? That was her best attempt at cheering her up?

Well, that was awkward. "Let's keep going." He led the way up the path. Victoria caught up to him and put her arm in his, making the comfortably one-person path a cozy two-person walkway.

"What the hell is going on this weekend?" she muttered. "We just watched them almost get crushed by a boulder, for God's sake. And everything's all awkward and weird, and I still don't know what's going on with Sam and Sally. Or you and Grace. That was pretty damn heroic, by the way, you should be proud of yourself. But you definitely have some explaining to do."

"I wish I knew."

"What do you mean? Are you even friends anymore? What's going on with you two?"

"I don't know, okay? Jesus. We went to school. We met other people and made new friends and I thought we were just… giving each other space. Growing up. And then her mom died and I didn't know what to do because she kept ignoring me."

"Join the club. She ignored all of us."

He felt instantly guilty. "We probably all would, if that happened to us."

She was silent for a moment and he listened to the dirt scraping under their feet. Suddenly he felt very tired. He didn't want to be having this conversation.

"Yeah, I guess. Sorry. But … God, Josh. You guys are best friends. You still could be. You're not that far from each other. Not that much has changed – for you, at least."

He sighed. "Everything's changed, Victoria. Everything's changed."

Alex

His knee throbbed and sweat beaded on his forehead. Damn. He didn't remember hiking to be this strenuous last summer. Of course, last summer he was an NCAA athlete.

Had he always taken being in shape for granted? Probably. Going to the gym was never a necessity – Coach Armstrong's brutal six-hour workouts kept him at a superb peak. His extra beach runs and weight-lifting with Erik just sculpted the already defined clay. Always extra. Always better.

After fall quarter he tried to maintain his form, but even though he spent hours at the gym he couldn't replicate the results of Coach's workouts. His knee burned as he attempted the Stairmaster but he kept going. Always climb up. Never look down.

"You need to slow down," his physical therapist told him during one of their weekly appointments. A blue UCLA barrette held back her curly hair, matching the blue of her nails. "You need time to heal."

"I don't work out that much," he lied.

She gestured towards the treadmill. "Let's go. Slowly."

He pulled himself up, trying to look effortless. He felt her eyes burning into him as he programmed a low setting – only five out of twenty, instead of twelve, like he usually started with – and started jogging.

The lingering soreness of yesterday's run built into a slow burn and he gritted his teeth. One foot in front of the other. He closed his eyes, pretending he was running behind Erik at practice. The mile lap. Grass under his cleats. Coach's whistle in the distance. Lightly panting. Erik bobbing up and down in front of him.

He glanced at the machine. He'd only run half a mile? How was that possible? He'd been on here for five minutes already.

He ran faster, feeling the ache inch slowly upward before it climaxed into a crescendo of pain. Sweat dripped down his chest and his clammy hand shot forward, desperately pushing the down button, panting until the treadmill finally stopped. Oh God oh God oh God. A volcano was going to burst in his knee and send blood flying and tendons whipping madly and oh God it hurt –

She put her hand on his shoulder and he realized that he was crouched in the fetal position on the edge of the treadmill. "Alex, I know it's hard. But you're not doing yourself any favors if you keep going at this pace." To his horror, he felt tears welling in the corners of his eyes. How embarrassing. She looked away tactfully and handed him a tissue. "I see it all the time. You have high standards for yourself. You're an athlete. You expect perfection. But Alex, listen to me." He glanced up at her, all knowledgeable and professional and confident in his failure. "You will never reach that level again unless you let yourself heal first. Do you understand?"

He nodded.

"Do you have any questions for me?"

"Can I still lift weights?"

She sighed and glanced at his chart. "You haven't been making the kind of progress that I'd like to see. I think the weight lifting that you do with me is sufficient."

He gestured towards the pair of purple weights on the table. "Those weigh five pounds. They're not doing anything for me." It felt so odd to defy an authority figure, but still. This was *his* knee. This was his life.

She looked shrewdly over the brim of her tortoiseshell glasses. She couldn't be that much older than him. Twenty-five, maybe? She probably didn't have enough experience to condemn him to inertia. She had no idea how hard he'd worked to get here, how much further he still had to go.

"Alex. You have to stop pushing yourself so hard, or you will never play baseball again."

He stood up and crossed the room as less-shakily as he could, and slammed the door.

He crossed the plaza and found himself in the middle of the gym. Again.

The cardio room was packed with people – skinny girls, athletic guys, even an old professor whose flabby flesh jiggled as he bounded easily up the Stairmaster. Two of his friends from the swim team waved at him from their treadmills and he forced a smile, ignoring the empty one next to them. He definitely didn't feel ready to run next to them.

He headed into the weight room, the walls of mirrors throwing his unwelcome reflection at him from every direction. Guys as built as he was lifted hundred-pound weights like they were pillows. His engineering friend caught his eye and grinned upside-down as he balanced his handstand against the wall. Jesus. No privacy. No opportunity to hide a shameful performance.

He quickly moved to the other side and found an unoccupied space between two strangers. Neither of them were UCLA athletes, but they easily could have been. Both guys put his baseball muscles to shame. Their bro tanks showed off the work of Arm Day. Their salmon workout shorts showed that they weren't as dedicated to Leg Day.

Envy coursed through him as he began lifting, realizing that he was only lifting three-quarters of what they were. His knee trembled as he pulled the weight up higher, overly conscious of the sculpted behemoths on either side of him, both probably judging him. I'm one of you, he wanted to tell them. I'm an athlete. I'm good at this.

He set the weight down slowly but the fire still burned. Sweat beaded on his forehead and he bit his lip, trying not to cry out.

He avoided eye contact as he fled the weight room.

Josh bounded easily up the path in front of him. Josh wasn't slowed down by self-consciousness or heavy breathing or his treacherous knee. He wished he could keep up that pace and still laugh and talk without panting. Victoria wrapped her arm around Josh and they led the line like the king and queen of fitness. Josh's muscular arms sparkled with sunshine, not sweat, and the cut of his tank top accentuated his shoulders, like the guys in the gym. How could one attain that look? How long did it take to master the intricacies of appearance? Josh and guys like Josh moved with an ease and effortlessness that Alex sorely missed.

Maybe it was confidence. Everything came down to confidence, in the end. Maybe he could get it back. Maybe he could be himself again.

He wished he could be Josh, who always kept his cool and seemed ready for everything. He wished he didn't have to go back to school so soon. Bracing himself for the school year always felt like holding his breath before trying to touch the bottom of a very deep pool. He needed more time. He needed to take a deep breath, he knew that, but everything just kept speeding up. He needed time to figure out his life and the person he was and the person he wanted to be.

Josh already knew all of that. Lucky him.

Sam

Grace slipped on the rock and caught herself before she could fall. His arms outstretched automatically and she smiled sadly. She always looked so sad. He wondered what happened between her and Josh. They'd been like brother and sister, and now it seemed like they barely talked to each other.

He wished he could feel angry. He should feel angry. But anger was not a typical emotion for him and he wasn't accustomed to feeling it; he was used to being happy because that was what people needed him to be. He was good at being happy.

He thought about the first few weeks after she broke up with him. He spent most of the time in his room with the door closed, staring at the ceiling, trying to drown himself in Coldplay and The Smiths. The songs had so much more meaning than they did before. He surprised himself by crying, realizing that he was now part of a sad, broken tribe that spoke the language of unrequited love.

"Are we almost there?" he heard Victoria ask.

Grace

Josh whooped and he ran to the end of the trail, arms outstretched. Sally and Victoria followed, screaming delightedly and she followed, leaving the path to gaze at the finally flowing waterfall.

How could you not appreciate such a sight? It drew her from the depths of her loneliness and for a wonderful moment everything was forgotten. The good thoughts toppled the bad and she couldn't feel anything but ineffable awe. She peered over the edge and felt a thrill of fear. Perhaps it was the day's near-death experience, but here, on top of a mountain, surrounded by friends, watching a brilliant force of nature exert its authority without threatening to destroy her, she felt truly alive.

She felt the wind ripple through her hair, cooling the sweaty parts that begged for water, and she thought she could feel a few flecks of spray kiss her face. She closed her eyes and she was Pocahontas, she was Rose at the helm of the Titanic, she was soaring and the wind was beneath her wings instead of beating her down.

Maybe this was why people loved nature so much. She thought she'd be in nature at Cornell, but Ithaca was a frigid and unfriendly sort of nature that froze the bad feelings, making them last forever, and numbed the good ones, keeping them from coursing through her and making her feel like a real, living, happy person. This was nature. Nature was supposed to be warm and nurturing and make you feel inspired instead of broken, alive instead of dying.

Had her banishment from warm weather really wreaked so much havoc on her personal happiness? College was supposed to make her feel alive, but it was nothing compared to this. Here there was wind and water and sun, glorious sun, that warmed and revived her after so many months of frozen exile. The warm glow swept through her, so much more real and beautiful than her short-lived respites from snow and sleet. She'd adopted an aversion to waterfalls but here waterfalls weren't the problem at all, were they? The problem was the chilling, empty loneliness and the tied-downness and the always-stuckness. This feeling, this beautifully pure and wonderful feeling, was the utter opposite of loneliness. Her friends were here and they loved her. She was in nature and loved it instead of feared it. There was so much to love and be thankful for. She *had* grown, hadn't she? She'd reached some point of self-actualization if she was able to be happy right now, right?

The waterfall crashed down, a euphony of force and beauty, and a thrill of wind slapped her face, and she recalled standing on a similar precipice on a very different day. She remembered her scared self standing on the bridge two days after her mom's funeral. Cornell had a scarily high suicide rate. Other students had stood where she stood and had the same fears and doubts and confusion that she did. They realized they just couldn't take it anymore and they gave up. They had nothing to look forward to and they knew it. Maybe their moms died, too. Maybe they'd also lost a parent or someone they loved.

Grace clenched the rail and realized how easy it would be to scale the gate and just jump. In movies they always showed people jumping, and falling, and screaming dramatically as they plunged to a fate that they'd chosen. Why would you scream? That wasn't dignified. But maybe there was something to that, to choosing your own fate. It showed a certain amount of control over your own destiny – or maybe no control at all. Maybe it was just surrendering to everything.

She closed her eyes and remembered that cold, awful day, and walking into her mom's room and the heels lined up mocking her on the floor and the Coach bag waiting for someone to pick it up and the black blazer draped like an omen on the chair that her mom would never sit on again. And then she walked to the other side of the bed and saw her mom's face and the bottle of pills and the note, the cold, awful note written in that perfect handwriting with those five little words that changed everything:

"I can't do it anymore."

She clutched the note and the pills, and didn't know how long she held them for as she stared at her mom's face, willing for this to not be real, for it to all be a dream, a horribly bad and real dream. It seemed so surreal, sitting on the floor of her mom's room holding a bottle of pills that her mom had swallowed and now her mom was dead and this note gave her no reason.

And then she fainted.

Eventually she woke up and sat on the floor for a while. At some point, she realized that she should call someone, and she made herself get off the floor and go in the kitchen and get the phone and call 911 and say some words. She sat on the kitchen floor and stared at the note and the pills in front of her, and when the paramedics came to the door she suddenly shoved them in her pocket. She didn't know why. She just knew that she didn't want them to have it, that she needed a little more time to figure it out. She very obediently did everything they told her to. They asked if she could call her dad and she tried to dial his number, but her hands shook too much. The paramedic called him for her. He helped her call Sally and Josh.

It was like a horrible, surreal soap opera and she watched it as if she were underwater. Her dad's car squealing into the driveway, Max crying, still in his soccer uniform, her dad, white-faced, babbling at the paramedics, Sally running through the door and holding her. Weird details stood out. She felt very concerned that Max was wearing his cleats inside and made him take them off. Her mom's sunglasses were on the counter and she felt like she should put them away but didn't know where to put them. She saw Sally's face through a haze and realized that Sally looked awful and vaguely wondered why. Her brother sobbed into her side and her dad paced around the living room calling people. She was amazed at how she felt nothing. She felt like she was watching herself standing in the middle of the kitchen. I should be crying, she thought as she wasn't. She just watched and waited to feel.

Death didn't stop for time. Time didn't stop for death.

When the paramedics were ready to take her mom out, Sally herded her and Max into the living room. Max sat on her lap as Sally put in the first DVD she could find and played it loudly, blaring out any noise of the paramedics moving her mom out of their house. She wrapped her arms around Max as *Toy Story* started playing and he kept crying, his pool of tears soaking her sweater. He was so little, only eight. He was too little to feel unloved. He was too little not to have a mom. Sally kept her arm around her and Max kept his head on her and she loved them both so much but she also felt trapped.

She was aware of activity in the foyer, and she held Max's head so that he couldn't turn to see their mom leaving their house for the last time. She closed her eyes. Sally's grip on her tightened and a small whimper stirred in her throat. Sally was crying and Sally's mom was still alive and Grace couldn't cry.

The note was still in her pocket.

"I can't do it anymore."

That was it, nothing else, no further explanation as to what "it" was. She'd brooded over this for months, writing the words over and over on her notes in class, wondering just what exactly she meant. Her mom was defined by her control and her domination of her surroundings, and that included the people around her. Right?

She mulled it over in class, in the shower, in bed in the hopeless hours when she wanted to fall asleep but was afraid to give in to the unconscious images that were worse than the conscious memories. She didn't want to remember, but she desperately needed to. Surely there was some key that explained everything, some tiny thing that she could think of and pinpoint and then everything would make sense.

Maybe it was the pressure of her mom's job, and being the youngest and first female partner, and the endless scrutiny that she constantly, bitterly reminded Grace that she was under. She didn't know the exact specifics of her mom's job, only that it sometimes involved multimillion-dollar transactions between huge corporations, and that her mom was in charge of writing the fine print that could mean the difference between a million and a billion.

But her mom loved it, and thrived under pressure, and lived for her career. Grace realized that a little after New Year's. Her job was what kept her going, what made her happy. She got the same sort of savage satisfaction from winning a case that she did when she won anything. She won a lot.

So it had to be something else, Grace decided. Max was so little and cute and certainly an occasional troublemaker, but nothing that she couldn't handle. It had to be her dad and his probable affairs and the arguments that had grown steadily in tempo and frequency, resulting in screaming matches that ended in her dad leaving early for his business trip… if they even were business trips. She'd never doubted him before, but maybe the endless excursions were actually to lovers instead of litigations….

Or maybe it was her. Maybe it was the sheer pain of raising an undecided failure of a daughter who was not particularly lovely or charming or attorney-like. Maybe trying to make Grace into a perfect replica of herself– which her mom had tried to do for eighteen years – was the "it." She could have prevented this. This was her fault. If she were better, Max would still have a mom.

She had no control over her life anymore. She could just end it and not have to think about her dead mom and her sad brother and her angry dad. She could just jump and not have nightmares about her mom's empty stare and that sinking feeling of knowing she was gone and wasn't coming back. She couldn't stand it anymore.

It was up to her to take charge of her life. She was the one calling the shots. She had to take care of herself now. Her fate lay in her hands.

I am the master of my fate. I am the captain of my soul.

She thought of her friends and wondered how they'd find out that she was dead. How would they feel when they learned how she died? What would her funeral look like? Her dad and brother, and family members, and friends, and teachers and coaches and everyone that had played a role in her becoming who she was. Josh's mom, the kindest maternal figure in her life, who had hugged her thousands more times than her own mom had. The principals of her schools would be there. Her old babysitter. Her aunts and uncles and cousins and neighbors. Maybe even regular community people that she didn't know personally but would hear about it and feel obligated to attend, like old classmates and her brother's friends' parents. They would all mourn her. They would all be sad. Her friends would be the saddest, she thought.

Of course they would. You couldn't choose your family members, but you could choose your friends, and for whatever reason, her friends had chosen her. They'd elected to bring her into their close circle, and even if she didn't deserve such special treatment, she'd received it. They were nice to her. They loved her.

She unclenched her fist from the rail and sank down to the ground. How could she even consider doing something so drastic? Her friends loved her. If she were to – to go through with it, they would see it as the ultimate betrayal. She would be choosing to leave them. It would be like showing them that she didn't care for everything they'd done for her, that all the times they'd spent together meant nothing. Climbing and jumping would be like saying that her friends' kindness and love that they'd so generously bestowed upon her was a waste. She would be throwing away a beautiful gift.

She remembered crouching on the ground for a long time. A few people walked by her and didn't say anything. She kept her head buried in her arms and just rocked back and forth. She couldn't believe she considered doing that.

It started to rain, a harsh drizzle that drilled onto her hands, and she buried them in her pockets. She'd forgotten gloves. She forgot a lot of things lately.

She felt like she should cry, but she'd been doing so much crying lately that she felt thirsty. Was it possible to actually dehydrate yourself through tears? If so then she definitely had. In the beginning she'd wept for hours on end, watching as water poured out of her body, feeling the huge gasps drag sickening amounts of air into her stomach. She threw up a few times from crying so hard and laid with her arms clasped around the toilet gagging. Her roommate left the room during these sessions and she didn't blame her.

She was so tired of crying. She hated it. She loathed it. She wished she could stop.

When she was done crying and throwing up she sometimes took a shower just to have a change of location and feel some warmth. The pipes got so cold in the winter and it took a few minutes for the water to get to a comfortable temperature. She turned it up as high as it would go and stood under the scalding stream, crying and feeling. Her useless tears ran down the drain with actually functional water and vestiges of vomit. Her nose ran and the snot joined the disgusting, shameful trail of emotions that could be buried in the Cornell plumbing. She wished everything else could be buried in the plumbing. She pictured all of her bodily fluids combining in a revolting amalgamation and causing a pipe to burst and her sadness would leak all over someone's dorm and they would know it was her and she would get kicked out of school and cry at home and burst their pipes and her dad would get mad.

Crying was such an odd act. Your body rebelled against you for a few days and used up all your water and then you found yourself standing next to a huge body of different water and contemplated leaping into it.

She wasn't sure exactly how long she stayed on the ground, but she completely forgot about her classes and wandered back to her dorm. Her roommate left as soon as she came in. Maybe Jessica was trying to give her space, and she tried to appreciate it. It was nice to have the room to herself but it also felt horribly lonely. Sally would have taken care of her.

Her own reflection caught her eye and she stared into Jessica's mirror. Looking at herself made her feel worse. Her eyes… God, she'd never seen them so puffy. She'd forgotten her winter coat and just wore her Cornell sweatshirt with jeans, and her sweatshirt was completely soaked. Her matted hair clung to her scalp, little tendrils wrapping themselves around her neck. She was glad she'd abandoned makeup because that would have been smeared and made her look even worse. Her face was a strange contrast between puffy and sagging; she sometimes forgot to eat, but the crying made her cheeks distended. She didn't even look like herself. She looked like a pale and broken imitation of someone she used to recognize.

She peeled off her sodden clothes and wished that she had someone to do her laundry. She hated having to re-wear her wet clothes all the time but she couldn't bear the thought of a close human interaction in the laundry room. She always saw someone she knew in there and they would ask her "how are you" and she would start crying and she hated crying in front of people. She didn't want to tell people about her mom because saying it out loud made it real. She'd emailed Jessica the day before returning to school, and she didn't know how many people Jessica had told, if any, but she hoped to keep that number to a minimum. If people knew then they might try to reach out to her or be nice to her and that would make everything so much worse because everything was her fault. It was bad enough that her home friends knew and kept texting and calling and emailing. She turned her phone off because she was tired of seeing it light up and hearing it vibrate with her friends' worries. She couldn't talk to them right now.

She wished they would understand why. When she was at her lowest she hated to be around people that loved her because she knew it hurt them to see her that way, whether she was lost in her poisonous self-loathing or drowning in confusion about her mom's … suicide. She knew exactly what they would do. Sally would be the main comforter. She would hold her and let her cry and comb her hair and tuck her into bed. Sally would act like a mom and that would make everything so much worse. Sam, funny, sweet, stupidly brave Sam, would do anything to make her laugh. Victoria, not wanting to show any emotion whatsoever, would tell Erik what to do because she knew he needed direction. Alex would embarrass her with attention and hold her until he was sure she wasn't broken.

And Josh… if she told Josh that she needed him, he would be there on the first train, and he would stay with her as long as she asked him to. He would be her friend and do whatever she needed. At the time, she felt like she didn't deserve the kindness that she knew her friends would bestow upon her. She couldn't bear the thought of being the recipient of such pure goodness. They would love her just for being her.

How many times had she picked up her phone and set it down without dialing? How many emails had she almost sent? She wanted to call for help. She almost did, so many times, and each one seemed like a message in a bottle thrown into a never-ending ocean. She so badly needed them. She wished to deserve them. A small part of her held herself responsible, and another part knew that it was ridiculous to think that way, that her mom was a grown adult who made her own decisions. But that tiny dark box lingered in the attic of her mind and she was afraid that if they came to her she would tell them everything. She didn't want to remember that her mom didn't love her. She didn't need to be reminded of that.

And here, on the edge of a waterfall, she remembered. On the edge of friendship and falling she was reminded and she didn't mind. And somehow, that made all the difference.

Sally

She peered over the edge. What a view. This completely made up for last summer's lack of waterfall. She closed her eyes and felt the wind ruffle her hair. God, this was amazing. She needed this. She missed this. She hoped her friends felt as happy as she did.

She remembered learning about the sublime in her Romantic lit class. After the lecture she printed out a copy of *Wanderer above the Sea of Fog* and tacked it above her desk. That painting seemed to sum up so much about her ideal life as she envisioned it: standing on a rocky precipice watching the tumultuous waves tossing below her. The first two quarters of college felt like she was thrown between the waves, dragged under by forces greater than she, but she would learn to swim.

She'd grown up so much this past year – the past six months, really. She'd almost drowned. She still felt like she was drowning, sometimes. But those first few months, when everything was topsy-turvy in the least expected ways, she found herself engulfed by the white caps of unfurling fate that tossed her in every direction and left her gasping for air. The swells beat mercilessly against her and pulled her under with their foamy relentlessness until she didn't know which was up and she felt ready to capitulate to the forces around her.

But she hadn't. She couldn't. She owed it to herself – to her family and friends – to learn to swim. She owed them that much. So she pushed and fought until her head was above water, and then she could swim to shore. She clung to the rocks and pulled her ragged body out of the water, dragging herself with every ounce of determination she could, trying to shake off the self-hatred of the past few months. It seemed an impossible task, but she did it. She certainly wasn't as well-dressed as the guy in Friedrich's painting, but she felt just as triumphant as he did, looking down at the waves below. Nature dazzled and defied and derided her and she respected it for it. She knew her place was to admire instead of conquer, but she felt a thrill of satisfaction knowing that she had lifted herself up from the metaphoric deluge.

Maybe she was done with drowning. Maybe this could be her chance to keep climbing and never look back. She could rise above her shame and her self-hatred and ascend towards a peak of self-reconciliation and acceptance. She would have to.

"Excuse me!" Victoria's voice jolted her out of her reverie. She was talking to a pair of hikers behind them. "Can you please take a picture of us?" She brandished her camera emphatically.

"Of course!" the elderly woman came forward kindly. She took her glasses from her fanny pack and Sally heard Erik snort. The woman was being kind to them and he was laughing at her fanny pack and Sally found herself extremely annoyed with him. Victoria showed her how to use it and turned back to the group, once again in the role of bossy visionary.

"Get in line!" Victoria yelled at them. Josh and Alex positioned themselves on either side of Erik, who dwarfed them. They stood comically entwined while the girls arranged themselves around them. Grace moved to her left side and Victoria moved away from her so that – oh, great. Of course. She should have expected this. She put her arm around Grace and could feel Josh's hand graze her back. It slipped a little lower than friendship level and she felt him hurriedly pull it back up. Just an accident, nothing noteworthy.

Sam stood next to her and wrapped his arm around her shoulders with surprising authority. She thought he'd be weird and hesitant but he held her with a firmness that she found both startling and gratifying. His hand lingered briefly on the curve of her waist and she felt the susurrations of something long-dormant and entirely unwelcome.

They wrapped their arms around each other, just like last summer. She could feel him next to her. She wondered what he was thinking. He smelled a little salty from the hike, but that was fine; she was used to the smell of their cross-country workouts mingling. His face was very close to hers. Grace's arm was around her. Josh's arm was on her. She was surrounded by people she loved.

"One, two, three!" The woman called. "I think I got it." Victoria freed herself from the line and ensured that the picture was of sufficient quality.

"Thank you!" Sally called. Her friends followed suit and the woman looked pleased. "No problem!" Sally waved goodbye to her and her husband as they continued down the trail. Victoria liked to solicit favors from strangers but she rarely thanked them, a constant source of consternation for her.

Grace looked slightly happier than earlier and Sally hoped she was happy. She hoped they were all happy. She hoped Sam – well, she didn't know what she wanted him to think. But she hoped they were good thoughts. In the dark recesses of her mind a little ray of light began to shine through again and she beamed out at the waterfall, not sure if she should let herself feel happy but enjoying it anyways.

Victoria

"I'm hungry," Erik said. Trust Erik to ruin a perfect opportunity to ruin a beautiful view that they hiked three miles to see.

"We just ate an hour ago."

"I'm still hungry."

Sally ruffled through her mini backpack and pulled out a grocery bag. She tossed him a granola bar. "How's this?"

He wolfed it down. "Do you have any more?"

Fucking boys. Fucking Erik. (Always an adjective, never a verb – at least in his case).

Chapter 5

Sam

Climbing down was easier. He definitely preferred it to going up.

He wished he had paper and a pen. He wanted to draw their little group clamoring down the rocks, trying not to skid. It would have made a funny cartoon.

Sally

Climbing down a mountain was not nearly as rewarding as climbing up. She loved conquering. She loved testing herself. She hated feeling like she was disregarding hours of effort by returning to the bottom.

At least this time she was going to the bottom voluntarily, she thought. Her downward spiral had been the opposite of voluntary. She'd been totally forced into it.

That wasn't true, she reminded herself, as she had countless times. She hadn't been forced into anything. She was a consensual and willing participant in her own destruction.

With a jolt she realized the date and remembered that today was the one-year anniversary of losing her virginity.

That night in the car in the woods, after they were done and laying naked in the backseat, she remembered feeling very happy. She'd wanted this for a long time. They were both eighteen. They used protection. She knew her parents wouldn't approve, but they had waited four years and she knew that he was the boy she was going to marry, so God would be okay with it.

She'd always imagined that she would feel tremendously guilty after the first time. She felt guilty just kissing him on her porch when he dropped her off. But she realized that this was something that she really wanted, because it confirmed for her that they would be together forever. Maybe she was a little young, but he was the only guy she would ever sleep with. She had told him that she wouldn't sleep with anyone unless she wanted to marry them, and he told her that he felt the same way. It seemed like a pre-engagement, like a promise that they were making to each other. She was going to marry the boy that was her first kiss, her first everything, and that was all she wanted.

Maybe we'll take our kids camping, she thought as they quietly headed back to the tent. When we're thirty and have kids we'll take them everywhere and we'll be the happiest family in the world.

She stayed in her happy state of mind as she prepared to move to school, and this confidence in her future eased the transition into the unknown. She thought about how lucky she was that she already had a boyfriend who wanted to marry her, someone that she knew would take care of her and love her forever. She could focus on academics and get perfect grades and not have to worry about finding a boy at a new school. The long distance would suck, but she would see him at Thanksgiving.

She called him as often as possible during the first few weeks, the only weeks of college that she'd really enjoyed. She told him about her new friends and classes and clubs. Everyone on her floor was her new best friend. Her roommate was amazing. Classes were fascinating. She loved everything.

Her Christian club wanted to go on a mission to Guatemala, and she excitedly told him all about their plans. All she had to do was get a quick check-up and she was good to go. She promised to call him after her doctor's appointment and she jogged to the health center, smiling to herself as she mulled over how much she loved Stanford. She was so busy, but she loved everything she was doing, and all of her new friends. She hoped the appointment would be quick so that she could meet up with some girls from her floor for dinner.

She waited a few minutes before they called her name. She smiled at the nice nurse who led her to the exam room.

"So you want to go out of the country?"

"Yep! My Christian group wants to go to Guatemala and build houses." She was so proud to be a part of her group. She loved meeting similarly selfless people that loved being selfless.

"That's wonderful!" The nurse said, beaming. "I'm just going to ask you a few basic questions and take a blood sample before I sign you up for any necessary inoculations."

"Of course!"

"Age?"

"Eighteen."

"Height?"

"Five-three."

"Weight?"

"One-ten."

"Have you ever had chicken pox?"

"Nope."

"Date of your last period?"

Sally thought. In all the hubbub of school she hadn't realized that her little box of tampons sat unopened in her closet. That often happened when she was busy and not sleeping, and she definitely was adjusting to a new sleepless lifestyle. When was the last time she'd had it? She closed her eyes and thought hard. The week before camping? She remembered feeling relieved that it wouldn't obstruct her plans to swim in the lake.

"August... fourteenth."

The nurse peered over her glasses at her. "Are you sexually active?"

"No." Sally said automatically. Then she remembered. "Oh. Oh my gosh. Yes. Just once though."

The nurse looked sternly at her, all traces of admiration for her charitable works gone. "When was that?"

Sally felt the blood drain from her face. "August twentieth." It couldn't be.

"Did you use protection?"

Sally nodded. "Of course."

"Are you usually regular?"

Visions of her calendar spun around in her head as she tried to remember disappointing lost beach days and particularly uncomfortable cross country practices. "I.... I don't know."

"Okay then, I want you to go in the bathroom and take this pregnancy test. Just to make sure." She pulled a purple box out of a bin and handed it to her. "Right down the hall, to the left."

Sally walked down the hall, not believing that she was holding a pregnancy test. She couldn't be pregnant. She was Sally Chandler, for God's sakes. She was not the kind of girl to get pregnant at eighteen.

This was so surreal. She held the box behind her as another girl came out of the bathroom. What if she saw someone she knew? What if she saw one of her new friends while she was holding a pregnancy test box? That would be horrible. She'd just met them. They thought she was sweet. Everyone thought she was sweet. She was Sally Chandler.

She sat on the toilet, too tense to pee. She held the stick under herself like she knew you were supposed to do from TV. She read the instructions on the box and waited.

There were two in the box so she decided to try that one too. She wrapped both sticks in toilet paper and carried them back to the exam room, feeling very odd and hoping that no one saw her.

The nurse was waiting, the friendly veneer replaced by professional concern. "Well, let's see it." Sally unwrapped the two sticks.

Two plus signs.

Her heart caught in her throat and she couldn't breathe and no she couldn't be pregnant her life was just beginning and the nurse was holding a paper bag to her mouth telling her breathe honey breathe and she laid back and cried and the nurse held her.

"Honey, you're not the first girl I've seen in here who got an unwanted surprise," the nurse said gently.

Sally rocked back and forth. She wasn't like other girls. This couldn't happen to her.

"Do you want me to call your parents, or do you want to call them? Or do you not want them involved?"

Sally sobbed harder as she imagined the look of disappointment on her mom's face, the betrayal her dad would feel. She was their good little girl. They'd both waited until marriage. They'd talked about it with her many times, once they realized that Sam was a permanent addition to their lives, and she knew that they'd expected her to wait.

"Please don't – they can't know. It would kill them."

"I won't call them, but I think you should. Maybe not right now, but later. Even if it seems like they'll be mad at you, they love you and want you to be safe. They'll forgive you."

Sally shook her head. "You don't understand. My parents are very – they won't. They'll hate me forever." She sobbed into her shirt.

"I'm sure that's not true." The nurse rubbed her back like her mom did.

"I'm a good kid, I go to church, I go to Stanford. I'm supposed to be...."

"Nobody's perfect, hon. Everybody has something happen that they don't plan for."

This couldn't be happening right now.

"Do you want me to call the father for you?"

She shook her head.

"I really think you should call your parents, talk about your options."

"Options?" Her nose dripped onto her sleeve.

"You could give it up for adoption. There are tons of nice, financially responsible people that would love a happy, healthy baby. They could take care of it, make sure it has a future."

This was not happening.

"I'm guessing that you're not in a position to raise a child right now. Do you think you could go through with a pregnancy?"

Sally sat frozen. Did she mean what she thought she meant?

Her parents were staunchly pro-life. They believed that if you got pregnant you were obligated to have the baby. "You might as well turn your mistake into someone else's miracle," her mom always said whenever abortion popped up in conversation. They knew so many nice couples that hadn't been able to conceive but adopted happy, healthy babies. Their lives changed forever.

Her life would change forever. Everything she'd worked for would be gone. All the years of studying, of making herself better... she'd have to leave Stanford. After only a few weeks of being there. Her parents' dream for her would be shattered. Their conception of her, their understanding of who she was, her perception of herself.... It would all go down the toilet.

She was supposed to be a role model for her little sisters. Carly would be an ... *aunt*... at twelve. Jenny would be an aunt at nine. She was the example for them. They looked up to her, tried on her clothes, tagged along as much as they could. They loved her and respected her and she hadn't realized until now how much their admiration meant to her. Maybe they were too little to understand... but they would, eventually, and they would feel the waves of judgment emanating from their parents and grandparents and they too would think that she was.... a slut. It was inevitable. It would come to that.

Everyone's perception of her would come to that. She imagined the surprise as her old teachers and youth group leaders learned of this unexpected twist in the life of one of their favorite, most studious, most ambitious pupils. They all had such high hopes for her. She'd flourished under the generous praise of the adults in her life, and they'd all expressed their excitement to see what she would become, the potential that she had to do great things, how she had already done so many great things at eighteen.

At eighteen her life would revolve not around school and friends, as it should – her life would revolve around... baking a baby for nine months and preparing herself to give it away. Spending the next seven months of her life getting fat and taking vitamins and sitting around her parents' house while they hated her, all so that she could give away the product of her nine months, and then try to return to her old, broken life?

"I can't have a baby," she whispered.

"Do you want some time to think it over? This is a big decision."

"No." Sally croaked. "No, I know right now. I can't have a baby. No one can know."

"Are you absolutely sure?"

"Yes." Tears spilled out of her eyes. She put her hand gingerly over her stomach. Sam's baby was in there.

"How big is it?" She imagined a little nuggety baby curled up inside of her, a tiny huddled mass of cells that had the potential to grow into a real person. She didn't even know if it was a girl or a boy. She didn't want to know. That would make it worse.

The nurse looked at the calendar. "Today's the sixteenth ... about the size of a kidney bean."

She looked down in wonder. A kidney bean. A little bitty kidney bean, half her, half Sam, was growing inside of her.

For a moment she envisioned herself with a baby at her chest, Sam and her parents looking on fondly. Then she realized that would never happen. It couldn't.

"A kidney bean." She whispered. Something the size of a kidney bean was going to change her life forever, no matter what she did.

Her parents would hate her. She would not be the daughter that dropped out of Stanford to raise a baby out of wedlock. Her grandma would hate her. Her church would hate her.

"Abortion is perfectly acceptable if you're not prepared to raise a baby," the nurse said softly. "You'd be doing it more harm than good if you brought it into the world before you can take care of it. You can always have babies when you have your degree and an income. And then your parents will love you even more."

She clung to the nurse and sobbed huge billowing sobs until the nurse's sleeve was completely soaked. "I'm so sorry," she said thickly, realizing it.

"Happens all the time," she said breezily. "It's just water."

Sally took a deep breath. "Can you please tell me…." She sighed. "Can you please tell me what to do next?"

"Of course, hon." She pulled some pamphlets from another cubby.

An hour later, Sally emerged, puffy-eyed, with an appointment confirmation for an abortion clinic the next week. She walked back to her dorm, crawled into bed, and cried for the baby that she couldn't have and her own childhood that she'd thrown away.

She isolated herself as much as possible for the next few days. She ignored her new friends' invitations and her old friends' messages. Sam called. Grace emailed. Her parents called. She texted them tiny, uninteresting tidbits, enough for them to know that she was alive, not enough for them to have any notion of her actual emotional state. She shut off her phone after Sam's picture flashed on it three times in a row.

She missed classes and told her roommate she was sick. Her Nikes lay abandoned under her bed, where she'd kicked them off after her life-changing doctor's appointment. They sat on top of the paper about the Guatemala trip.

The Wednesday after the appointment, she got on the bus with a book that she did not read. She looked out the window and wondered if she'd ever be the same. She thought about the kidney bean inside of her. She'd always felt strangely removed from the abortion debate – she always assumed it wouldn't apply to her, that premarital sex wasn't an option. When she had envisioned herself telling her parents that she was pregnant, she was in her late twenties at least, and seemed tall and cool and mature and financially stable. She would buy her parents matching "Grandma" and "Grandpa" t-shirts and her whole family would celebrate.

That was how it was supposed to be, she chastised herself. This was her punishment for not waiting as long as she was supposed to.

And Sam... she couldn't even think about Sam.

She got off about twenty minutes later and followed the directions she'd printed out. She walked past the clinic before realizing that it was the right number – it was so tiny and unassuming. How could such a life-altering process take place in such a tiny building?

She took a deep breath and went in.

She waded towards the front desk, still feeling like she was underwater. The entire week seemed like a bad dream. She muttered her name – what if someone she knew was here? – and sat down, rubbing her knuckles together nervously as she waited to be called. There was one other girl in the waiting area. She looked about Sally's age, very pretty, curly red hair and blue eyes that looked like they were full of tears. Her friend held her hand. "You can do this," she heard the friend say.

She needed a friend right now. She needed someone to be here with her. She hadn't talked to anyone besides her roommate in a week. She needed a real friend. She needed someone that loved her.

She needed Sam.

She took out her phone and held it uncertainly. What would she say to him? How could she possibly explain?

The words would come. Or maybe they wouldn't. Just hearing his voice would be enough.

She scrolled down to his name and was about to call when she heard her own name.

She put her phone back in her purse and followed the nurse down the hallway, feeling a strange déjà vu from last week. Except this time she'd leave here with a little piece of her gone.

Grace

Everyone thought that climbing down was so easy, but it wasn't really. She clutched a rock as she started skidding down. God. At least when you were climbing up you felt like you were going somewhere, like you were achieving something. When you were going down you just… erased all of your effort.

"Told you we'd find it." Josh grabbed her in a side hug. It startled her and she skidded slightly, sending little rocks cascading down in front of her. She peered over the edge and wondered how far down it was. Imagine… climbing to the very top of a mountain and jumping off the top of it.

She skidded again, suddenly mad at herself. Her mom still had so much power over her. Her friends had no idea what was going on inside her head. None of them could possibly understand how it felt to become a completely different person in a single school year.

Victoria

She waded into the weird darkness of the wooded exit. After the bright openness of the valley of rocks it was somewhat jarring to be back in this claustrophobic little cove. She couldn't believe how dense it was, how closely packed together the trees could be this close to the edge of the woods. Maybe it was her recent unwelcome recollection, but everything seemed so much more… threatening now. Disjointed and menacing. She didn't fancy inserting herself into a dark, nature-filled hole, but what choice did she have?

Her hands rose hesitantly, unsure of what they would touch.

Memories rose in her like bile and she swayed nauseously in the darkness. First her broken arm, now this…. She couldn't stop it from coming, it was welling up inside her and she tried to shut it out…She was always so good at repression, why were these coming back now –

It was move-in weekend and, in typical Victoria fashion, she had dumped her boxes unceremoniously in her undecorated dorm room before setting off to attend a foam party that she'd been invited to by some guy in the quad. Other freshmen were still milling about, saying goodbye to their families and meeting their roommates, but she wasn't interested. There would be plenty of time for that later. She smiled at her neighbor, laden with boxes, and dodged the parents still lingering in the hallway, who looked questioningly at her scantily-clad form darting between them. Her mom had not accompanied her on the train, and that was just fine with her. She had bigger fish to fry than her incompetent mother.

She'd fantasized about the Berkeley guys that she would meet, charm, ensnare, and abandon when she got bored. She made the mistake of assuming that she was still smarter than all of them.

The guys at her high school were dissatisfying and dull. She never dated a resident of Little Cottonwood, deciding long ago that the members of their sleepy little town, though kind and wholesome and blah blah blah, were simply unworthy of her limitless charms. She knew she was hot. She knew she deserved better. They had to be equal to her in either intelligence or attractiveness – a fellow pre-med, or an athlete, or something. She deserved a charming entrepreneur or a passionate Poli Sci guy who would become president. She deserved the triangular, tanned members of the Berkeley water polo team, who, hopefully, would possess a few more modicums of intelligence than the brainless goobers that donned LCHS Speedos. Maybe one of these Berkeley guys would finally be worthy of taking her most prized possession.

She sped up as she planned out her perfect courtship. He would be super hot, of course. That was non-negotiable. The guy she was about to meet was a solid 8.5, but she was a 10. She wanted a 10. In addition to being a perfect physical specimen, he would also be intellectually stimulating enough to converse with, and of course completely dazzled by her. She'd watched her own mom go through enough crappy guys that treated her horribly. Her V-card was at stake here, and she wasn't about to trade it for anything less than a king of hearts.

She smiled in anticipation as she headed up the stairs to the front door of the house. Guys were always shocked to find out that she was a virgin. "I can afford to be picky," she told them, laughing as she turned them down. In her nighttime excursions to neighboring cities she'd strutted through house parties and frat parties and lame clubs. She combed the beaches of southern California, one eye always open. She'd had fun, of course, and she'd perfected her caresses and her everything-buts in the backseats of cars and movie theaters and under the bleachers at football games. Those had all been boys, she thought to herself, smiling at the shirtless guy opening the door for her. College proffered an endless and far worthier selection of men. They grinned down at her and she was quickly absorbed into a group surrounding a keg stand.

She'd never been to a foam party before, but a quick Google search prepared her for the debauchery in the backyard. Thankfully, it also prepared her to wear plastic flip flops and a bikini. The entire yard was lined with bubble wrap and trash bags, protecting the columns that kept the back roof up, and bubble wrap chains cordoned off a huge dance floor. Hundreds of people crammed into three solid feet of bubbling foam, wading and yelling and splashing their drinks as they danced. A hose connected to a giant bucket of bubbles that tipped forward every minute or so, dousing the dancers under it and evoking a collective roar of approval as the yard slowly filled with more foam. She laughed at a girl with her iPhone in a Ziploc dancing with one arm in the air, protecting her phone from the bubbles.

Her keg partners yelled and passed her a shot. She downed it, enjoying their approval, and took another one.

"Nice! Wanna dance!" The guy who asked her was tall enough to maybe be on the basketball team. She scanned his abs. Definitely some sort of athlete.

"Yeah!" She let him pull her out to the dance floor and let him grind his crotch into her. Ugh. This kind of dancing was so droll. She turned so that they were face to face and he ran his hands down her, covering her in foam.

"You're hot!"

"I know!" she grinned and tossed bubbles at his face. Well, this was mildly disappointing. He was super hot but clearly no more intellectually stimulating than the high school losers with whom she'd replicated this exact conversation.

She grabbed a Jell-o shot from some guy's hand and swallowed it, savoring the sweetness. She'd have to be drunker if she was going to do anything with this guy.

She put her arms around his neck and danced into him. She was thankful that the alcohol finally hit her just before his hands grabbed her butt. God, they were all so textbook. She could predict everything they did. Every move seemed to come from some weird Man Bible for Guys Who Want to Get Laid. Was there a male equivalent of Cosmo that they all read and memorized tips from? Articles like "Seduce Some Girl in Three Simple Steps?" Next they'd start making out, and while they were he'd feel her up.

They made out. He felt her up.

She gradually relaxed as the alcohol coursed through her slight frame and she began to appreciate her partner's physique. He *was* really hot. Maybe even a 9.

The bell tolled and she joined in the cheering, laughing as the girls under the bucket squealed, shielding their eyes.

He pushed her up against the bubble wrap wall and leaned in, kissing her harder. The bubble wrap bubbles popped under her and the foam tickled her arms and she raised sudsy fists above her head and they glittered like soft smoky diamonds as she stuck her tongue into the mouth of some guy she'd just met.

His hands gripped her hips tightly, and she gave a little cry of pain as he squeezed her. Okay, that really hurt. She stiffened as his hands moved down into her bathing suit bottoms.

Not okay. She pulled them out, trying to admonish him with her eyes, but he leered and tried to untie her bikini. Um. Not cool, bro. She felt a surge of panic as he pushed her into a corner and his hands scrambled fiercely and it wasn't good, it hurt and she screamed–

An equally muscular guy pushed her guy away. "Dude. Get off her."

"Fuck you, man." He turned and immediately grabbed another girl, who happily gyrated into him.

Her savior turned back towards her. "Sorry about that," he yelled.

"It's fine," she said, shaking a little. It definitely wasn't fine. She wasn't going to let some guy finger her in a dirty pool of foam filled with hundreds of people and God knows what kinds of germs.

"Do you want to dry off in my room?" He asked. "I'm sober brother tonight. I'm the responsible one. No funny business." He raised his palms and she decided to trust him.

"Sure."

"You can borrow a shirt if you want."

She smiled gratefully and let him lead her up the stairs past hordes of super attractive (and even more inebriated) kids. This was hardly her first frat party – she'd been going to LCCC's since she was fifteen – but it was definitely the largest. Girls in bikinis danced in groups bordered by guys in Speedos. The DJ was actually playing good music. She accepted another Jell-o shot by some guy on the stairs and followed her new friend down the hallway. She shoved past contorted couples, desperate, less-hot-than-her girls, and overly confident tank-topped guys before finally reaching her friend's room.

He opened the door and gestured for her to go in first. Two beds made up a clearly makeshift bunk bed, leaving just enough room for a giant beer pong set-up. Two guys were already playing.

"Hey!" They looked her up and down and smiled approvingly at her friend.

"Guys, this is – what was your name?"

"Victoria." She smiled at them. "Who's winning? I'll be on your team."

"We are!" both sides yelled. They laughed. She walked to the side with the taller guy. He looked her up and down, smiling with approval. His blue eyes were too pretty to squint so meanly.

"Nice, bro, she's super hot," he said, like she wasn't even there.

"How drunk are you?" asked her other teammate.

"Barely. Three shots." She said, grinning. Being a natural lightweight was a pain in the ass, but she'd pushed herself to acquire a reasonable tolerance. She wasn't going to let her fatless body betray her in a moment of proving herself.

"Dude. Have this." He handed her a nearly full red cup.

She sniffed it. "What is it?"

They all laughed. "House recipe. Top secret. But I promise you, it's delicious."

Someone knocked on the door and she looked up to see the first guy open it slightly. "Room's full, sorry!" She heard the disappointed groan of some lame girls and felt glad to have them all to herself. Blue Eyes handed her the cup.

"Well boys, I guess I have no reason not to enjoy it. Bottoms up." She chugged the contents, tasting beer, vodka, and something else that she couldn't quite place.

She held in her disgust and pretended to enjoy it, feeling the room sway a little. "My turn!" She grabbed the ball and cheered when it landed in the cup. Blue Eyes lifted her up in mock celebration and pretended the boob graze was an accident. She laughed and kept playing.

The next thing she remembered was waking up in a dark, tiny space. Something was loud. Something outside? It didn't matter. It made her dizzier. Her head pounded. She wanted to throw up. Everything hurt. Something stabbed.

She tried to stand up and felt something wet between her legs. Everything felt wrong.

She realized that there was a blanket on top of her. She pulled it off of her head. Her bikini top was missing.

Slim rays of light illuminated the room, which held a few beat-up couches, a fridge, and a pool table. It looked like a basement of some kind. She was the only one there.

Standing up was a nightmare. Her head hurt to move. Her – stomach? – hurt worse. She looked down. Even in the faint light she could see the dark bruises already clouding her thighs. Shaking, she pulled down her bottoms and bit her lip to keep from screaming. The bruises grew darker as they crawled up her legs, dotted with blood.

She leaned over and vomited on the floor.

The room swayed as she staggered to where the light was coming from. She had to get out of here. The handle on the back door was stiff but she shoved it and nearly fell out when it swung open.

She ran out gasping into the cool morning air, still clutching the blanket around her. She refused to believe it. The pain told her it was true.

Victoria refused to cry in public. Crying was for the weak. It broadcasted your emotions to people who didn't deserve to know them. If people knew your actual emotions they could destroy you.

She held in her tears as she hurried across campus. Judging by the light, it was only 5:30 or so, blissfully early enough for campus to be empty. She took the stairs to her dorm room and found her key where she'd hidden it earlier.

Still wrapped in the blanket, she entered her new, unfamiliar room as quietly as possible. Thankfully, her makeup bag had been in the box with her towels, so she remembered where that was. She grabbed her thickest, most comforting towel and padded silently down the hallway to the bathroom. She checked under all the toilet stalls and pushed open every shower stall, making sure she was alone. She threw the blanket in the trash can.

Under the low-pressured but thankfully warm jet of the dorm shower, Victoria cried for the first time in eleven years. She threw up again and watched in disgust as it whirled around the drain. This couldn't be real. She hadn't even been here for twenty-four hours.

She'd forgotten to bring in her shampoo and soap but some girl had left hers in the stall and she scrubbed herself until the gray-purplish marks were red. She stayed in the shower for well over an hour, washing herself as best she could, throwing up until there was nothing left inside of her.

Finally she was too tired to stand and she sank to the floor of the shower, letting the water pound her head, trying to beat out the memories. Maybe it was a good thing that she couldn't remember everything.

She needed to do something. She always had some plan of action, some way of getting ahead. She was hardly the first girl for this to happen to.

Okay. You can handle this, she told herself. She thought of her mother. She'd watched her mom go through this countless times, she realized. God. After all the time she'd promised herself that she would not become her mother, after all the measures she'd taken to ensure that she would be a strong, independent, life-saving woman… she'd been reduced to the same, quivering, beaten woman that she'd sworn she'd avoid. She had become her mother.

She tried to remember the r- no, she couldn't think of the word, because that made it real. She tried to remember what you were supposed to do if you were attacked. She couldn't.

Who would take her side? She wondered. She'd wandered into a frat house in a bikini. She'd voluntarily gotten drunk. She knew it didn't look good, from the outside. She couldn't believe she'd been so careless, so overly confident.... But something horrible happened to her and she sure as hell didn't ask for it, even if some people would think she did.

So she would do what she had to. She would go to the campus police tomorrow, and give her name, and the guys' names –

She didn't know their names. It couldn't be that hard to find them though, right? She sort of remembered what they looked like. She felt another swoop of nausea as she recalled Mean Blue Eyes. She could identify them.

Okay. It was the second day of move-in weekend. She still had time before class started to –

It was the second day of move-in weekend. She cursed herself. She'd already fucked up on her second day of college.

She'd spent eighteen years cultivating the image that she would present in college. Her apathy towards her high school classmates gave her confidence; she really did not care what they thought of her, but she realized that she really did care what her college friends thought of her. They were the ones that mattered. She'd spent her whole life dreaming of the friends she'd make her, and the guys she'd date, and the person she'd become here. She wanted people to meet Victoria, not Victim.

If she went forward, she would always be known as a victim. Berkeley was her prize. She was not going to let three assholes take that away from her. She could get over this on her own. She would work out some way to punish those guys later. Vengeance was always sweeter when you let it simmer.

Control. She was the master of control. She'd overcome the psychological scar tissue left by her fucking dad. Those wounds had healed, nestled comfortably under years of careful self-preservation and her steady confidence in her ability to take care of herself. At seven years old she'd proved to herself that one man could not control her, that she could be an independent individual and free herself from the burden of a traumatic childhood. Her past did not define her. The person she chose to be defined her.

She would not let this ruin her life. She would not let them affect her. She would keep going, and conquer everything in front of her, because she was Victoria and that was what she did. She'd waited to get to Berkeley for too damn long and she was not going to miss out on it. She was going to be a surgeon. She would be unstoppable.

Maybe she had made a mistake. But she would make it once, and wasn't that kind of the point? She wouldn't ever make the same mistake again. She could use this to make herself better.

She stood up less shakily, turned off the shower, wrapped her towel around her, and walked back to her room. Her clock read 7 a.m. Time to start a new day.

Her feet padded slowly down the steep incline and she felt her way out, blinking in the sunshine as she emerged back onto the sidewalk. She still didn't feel totally comfortable in tiny, dark spaces. Sunlight felt so much healthier. Her hands drifted unconsciously to her thighs and she remembered watching impatiently each day, waiting for the bruises to shrink enough for her to wear shorts. She threw herself into her new life, regaining control as best she could, keeping up her impenetrable façade. She rebuked Sally's early invitations for her to visit, but those stopped suddenly in October. By then Victoria had already established herself on her floor and collected a coterie of harmless, interesting male friends. She told no one of her first night. That next morning she'd bought Plan B at the pharmacy, and hadn't contracted any STDs, thank God. She could move on, with no token of the incident except for the shadows of bruises and her already scarred psyche.

Josh emerged, squinting, and she smiled at her best male friend. He would never hurt her, and she was grateful for that.

Erik

The sidewalk was bumpy under his feet. His stomach grumbled and he glared at Victoria in front of him.

He did not want to go to the lake. He hated the lake. The lake reminded him of his dad. Everything here reminded him of his dad.

The air pressed down on him and he remembered and it was twelve years before and he and Alex hopped out of his dad's truck.

He stumbled out of excitement as he ran to the lake, Alex close behind him. His dad pulled the kayak off the top of his truck and made them push it into the water. He picked Alex up and set him inside, then got in himself.

"Dad, can you help me?" He lifted his arms up.

His dad shook his head and the kayak drifted out a few feet. Alex watched him, worried. He waded into the water, panicking slightly as the kayak glided faster than he could walk. His tennis shoes squished on the silty ground and the water came up to his neck.

"Coach, can we help him?" he heard Alex ask. He abandoned walking and paddled, arms desperately whirling, anything to keep himself afloat.

"He's a big boy. He can do it himself." He realized how far away his dad's voice was and he swam harder, arms determined to get him there. His jeans felt so heavy but he kept going, watching the kayak drift slightly farther away. A big pink fish swam under him and he hoped it wouldn't touch him.

"You can do it, Erik!" Alex yelled in his high-pitched voice. He paddled harder. Just like the pool at home. He could do this. He was only twelve feet away now.

He gasped as something grabbed his foot and he felt himself sinking. He turned to see what it was and surprised bubbles floated to the surface as he saw that his foot was caught in a huge plant thing that looked like a big green underwater monster. He tried to kick off his shoe but his hand got stuck too and he tried to wave his other hand or splash or something and he looked out at the big empty underwater world and the water stung his eyes and he sank a little further.

Something much stronger than he was yanked him out of the water and he gasped as the back of his head collided with the floor of the kayak. Water shot out of his mouth and he coughed until he could breathe again.

Alex sniffled and he watched his dad turn to him. "Why are you crying? Erik is okay, see! He just has to get better at swimming, that's all." Alex's sniffles grew louder and he watched

170

his dad above him, darkening. "He's fine. He's just a little kid. Look at him." Alex glanced down obediently and Erik tried to tell him with his eyes, tell him to stop crying because that was the only way to stop the anger. He breathed deeply, trying to look as alive as possible, anything to make Alex stop crying.

He stopped.

"See, boys? That's why you have to be as strong as possible. Erik, take the other paddle. This is a great arm workout." He whistled as they rowed around the lake.

"Let's just take one car," Victoria's voice broke into his thoughts and he realized they were already back at the cabin. She climbed into the front seat. "Three up here, four in the back."

Josh got his keys from Sally and hopped into the driver's seat. "Erik, you should probably sit up here too, since you're the largest."

He opened the passenger door and Victoria glared at him. "I'm not sitting on your lap."

"Good. Don't. Move over."

She rolled her eyes and budged over just enough for him to cram his considerable bulk into the passenger seat. At least she was skinny.

Josh

They pulled into the parking lot and he hopped out of the truck. The lake was stunning, green instead of the blue they were used to, and it seemed somehow earthier than the ocean. It felt so good to be near water after getting used to urban landlock. The wind ruffled his air and he felt energized, back in his board shorts with girls in bikinis and water to ride on and oh, it felt right.

"Come on, guys!" How could they not be as excited as he was? Alex leapt out of the car and pretended not to wince as most of his weight landed on the bad knee. Ouch. The girls ambled out with the unconscious knowledge that their exit was watched. There was something so cute and delicate about watching girls in flip flops get out of a too-high truck, he thought. Victoria leapt out of the car, Sally hopped down lightly, and Grace looked like she hoped the ground would rise to catch her.

The girls made their way down the dock as he got the cooler out of the back. Alex moved to grab the other end but he waved him away. "No heavy lifting for you. Sam?" Alex's face darkened for a moment but he smiled and grabbed the pile of towels instead. Sam hefted the other end and they climbed down the stairs, which were obtusely not designed for boaters carrying large things.

Finally they reached the bottom and he watched the trio, now far ahead of them. They used to look like girls. Now they looked like women. In just a year they'd transformed from his childhood playmates to … adulthood playmates. Victoria with her blonde curls and tiny waist and disproportionate chest. Sally with her toned, tanned everything and soft hair and musical movements. Delicate Grace with her long legs that gleamed white from beneath her red shorts. It was nice to see her in sunshine again. All so different, so beautiful in completely singular ways, and as the line of girls pranced down the dock he felt very, very lucky.

Wally opened a well-worn ledger and scanned the list of names. "Let's see… are you kids the Victoria party of seven for four o'clock?" He scratched his bald head.

"Yep." Victoria flounced forward. "Sally, credit card." She handed it over, looking annoyed at being commanded. Wally carefully locked it in a drawer beneath the desk and placed the key in his shirt pocket.

"Let's get you set up!" Victoria rolled her eyes at his enthusiasm as they followed him out the back door onto the dock. Wally hopped into the boat and they climbed down after him.

"Who wants to drive first?"

"I want to try!" Erik looked like he was ready to object but Josh took the post behind the wheel before he could. Wally turned the key and the ignition roared to life.

"Push this up to go faster, push it down to slow down, and you look like you know how to turn a wheel. Have fun, kids!" He leapt spryly onto the dock and waved. Josh pulled out of the slip, avoiding kayakers. He passed the five knot safety buoy and sped up a little, feeling the purr of the engine under his feet. He accelerated more and the girls giggled as they slipped backwards.

"You guys might want to sit down!" He yelled as he continued to speed up.

"Slow down for the corner!" Sally yelled and he obediently slowed two knots, dragging them around the edge of the last line of trees. The branches reached right over the water and scraped the top of the boat.

Now that they were out of the little cove they could see just how large the lake really was. The lake unfurled before them, a glorious sheet of aquamarine that stretched against the border of trees. Other small boats zoomed off in the distance.

He grinned at his friends and accelerated to twenty-five knots. Erik and Alex high-fived. Victoria screamed out of pure pleasure and Sally giggled, holding onto Grace. Sam whooped.

Driving a boat was so much better than driving a car – no stop signs, no traffic lights, no worrying about merging or changing lanes or other drivers. He felt the wind pick up and watched light swells forming. He loved that the lake was big enough for actual swells to form.

"Speed bumps!" Sally yelled.

"Get ready!" He took it down a knot or two, but as they bumped over the swells they still shot upwards. They giggled as they fell back down, only to be thrust in the air again.

"Slow down!" yelled Grace.

"Speed up!" yelled Sam.

"Josh, I swear to God, if anything happens to my face I will kill you!" yelled Victoria, laughing.

He slowed until the swells stopped and drove more towards the center of the lake. No other boats or kayaks zoomed around and it felt like they were the only ones on the lake, like they owned it, like this afternoon was created especially for them. The air was still and silent and he couldn't remember the last time he felt so tranquil. The line of trees around the lake obscured the streets and houses behind him. They could have been in the middle of nowhere and he wouldn't have cared. It was absolutely perfect.

Alex

He kind of wanted to drive the boat, but Josh snagged it before he could. Of course. He still felt a little miffed about the cooler thing.

Get over it, he told himself. But it was hard to push the thought out of his head. Was that how people saw him now? Damaged goods? Incapable of carrying a cooler, much less starting at catcher?

Erik spread his arms on top of the bench and his wiry hands grazed his back, brushing the taut muscles. At fifty, Coach Armstrong was still in the same shape he was at forty. He could still hit farther than most of their team. Only Erik beat him consistently when they ended practice with a home run derby. Erik's perfect genes would never let him down. *His* knees would let him play as long as he wanted.

Although it couldn't be genes, could it, he thought as Josh killed the motor. Alan's golden arm was still mowing down batters. Alan, who followed Coach's orders exactly and never pushed himself further than necessary. Alan, who listened when Coach warned them against the dangers of overworking their bodies.

This had never been part of his plan. Getting injured his freshman year was – unthinkable. It wasn't supposed to happen. He was going to graduate from UCLA, the only engineering major on the baseball team, and then when he had his degree he'd get drafted, and announcers would talk about how smart he was, and his parents would be prouder of him than of Alan.

Josh killed the motor and they drifted. He didn't like being out in the middle. He didn't like not knowing what they were doing next. Is this what relaxing was supposed to be? Not knowing where you were going? It was disorienting, really, floating with no purpose, with no direction. He leaned over the side and felt the tentacles of agoraphobia clench his heart as he realized how far they were from the shore. What if something happened to the boat and they began to sink? He hadn't gone swimming since his injury. What if Josh tried to help him? That would be embarrassing. Erik would laugh at him.

He didn't like floating. He didn't like it at all.

Grace

They bumped over a swell and mist sprayed into her face. She giggled as she slid down the bench into Sally. "Sorry!" They collided again, giggling and clutching each other. It felt wonderful to laugh.

She loved the feeling of the wind dragging through her hair as Josh zoomed around the lake. Goose bumps tickled the nape of her neck and Sally's hair flashed across her mouth and she giggled as she was pulled once more into the air. She kept laughing, even after the swells stopped and Josh slowed, and she didn't know why but it didn't really matter. Sally joined her and they clutched their stomachs, unable to stop, not knowing why, and laughing harder at their mutual inability to stop laughing.

Finally her giggles subsided into hiccups and Sally leaned her head against her shoulder, like she used to. This felt familiar. This felt right.

As the last whirs of the engine died and they began floating, she realized how lovely it was to do nothing. She hadn't thought that she would like it. She surprised herself by liking it.

They bobbed peacefully and she hoped that everyone felt as happy as she did. Sam leaned over the edge like a dog sticking its face out the window. Victoria kicked off her shoes and sprawled across the back of the boat, the sun kissing her legs. Even Erik looked less angry than usual.

They were quiet but it wasn't an awkward silence. There was nothing awkward about being comfortable with each other. They just soaked in the mutual delight and found solace in each other's love of sunshine and she thought that was beautiful.

She hadn't felt this content in a long time, she realized. Here, in the middle of the lake, she wasn't isolated. She was with friends. She wasn't alone.

Sally

This was how summers should be spent, she thought as Josh killed the engine and they melted into the gentle rhythm of the lake. Perhaps you had to get lost to find yourself. Maybe it took the incredible loneliness of nature to make you discover who you really were and why you were there. Maybe that's why Thoreau went to Walden and Buck stayed in the Yukon and that guy from *Into the Wild* went into the wild.

It was almost silent and they could have been in their own little world, their own little pocket of nature carved out especially for them. This was the closest she'd felt to childhood in a while, the closest she'd come to feeling the sanctuary of an enclave of people that really knew her and cared about her. How rare was it, she wondered, to get to spend three entire days with people that you'd known since elementary school? How often did those friendships last?

With a pang she realized that this was probably the last summer they'd get to do this. They had three more school years in which they could still call Little Cottonwood their hometown, the place they returned to for Christmas and part of summer, but they'd grown and changed so much in one year that it seemed impossible that they would continue coming home for long. God, she was a completely different person than she was ten months ago. She couldn't even imagine what she would be like in three years. She couldn't imagine what her group of friends would be like. They were brilliant and hard-working and talented and she loved them for it, but she also knew that soon enough the lure of internships and summer jobs and research opportunities would keep them grounded to their respective campuses and states and then the summers would be gone and maybe even the Christmases.

It was natural. It was inevitable. She accepted that. But that didn't mean she had to like it.

They would have to make the most of their time together, she realized. They would have to take advantage of these moments, this time right now, because soon enough summer would be a hazy memory lost in the hustle and bustle of school and new friends and new experiences. These three days together would probably be the last three days for them to spend together until… until when? Josh and Grace probably wouldn't come home for Thanksgiving this year – air fare was way too expensive. Next Christmas, hopefully, though her dad was already talking about spending Christmas with their family in Georgia. So when would they all be reunited again? Next summer? A whole year from now? And that was assuming that no one stayed at school to be a camp counselor or volunteer somewhere or study abroad. Ambition bound them together, but it was also pulling them apart.

So this was it then, she thought as she watched the light dance on the surface and glint off of Josh's sunglasses. He looked either asleep or just incredibly relaxed in the driver's chair. These next two days – today and tomorrow, really – will have to satiate us for the next 365. So little time together to compensate for so long an absence. It felt unfair, but that was life, wasn't it? You could only make the best of it.

She wanted this weekend to be memorable. She needed this weekend to be important and wonderful for them. They all needed it, she thought as she looked around her circle of friends. They deserved more than a weekend of happiness. They deserved more than what she could give them. They deserved something magical.

She stretched her head over the side and peered down, delighted by its clarity. She had no idea how deep it was. It looked warm and inviting and … memorable.

She looked around. There were no other boats in sight.

"Let's jump in," she said suddenly, surprising herself.

Spoken words broke the reverie of their sleepy contentment.

"Hmm?" asked Josh, stirring in the driver's chair.

"Let's go swimming."

Sam turned and she averted her gaze before he could meet hers. Victoria peered up at her skeptically. "*You're* going to jump in a lake?" she asked doubtfully.

Emboldened by her friend's doubt in her capacity for spontaneity, Sally leapt up. "You bet I am." She unbuttoned her shorts and kicked them off quickly. She felt the pressure of her male friends as she slipped off her t-shirt.

The little voice in her head was screaming at her that she was standing in front of four boys in her bra and underwear. A new voice told it to be quiet and let her do her thing.

She liked this new voice.

She stepped to the rear of the boat and looked down at the water. She really hoped there were no big fish in there. She had a sudden image of herself jumping into the jaws of a giant lake creature. That would certainly be memorable: the camping trip where Sally tried to be spontaneous and got eaten by the Loch Bear Lake Monster.

She giggled and made herself stop thinking. She'd never been able to do that before. She'd never not analyzed something, not calculated a million ways it could go wrong or a million ways to make it better. She was surprised by how empowering it was to not think.

The new voice in her head – it wasn't really a voice, was it, if it was more actions than words? – lifted her feet and tossed her into the air in a straight pencil dive and she slipped under the covers of the lake with a small and un-intrusive splash. The cold enveloped her and she let herself sink into its soothing embrace before kicking up and kissing the surface. She laid back and felt the sun dance on her chest as she floated and enjoyed, for the first time, what it felt like to be spontaneous.

Sam

He leaned his head out over the lake. God, it was quiet here. It was kind of nice. Kind of weird. He wasn't sure if he liked it. It felt wrong not to have an ocean breeze stirring his hair when he was so close to the water.

He wasn't sure if he liked this trip, to be honest. He always felt like the odd one out anyways, but here he was even more out of his element. The distance from the ocean pained him. He rubbed his St. Christopher necklace.

"Let's jump in." Her voice startled him before he realized the implication of her words. Spontaneity was his thing. He was delighted to hear it from her. She still surprised him.

Sally stood up and he felt the need to look away as she slipped off her shirt. He felt like he didn't deserve to see her do that but he really wanted to. He heard the soft thud of her shorts hitting the bottom of the boat. He tried to avert his eyes as she turned around but he couldn't.

Sally stood at the edge of the boat and he wished she could stand like that forever. Sally, who always kept her clothes on and never ran in just a sports bra, even on the hottest days, was standing in her underwear in front of him. Sally, golden and perfect, silhouetted against the lake, which was beautiful but no match for her. She took out her hair tie and her soft hair floated down her back, covering the blue bra.

She jumped precisely, flawlessly, in the way that only Sally could, and she made the tiniest splash as she entered the water.

They watched the ripples smooth out and finally she burst back into the air, graceful as ever, and he thought she looked truly happy as she leaned back and let the water take her. She laid her arms back unselfconsciously and he admired the languid curve of her golden form against the water. She smiled to herself and closed her eyes and he realized that it had been so long since she smiled like that. He missed it.

178

She could still surprise him.

Victoria

She watched bemusedly as Sally slipped off her clothes. Modest, conservative, occasionally prudish little Sally was taking her clothes off in front of *boys*. She smirked. Sally must be growing up, or finally getting some confidence, or just not caring any more. She looked different than the last time Victoria saw her in a bathing suit – same perky little boobs and butt, just more toned, the childish edges turned into nimble musculature. Her tan illuminated her tiny frame, interrupted only by the white negative of bikini straps. She stole a glance at the males of the group. Josh's tongue was practically hanging out of his mouth. Alex looked away, embarrassed. Erik watched her, frowning – probably comparing her to someone hotter and preparing complaints for later, she thought, and wanted to laugh – and Sam – oh, poor Sam. He wanted so hard not to look but he just couldn't

She wanted a boy to look at her the way Sam looked at Sally: like she was rare and precious and he would do anything to keep her from breaking.

She was broken. Sally seemed broken, too, in ways that Victoria would never have thought possible. Sally, with her unflagging spirit and maternal optimism and sometimes annoying cuteness. Maybe she had to be a little broken to get a little naked.

She hovered at the edge and Victoria wondered if she was really going to do it. Taking off her clothes in front of all of them was already such a big deal for her and she looked like she hadn't thought out the actual jumping-in-the-water part of it. The beach days of their youth were padded with Sally's towels and sunscreen and warning them about rip currents, for God's sakes.

Just when she thought she was chickening out, Sally jumped and slid gracefully into the water. Even her splash was neat and unobtrusive.

She counted the seconds and marveled at Sally's lung capacity. Victoria herself had never been that into swimming - she much preferred tanning, when you could be the envy of everyone on the beach. How many summer days had she spent perfecting her bronzeness, she wondered, while Sam and Sally splashed around and acquired an actual ability?

Of course, running cross country was probably part of the ridiculously excellent lung capacity. Sally was one of those weird people that liked running for fun, and judging by her new and improved physique, it looked like she'd been doing quite a lot of that this year. Finally her absurd oxygen supply ran out and she emerged in a fountain of bubbles, looking actually happy for the first time all weekend.

They all watched her for a bit, transfixed by the glow of Sally swimming in the sunshine. There was something magical about seeing a pretty person happy. Not a hot person, like she was, but a legitimately pretty person, like Sally, someone whose smile brightened the world for everyone around them. That kind of beauty was the best kind, and not for the first time, Victoria found herself wishing that she had turned out more like Sally. The smile and the cheeriness and the lightness weren't something you could just attain. They were natural gifts and Victoria really, really wished she had them.

Josh pulled off his tank top and set his sunglasses on the steering column. He grinned around them, settling his eyes on her. "Aren't you guys going in?" He ambled towards the back of the boat and launched himself into the air, pulling his legs into a cannonball. She laughed as his "woooo!" echoed around the empty lake.

"You're so fratty!" she yelled at him, teasing, and he grinned and splashed water up at her.

"Get in here!"

Sam slipped off his shoes and pulled off his shirt – wow, Sam really grew up this year too – and jumped into the water.

"Jesus, it's cold!"

"Yeah, but it feels great!" Josh said, reaching for the sky. She loved his arms. Why did such nice arms have to be on such a nice guy? And a childhood friend, no less. Wasted.

Erik followed suit and Victoria tried not to stare at him either. His excellent baseball body was so difficult to appreciate when it housed such a horrible personality. She averted her eyes from his perfect triangular back, but any glimmer of attraction to him was dashed when he didn't bother jumping far enough and his enormous splash soaked her hair. Jerk.

"I'll go in!" chirped Grace, and they all turned towards her. Well, wasn't this a day for surprises? First Sally and now Grace were stripping and Victoria was fully clothed. This was probably the first time in the history of their friendship that she was more clothed than the other females of the group. Of any group, for that matter.

She sized up pale Grace, who was no match for her physically. She was slightly pudgier and whiter than Victoria remembered.

"God, isn't there sun in New York?" she blurted unthinkingly. Grace looked hurt and she felt stupid for ruining her moment. "I wish my skin looked like yours. Purple looks amazing on you." She tried to cover it up and Grace looked confused. She tugged at her purple underwear self-consciously.

"Uh, thanks?" She pulled off her shirt and crossed her arms over her chest, covering what little boobage she had as she jumped.

Now it was just Victoria and Alex on the boat and she felt a pang of jealousy as she watched her friends splash around in the water. They looked innocent. They still deserved the joy of acting like kids.

She peered over the edge of the boat and considered jumping in. It seemed like a good idea, judging by her friends' ecstatic reactions, but…. she wasn't feeling it. She used to connect to nature. She liked finding herself in it and dominating it. Mountains could be climbed. Waves could be cruised over. Just surviving in a forest could seem like an act of conquest. But a lake… a lake was static and gigantic. It didn't change and it wanted to swallow her. There was nothing to be gained. There was only more of herself to lose, if she had anything left. She couldn't even tell anymore.

The edges of the lake stretched away from her and she suddenly realized how little control she had of the situation. She was one of two people on a boat while five others frolicked in the water. She didn't know how to drive a boat. Figuring it out wouldn't be too difficult, obviously, but still. New fears of a lack of control clouded her vision and she buried her face in the crook of her arm, closing her eyes, blocking out the unhealthy sentiments of this past year that swam uninvitingly into her consciousness when it was least convenient. Feeling out of control was never convenient. It had never been a problem until this year and she supposed that was her fault.

She hated this feeling. She hated feeling less than powerful. Impotence was not impressive or awe-inspiring and it damn well wasn't sexy. For the first time in months she realized how much she was slipping away from her former self. The exterior was fine, of course. Maintaining a façade was easy when the foundation was flawless. Interiors were much harder to maintain. They could be demolished so easily.

She wished she knew what it was like to be a kid. Wasn't being a kid supposed to entail some sort of sweet innocence, some idea of serenity that you could return to in your darkest moments? Childhood grounded you and reminded you of how you once were. She couldn't remember ever feeling like a kid. Her childhood had not been one of banal sweetness like Sally's had. She did not remember the scrapbookable summers and dolls for Christmas that Sally sometimes reminisced about. She was not borne of such simplicity. She was not meant to be innocent. She'd known that for a long time but the events of this past year confirmed that.

She watched her friends swim and she wished that she could join them. They looked so... young. Younger than they actually were. They all had it, that same childlike wonder, something that she couldn't touch, some secret magic that didn't belong to her. She wished it did. She sorely, desperately, maddeningly wished it did, but it didn't. That sort of happiness was not open to her.

Sam splashed Grace and Erik egg-beatered. Sally duck-dove and Victoria watched her kick her way down, seeing how long she could hold her breath. Josh laid chest-up, tanning and grinning. They were still themselves.

She leaned her head against the edge and wished to be better.

Grace

She was delighted at her uncharacteristic bravery. Even Victoria's snippiness couldn't dampen her mood, she thought as she kicked back and let the top of her scalp dip into the water.

She'd felt the pressure of the others' eyes on her as she peeled off her clothes, but not in the same way that they looked at pretty Sally or athletic Erik. They didn't look at her in lustful admiration. Was that a good thing? Maybe. Envy was a weird sentiment to evoke from your friends. She watched Alex's eyes skim over wholesome Erik and his hand drifted to his own knee. Poor Alex. He thought he was broken.

Erik was definitely not broken. Erik was all man muscle and baseball shoulders and veins that popped when he flexed. Girls were competitive enough with each other's looks. She definitely knew that. It was so odd to see the shifting standards of appearance from coast to coast. Nationally there was an emphasis on skinniness, obviously, but it had to be the right kind of skinniness. She knew that she was (had been) skinny, but not in the attractive, sunny, athletic kind favored in their hometown. Hers was (had been) of the gaunter variety, the kind that came from pacing endlessly and worrying until her stomach hurt. She didn't loathe food so much as forget about it. She came to associate food with her mom's criticism and her own subsequent self loathing. Since December her appetite for everything had fluctuated in the oddest ways. She didn't want anything. The thought of consuming something sickened her, then she couldn't stop eating. Fat piled up clumsily until she stopped eating again and her stomach melted away and her shoulder blades turned poky again. Was that what being feminine meant?

So was the opposite of that – her old boniness and smallness and paleness – what masculinity was? Was Erik the epitome of masculinity and that's why Alex stared at him like that, because Alex wished that he was still a college athlete? Were Erik's muscles the masculine equivalent of waists and boobs and everything else that girls used to measure themselves against each other? It seemed so silly, so antiquated to gauge their value of themselves based on the physical attributes of other girls. She had no control over the parts of Victoria and Sally that made her envy them, yet she did. She could not stop. There was some intrinsic part of being a girl that made her examine herself critically and compare to those around her and then examine herself more critically. Self-awareness was crippling. If it was such an inherent part of being human then surely her male friends were subject to the same deleterious demons.

Alex leaned forward on his still-powerful arms, watching his more active friends. Well, watching Erik, whose large arms propelled him to the little outcrop of rock in the middle. Foam jetted behind him as he surged through the water, kicking off the rock and shooting backwards in a glorious whirl of motion. She and Alex – was no one else paying attention? How were they missing this? – watched his athlete's progress, conquering nature only in the way that a 225-pound third-baseman could. For a moment she was able to forget that he was kind of mean and just appreciate the aestheticism of it all.

Alex appreciated it too, she could tell. Alex, the other lost soul of the group. It was too bad that their mutual proclivity for masking their actual feelings prevented them from bonding over this. She was no Sally and he was no Erik and because of this they had no way to vocalize the pain of having a best friend who was better than you. You admired them, of course. You were proud of them. Their successes became your successes. But every wonderful thing that they did was also a reminder that you were not nearly as fantastic.

Alex

He watched Erik dart through the water. Drops glistened in his hair in a way they never did in his. Black hair was so boring, he thought, watching his best friend's golden hair, dewy with conquered spray. Erik even looked good when he was sweating.

Watching Erik's golden sweaty head… hadn't he stared at and envied the same head last summer? He remembered the hike, and Erik getting frustrated with how slow he was and tried to cut in front of him. He accidentally brushed against him and a drop of his friend's sweat lingered on his arm. Erik shoved past him and he felt awed by the force and power of the heir to one of USC's favorite baseball dynasties. Erik turned and smirked at him as he barreled passed Sally and pushed in front of the group.

Alex felt something long-dormant stir inside him and the need to compete rose, dazzling, sizzling inside him, and he thrust himself up the path, not even noticing Victoria's "ow!" as he shoved past her. He hadn't experienced this level of focus since their championship game months earlier... he wanted to win, he had to win … he was only conscious of Erik's golden, sweating body in front of him, challenging him, pushing him to go faster. The path grew steeper and he almost slipped as he leapt over a rock, propelling himself, fingers trembling with adrenaline as he seized and shoved handholds. He felt like he was on fire. He felt... aggressive. In control. Unusually powerful.

He liked it.

He watched Erik bounding along above him and he marveled at his total dominance of his surroundings. He didn't have to stop for anything. Nature was completely conquered by him. Rocks and cliffs and bunches of boulders were no match for the only freshman to make their high school's varsity baseball team in the last fifteen years. The soles of Erik's red and gold shoes (part of the endless collection of pimped-out regalia that showed everyone he was a fixture of an indomitable legacy) disappeared and he sped up, climbing over the rock wall that shielded him from his friends' eyes.

Erik stood on the edge of the cliff, arms crossed, impassively overlooking the valley, and he was struck by the godliness of his friend's physique. This was the perfect setting in which to admire him. Something about the layout of the forest, about how it beckoned with secrets and hidden explanations and dark little corners where anything could take place, niggled at his consciousness and he realized that he were completely alone, separated by distance accrued through athleticism and competitiveness, and it seemed like such an accurate representation of their friendship. They would always be further ahead, wouldn't they, separated from everyone else by sheer talent.

Erik turned and grinned at him. "I beat you."

"Not by that much."

"By a full minute, at least."

"Better luck next time."

"Okay."

The sun dripped over them, throwing golden arcs across his eyes. He raised his arm over his face and stared out over the canyon.

They were quiet.

Sally

She wished she could live in water. She was barely aware of her friends as she pushed herself deeper down, loving the feeling of entering colder zones. She could always breathe better in the water when she was drowning in the air.

Her legs kicked emphatically and she erupted from the surface, giggling as she crashed back down. Goodness, this felt fantastic. So cathartic. She definitely needed this.

She laid back and floated gently, enjoying the lapping water tickling her ankles. Her arms drifted out and she closed her eyes. Perfect. Just the way she liked it.

Grace

How much time had passed? She had no idea. Time stopped for them. The ethereal circles of dives dissolved in the water. The boat floated. They floated. They splashed. They laughed. The sun slid down. She swam down as far as she dared, until the iciness clasped her chest and she kicked her feet as hard as she could and burst out of the water sputtering.

"You okay?" Josh asked as he bobbed. So casual in everything. So maddeningly casual. Like nothing mattered.

"Yeah, just cold." She swam back towards the boat and held lazily onto the rungs of the ladder, enjoying not having to kick herself upwards any more. This felt much better, just hanging, just floating, knowing that she couldn't drift away. But the water was getting colder and the sun was still sinking and she was getting kind of hungry.

She pulled herself up rung by rung and collapsed on the seat next to Victoria.

"Aren't you freezing?"

She hadn't noticed until Victoria pointed it out. She looked down. Goosebumps spiked their white heads up on her arm. "Yes."

Victoria handed her the towel and she wrapped it around herself. "Thanks."

Josh

He perched on the rock and watched Grace swim to the boat. She'd never been that great of a swimmer, much to the chagrin of her triathlete mom and baseball champion dad. He still found it hard to imagine his dad being teammates with Mr. Hastings, bound together by something that only real athletes could understand.

He wondered if his own dad was an asshole already when he was in high school. Probably. It wasn't exactly an acquired talent.

Grace held on to the ladder and he watched her legs drift out behind her. Floating came so much more naturally to her than swimming did. She looked more relaxed this way, untroubled by motion and the business of asserting her presence. She was so much better at being conquered than conquering. He worried about her.

He should have worried more about her during the school year. He knew that he should have made more of an effort to reach out after... well, after December and everything happened, but it was so damn hard to do. How do you anticipate another person's emotional needs when she clearly doesn't want you reaching out? Or does she just say that as some sort of defense mechanism, some shield against getting hurt even more? He didn't know. He doubted that she knew.

She looked better in the water – still too empty, but the water colored her in and took away some grayness. Light danced on her sparkling pale skin and she brushed a strand of hair out of her eye before beginning to climb.

The spell was broken; she was the first of their number to get out. Some silent chord had been struck, jolting them out of their silent watery trance, and he realized how far the sun was going down. He glanced around. Sally was already swimming in. Sam jumped off the boulder one last time. Even Erik kicked off the rock and jettisoned towards them. Bound by the same unassuming, silent knowledge of the ways of water, they responded automatically to the pull of each other's actions. It was time to go in. It was time to return to reality.

Grace wrapped herself in a towel and laughed at something Victoria said. He wished they could stay.

Alex

He felt his eyes closing as soon as he climbed into the passenger seat and his struggle to stay awake lasted the solid duration of backing out of the lake parking lot. The truck jostled bumpily up the driveway and he awoke with a jolt, feeling a momentary panic before remembering where he was.

"Dude, wake up, we're back!" Sam patted him on the shoulder kindly.

"Sorry I fell asleep," he said automatically.

"No need to apologize!"

Erik laughed. "Why do you always apologize for everything?"

He shrugged and trudged up the path after the rest of them. It was barely eight o'clock but he could barely keep his eyes open.

"God, your hands are so pruny!" Victoria grabbed Josh's palm. "Look how gross that is!"

He noticed Grace look away from Victoria's long red nails tracing Josh's hand.

Josh laughed and batted her away. "Are you going to help make dinner?"

"Pssh, no! I like to be cooked *for*, not coo*king*." She smirked and flounced upstairs after Sally and Grace, presumably to… do girl stuff. Comb their wet hair? Change out of wet clothes? He blushed at the thought.

He hovered in the kitchen, lethargy rendering him even more useless than unusual. How do you cook for seven people? He never cooked. He couldn't cook for himself, let alone for six others. His mom did the cooking while they practiced.

Josh searched through the grocery bags. "I'm going to make you guys my famous spaghetti. We got bread and salad and brownies for dessert, sound good?"

It sounded wonderful. He'd never possessed any desire to cook, but he wished he knew how to help just so that he could look as cool and manful as Josh. Josh opened cabinets like he lived there, wiping down pans, humming with the happy ease of someone well-versed in the ways of kitchens. Alex opened a cabinet at random – oh. Alcohol. They shouldn't be messing with that. He closed it hurriedly, but Josh caught a glimpse of the bottles.

He grinned. "Don't worry, I brought more stuff."

More than last night's beers? "Oh, okay. Cool."

Josh patted him on the shoulder. "We're on vacation. You can have fun tonight – we want you to. But I totally don't have to bring it out, if it makes you uncomfortable." He looked at him expectantly.

How easy it was for Josh, he thought. He hated feeling envious but he certainly felt envious now. Josh, with his cool frat top and his real Ray Bans and his toned arms and his alcohol and his wasted baseball body.

"I don't mind." What were his friends like drunk? he wondered. He'd never seen them drink before. He couldn't imagine Sally drunk. Victoria, definitely. Josh, obviously. Erik? He was forbidden from drinking during the season, and for him the season was year-round. What would Erik do when he was drunk? Probably something awesome. "It's fine, go ahead. Really."

Josh grinned and patted him on the shoulder. "Well done, bud, I'm proud of you." He continued humming and making his way around the kitchen, coaxing out the secrets of a culinary world that Alex did not understand. He didn't care to find out. It wasn't his sphere.

He watched Josh get out the... bowl with holes in it. What was it called? A calendar? He was so bad at this.

"Um... do you need help?" Please say no, please say no.

"No, I got this! You can go chill or nap or whatever, it'll be about half an hour."

"Uh, okay. Thanks."

The couch was much more welcoming than the kitchen was and he laid on the smaller one. Sam was already sprawled out on the long couch and he looked asleep. Erik was – somewhere. He wondered where, and that was his last conscious thought before he drifted off again.

Josh

He smiled at each Dodgers kitchen utensil he discovered. Spatulas, oven mitts, silverware, even the turkey baster were covered in the blue and white insignia. Even the most feminine area in the cabin wasn't free from the influence of its self-righteous financer. Sure, Erik thought he was an asshole, but at least he'd more than provided financial stability for Erik. Erik Sr. was a great coach and had definitely made Josh a better player. Josh just wished he hadn't.

Once he hit middle school he began wishing he was just a little bad, just a little more average, in the hopes that it would make his dad leave him alone. The better he was, the worse the ramifications of his occasional failures. The price of failure was too high.

He remembered one of his first all-star games. They were in San Diego. His mom sat with his baby sister on her lap and waved to him when he was on-deck. In the fifth inning he hit a three-run home run (a real home run that cleared the fence, not one of the "fake" ones his dad teased his teammates about). As he circled the bases he watched his dad's smile of ugly triumph and he felt himself relaxing a little. He'd done one thing right today. Maybe Dad would be nicer on the ride home.

In the eighth inning, their pitcher, Mark, gave up six runs. He watched Mark's dad yell words of encouragement while his own dad stomped around the field, shouting at his team. "Get your shit together! This is a disgrace!" The umpire kept warning him to move away from the field. He walked to left field and crossed his arms on top of the fence, a soda can gleaming brightly in his clenched hand. Josh was afraid to turn and look at him. He tried to pretend he wasn't there but he could feel his dad's angry presence emanating from the outfield in livid waves.

"Don't screw up, don't screw up," he thought to himself over and over, barely registering that the batter just made contact. He realized that the ball was rolling towards him and fumbled his glove and watched as it rolled under his legs into right field. The runner on third scored. The batter rounded first as he ran out to cut off. He threw to Erik, but the runner was faster and landed safely at second. His dad chucked the can of Sprite against the fence and stormed out to the parking lot. He watched his car peel out as his mom looked back worriedly. She looked out at him and even though she was far away he knew exactly what she was trying to say with her pleading eyes: It's okay, it's not your fault, you did nothing wrong. The game dragged on another twenty minutes as the other team circled the bases in a parade of RBIs.

After the game his mom told Mark's mom that his dad got an emergency call from work and felt terrible about leaving his family in San Diego but had to go immediately. Mark's mom said of course she understood and of course they'd be happy to give them a ride and he and Mom and baby Megan climbed into their SUV with Mark and his nice dad who wasn't even mad at Mark even though he'd pitched so badly and Josh wondered what it was like to have a dad like that. He enjoyed the two-and-a-half-hour car ride with Mark's family – they even stopped for In N Out and Mark's dad patted him on the head like he was his own kid.

The ride was over way too soon and when Mark's dad pulled up in front of his house he wanted to ask if he could sleep over at their house but didn't want his mom and the baby in the house by themselves. Mark's family said cheery goodbyes and drove off. He could hear the tremor in his mom's voice as she carried the baby and his bags inside and tried to make it seem like everything was okay, but he knew it wasn't.

When they got inside his dad was waiting at the kitchen table with the lights off, a half-empty glass of something brown in front of him. Waiting. Just waiting.

"You fucked up," he said quietly.

Josh stepped in front of his mom. "Dad, that was my fault. I made an error. Don't be mad at mom."

His dad turned to him with angry, bloodshot eyes and Josh realized that the situation was more dangerous than he originally thought. "Shut up, you little prick."

"Don't talk to him that way." Mom's voice shook but her words were firm. "It's just a game. Let him go."

"Mom, go put Megan in her room," Josh said, trying to keep his voice even. "She's sleeping."

"No, stay here. I want you to see this." Dad stood up, one gnarled hand clasping the chair as he swayed slightly. "I want you to see what happens to fucking failures."

Josh braced himself but it didn't stop his face from stinging as palm slapped cheek. Megan started crying.

"Shut that baby up!"

"Do not hit him." She tried to stand in front of Josh but she was holding the baby and Josh realized how close the knives were to Dad. He took a step towards her and she shrunk but maintained eye contact. "If you're going to hit someone hit me instead."

"No!" Josh ran forward and slammed into him as hard as he could as his dad raised his fist. His dad looked down and laughed.

"What, you think you're going to stop me?" He hit him again, harder, with a closed fist this time, and everything went a little dizzy. He felt his mom's hand on his shoulders. Megan howled.

Dad leaned down and he hated the feeling of his hot, bitter whisper on his skin.

"Next time you let a grounder through your legs it's going to hurt a helluva lot worse than that. Do you understand me?" His head was swimming but he forced himself to nod.

He was seven years old.

The trend continued throughout Little League and into high school. He was left at more parks around the state than he could count. His mom made sure to be there as often as she could, which got a little harder when Megan was old enough to have her own games. But Josh would never even consider asking his mom to come to his game while his dad went to Megan's. He was determined to protect his little sister as much as he possibly could.

Under the tutelage of Erik Sr. he felt himself improving and hated it. He almost hoped for an injury, anything to keep him from subjecting himself to the stage in front of his one-man audience. He considered quitting but hated thinking that doing so might make Megan or Mom the main target. As long as he played, his dad had something to watch and criticize. If he could take the blows, they wouldn't have to, and that was all that mattered.

He remembered getting ready in the locker room before the first varsity game sophomore year. Jason blasted rap and they pretended to know more words than they did. Coach passed around the eye black and they fed off each other's energy as they transformed from a group of mostly-blond beach kids into legit BAMFs. He buttoned his jersey with shaking fingers, barely recognizing the voice chanting from his own mouth. Alex climbed on top of the bank of lockers and led them in their cheer that crescendoed into a roar as they ran from the locker room to the field and parents clapped and girls squealed and he joined the tribal roar and he was so ready to get on that field and kick some ass and show Dos Pueblos who was fucking boss.

He sprinted to second and Erik sprinted to short and they grinned at each other in spite of themselves. The specters of their fathers and the legacies they'd reluctantly inherited melted away as Doug tossed them warm-ups. His arm sizzled and the ball thumped sweetly in his glove. Everything felt right.

He couldn't help but notice his dad hovering behind the backstop talking to a dude he vaguely recognized as a Dos Pueblos dad. What the hell? Why was he talking to the enemy? His dad hated Dos Pueblos and had hated them ever since he played on this very field. The DP dad handed him something and they shook hands. He watched them uneasily – surely this couldn't be a good thing – for a moment before forcing himself to focus on the game. He returned to it slightly less enthusiastic than he'd been a few minutes before.

He managed to push it to the back of his mind until after the game. They won 2-0 and made their way in a triumphant train to Hurricane, the burger place across the street. The entire baseball team, a mass of dirty jerseys and eye-black-stained faces, crowded around the tiny tables rehashing every detail. Fan girls hovered around them squealing congratulations while they ate cheeseburgers.

Maybe high school baseball isn't be so bad, he thought as he made out with Lexi in the parking lot. Maybe it's finally happening for me.

As soon as he walked in the door his dad actually patted him on the back. "I knew you could do it!"

Holy crap. His dad was finally proud of him. His dad was *smiling*. That never happened.

"Thanks, Dad." Wow. When was the last time he said that?

"Between LC's offense and pitching, you guys are definitely going to kick DP's ass this year. The ginger pitcher's having shoulder surgery in two weeks. They won't stand a chance." Dad hummed as he poured himself another drink in his Cottonwood mug.

He should have realized it then, he cursed himself. It was so obvious.

Throughout the season his dad grew briefly ecstatic after wins and moped around the house dangerously after losses, just as he had all through Little League and travel ball. But this year the anger and the bruises intensified to a new level. He assumed it was because now he was on the LC field where his dad enjoyed his short-lived prime. Surely his dad was just trying to relive the glory days.

Despite his dad's predictions, DP managed to hang on after their best pitcher was out and both teams clung to first place. The showdown at Dos Pueblos was set for April 30. (He still remembered every detail. He wished he didn't). With both teams at 8-1 in league play, this game would decide who advanced to the playoffs.

The ball of anxiety in his stomach grew heavier as they warmed up in enemy territory. Both sides' bleachers were packed with orange- or blue-wearing parents, friends, siblings, grandparents, teachers, girlfriends, wide-eyed Little Leaguers, everyone who mattered. Pump-up music blared from the speakers above the snack shack and he mouthed along to "We Will Rock You" and hoped it was true.

It wasn't. Quite the opposite, actually.

He took his time getting home, knowing what was waiting for him. He felt like he was seven years old again when he walked in around midnight. All the lights were off, thank God.

"That was the shittiest game I've ever seen."

His dad's voice shattered the dark quiet and he almost dropped his phone. "Jesus, you scared me."

"Do you know how much your strike-out just cost you?"

"The playoffs. I know. You don't have to remind me."

"Your college fund."

He stopped short as he was taking off his cleats. "What are you talking about?"

"I had it all riding on this season. Thought you guys had this one in the bag for sure. Playoffs should have been no problem." He drummed his knuckles on the table next to his glass.

"Dad. What are you talking about."

"8-1 and you guys still couldn't hold onto it."

"No, I mean – my college money. What about it?" The lump in his throat grew heavier.

"You and your fucking teammates just lost you ten grand. Plus everything I won from this season." He pulled a piece of paper from his pocket. "A grand total of $11,050."

This couldn't be happening. "Dad. Mom saved up that ten grand. That's for school."

He gestured lazily towards the piece of paper. Josh could just make out two signatures under a short block of text. "And now it's Evan Fucking Berry's. I'm a good man. I keep my word."

He ran to his room and slammed the door and laid on his clean bed in his dirty uniform and cried big fat defeat tears.

He turned in his jersey the next day. Two more years of this... he just couldn't. It wasn't fair to him and it damn well wasn't fair to his mom, but that was life, wasn't it? What new lows could his dad descend to? He didn't want to find out. He couldn't risk that.

He still missed baseball every day.

Sam

Josh was so lucky, he thought as he watched him whirling around the kitchen. Good at everything, universally liked, and the dude could cook, too.

He turned to face the couch and tried to fall asleep. He'd never had trouble falling asleep before this year. It came naturally to him whenever he wanted to sleep, and he was thankful for it. His had been a blessedly stress-free existence (until this year, of course) and he missed it.

But now, in the soft and dangerous moments before falling asleep, his thoughts were full of Sally. He had to tell her, right? He couldn't just show up to the Bay Area with his mattress and a suitcase full of dreams. He was moving for her, for Sally in her blue underwear and pink t-shirts and yellow hair and green eyes that failed to meet his.

He would tell her. He would tell her... tonight. He had to. He would.

Decision made. He curled up further into the couch and drifted.

He was walking on the Golden Gate Bridge, carrying his suitcase and his banjo. Cars whizzed by him and he tried to remember where his new apartment was. He tried flagging down a car but they soared past, blue and yellow blurs with faceless drivers.

"Slow down!" He waved frantically, trying to get someone to notice him, but they all drove past him, ignoring him like he wasn't even there.

The stream of cars thinned out and he looked down the road. Sally's car was approaching. He waved with one arm, then dropped his suitcase and began jumping up and down, waving both arms recklessly. She was still far enough away that he couldn't see her face. She wasn't slowing down. He had to make her slow down before she drove past him forever.

He jumped into the middle of the street, arms pumping, preparing himself to get hit. She was going too fast and he saw her face and her look of surprise and her car was careening towards him and he clenched, preparing for the worst –

He gasped as he thudded onto the carpet face-first. He laid there for a few moments, letting his heart rate go back down. Jesus. Talk about realistic. He pulled himself back up on the couch and tried to shake the image of Sally hitting him with her car out of his head.

"You okay, man?" Josh called from the kitchen.

"Yeah, just… just fell."

"Dinner will be ready in a few minutes, can you go tell everybody?"

"Sure." He stood up, slightly disoriented. Alex was passed out on the couch and Josh was in the kitchen and everyone else was – where?

"Hey, uh, food's almost ready!" he called from the bottom of the stairs. The girls were probably changing and he didn't – well, he shouldn't go up there.

Sally's head popped out from the bedroom door. "Josh, I was going to help you! You should have told me!"

Victoria brushed past her. "I don't care who made it, I'm hungry."

"There's food?" Erik popped out from the other bedroom door and barreled downstairs. The girls followed. Victoria slapped his butt as she went by and Sally carefully ignored him. Grace gave him one of her small, sad smiles, and he followed her into the kitchen.

Grace

It felt so nice to be sitting around a table together. She couldn't remember the last time she'd had a family dinner.

Josh brought down the giant colander of spaghetti and walked around the table, serving them. Grace giggled at the formality. Victoria rolled her eyes but smiled. They piled bread and salad onto their plates and ate in silence for a few minutes, collectively hungry and exhausted and satisfied.

"Today was a good day," Grace said, surprising herself. She hadn't had a good day in a very long time. Everyone looked up at her.

"I'm glad you had fun," said Sally, genuinely happy that her friend was happy. Sally also looked far more content and relaxed than she had earlier, Grace thought.

"Josh, you're amazing," Sam said through a mouthful of spaghetti, scooping more onto his plate. "Like seriously dude, your spaghetti is so much better than mine."

Josh grinned appreciatively. "Thanks, man, but it's really not that hard. I'll show you sometime."

"What's your secret ingredient?"

Josh leaned forward conspiratorially. "Swag." Erik high-fived him. Victoria rolled her eyes.

They laughed, lulling into relaxed silence as they ate. Alex demolished his three servings and twirled his last forkful around lazily, head propped on elbow.

Victoria looked impatient at their lethargy. "Guys, please drink caffeine. It's like, nine o'clock. We need to wake up more if we're going to have fun tonight."

Alex obediently chugged the rest of his Coke and Victoria clapped. "Well done, you. Everyone follow Alex's example."

Josh brandished his Sprite sarcastically. "I'm going to drink all of this, but not because you told me to."

"Save that attitude for the vodka," she said, winking. She stood up, leaving her plate on the table. "I'm going to shower. When I come back I expect you all to be ready to have *real* fun." They watched her flounce up the stairs, fixated by the presence of beautiful confidence. Grace envied that. Boys wanted her. Girls wanted to be her. Victoria had it all.

Sally

She put the last clean plate away and looked around the kitchen. God, that was a satisfying feeling, everything put away, tidied up, neatly filed back into its own little corner of existence. She wiped down the counters and felt a warm glow of pleasure at the shininess of the granite. She attacked a stubborn stain and rubbed until the spaghetti sauce was no longer an offensive blight on her perfect landscape. It was bad enough leaving a mess at her own house; it was far less excusable to do so in someone else's.

She leaned against the sink. There was something so relaxing about standing in a completely clean kitchen. She missed that feeling in the dorms. She missed a lot about home.

She watched Victoria strut gracefully down the stairs and felt the little green monster of envy gnawing at her. Victoria fit in wherever she was. Victoria would never feel homesick.

Grace

Victoria returned to the living room, her tiny pajama shirt stretched unnecessarily taut. Grace watched Josh's eyes flicker over her as they arranged themselves on the couches and floor and waited for Sally to finish cleaning the kitchen. Alex squatted, wincing as his knee cracked. Erik spread his arms impassively across the whole couch. She sat on the floor cross-legged next to Sam. Poor Sam. He'd changed this year, too. She hadn't expected him too, she realized. She expected him to stay the same. She wanted to come home to the same familiar cast of characters that had narrated and entertained and performed during her whole life.

And now her mom was gone.

They all needed some things to stay the same. You could change. College changed you. You wanted to go have adventures and become a whole, real person, but you wanted to come home for Christmas, and you wanted home to be exactly the same. If your friends stayed stagnant, you could dance around them, rising higher and higher like a well-hit tetherball in orbit. But that tetherball relied on the solid pole to let it fly as high as it wanted. If the pole was suddenly cool and different and... fratty, the ball couldn't go as high as before.

Victoria laughed at something that Josh said and she concentrated on her fingernails. Her mom would hate how her nails looked, rigidly not uniform and desperately in need of a manicure. Remnants of her cracked blue polish from a few weeks ago stuck in random areas. She'd forgotten about it. She hadn't bothered.

Her mom's nails were always flawless. She'd spent her life wondering how her mother's nails were so perfectly rounded, so long, so perpetually chip-free. She watched her fixedly whenever her mom whipped out her ever-present emery board. Was there some secret to her mom's routine? She couldn't tell. She tried to replicate the same fast, painful-sounding movements on her own nails and usually just ended up with powdery stuff on her still-ugly fingertips.

Sally came in and tucked herself in next to Grace. Sally's nails were usually almost as flawless as her mom's were – as her mom's had been. Now Sally had multiple chips and cracks that made her neat, cookie-dough-rolling, piano-playing fingers look like normal people's fingers.

Victoria's laugh trailed off and Josh looked around. "Are we all here?" They murmured their assent. "Awesome." He got up and ran into the kitchen. She heard a cabinet door open and close and the shuffling of grocery bags.

He emerged a few minutes later with a column of Solo cups, two large clear bottles, two six packs, and orange juice. "'Kay, I brought vodka, rum, and beer."

Victoria sat up. "Nice! Did you finally get a fake?"

"Of course! And it's from Massachusetts so California people have a harder time with it." He grinned and flashed his wallet.

"Lemme see that." Josh tossed Erik his wallet and Erik pulled out the plastic. "Looks pretty fake to me."

"The guy at Ralph's obviously didn't think so, and that's all that matters," said Victoria, opening the vodka. "Who wants me to serve them?"

Sally stiffened. Erik and Sam raised their hands simultaneously. Alex shrugged.

"Alex. You are nineteen years old and you've never had a drink. You're with people that you trust. You're drinking tonight." Josh smiled and handed him a rum and Coke. He held it uncertainly. She could almost see the gears whirring in his head.

His friends wanted him to drink and he wanted to make them happy. His parents didn't approve of drinking and he wanted to make them happy. His brother… his brother drank a lot and his parents still loved him. Erik wanted him to drink. He took a tentative sip.

"You too, Sally." She crossed her arms but Victoria shoved the cup at her. "Screwdriver. It's a good one to start out with – the juice is so sweet you can barely taste the vodka."

Sally glared at her and took the cup.

Victoria poured Grace the same thing and held up her own cup ceremonially. "We are gathered here tonight to witness the most enjoyable loss of virginity a person can experience. Sally, Grace, and Alex are finally going to leave the realm of childhood and start acting like fucking college students, and they're going to do so in pretty damn awesome company, and I don't just mean myself. So drink up, guys, this is the start of a long and very pleasurable night." She threw back her head, hair streaming magnificently, and gulped down her drink.

Josh laughed and took a sip of his. "Do not learn about drinking from Victoria. She will kill you. Learn from me. Pace yourselves." He nodded at Alex, who obligingly took a longer sip, sputtering. Josh cheered. "Welcome to manhood, brother!"

Victoria cackled. "We're not in a fraternity, Josh."

Erik laughed. "Have you ever been to an athlete party? I'm sure ours are better than yours."

Grace realized that she'd just been sitting watching her friends drink. She took a sip of hers, expecting orange juice, and almost spat it back out when she tasted the vodka. The second sip was better, and the third almost tasted good.

"I don't doubt it!" Josh finished his and began pouring himself a second cup.

Sam wrinkled his nose. "You guys are so competitive about everything."

Victoria cackled. "Oh, Sam. Wanna know what I learned this year?" She leaned forward conspiratorially. "When someone calls themselves competitive, it means one of three things." She held up a red-taloned finger. "One. They like winning, pure and simple." She ticked a second finger. "Two. They hate losing." She nodded towards Erik and Josh stifled a laugh. "And three. It's not even a choice anymore. They have to win because that's all they've ever done, and they don't know any other way." She settled back against the couch and took a long sip of her drink. "I am definitely type three."

"You got that right." Josh high-fived her and she laughed.

"You'd be surprised how few of us there are in this world. Even at Berkeley, but I've met the *coolest* people there, so I don't mind. They've traveled the world. They've *done* things and *seen* things, things that people in Cottonwood can't even imagine. There's so much more to life than just – than *surfing*," she said with mock disdain. "My friend Chris volunteered in Ghana last summer and shadowed a doctor at a clinic. He got to assist on an appendectomy. Nat spent a month by herself in Florence and just *lived* and drank wine and went to museums. Raj is on an archeological dig in Turkey right now. They're so *cool*."

Grace felt a twinge of annoyance. Typical Victoria. She collected friends the way some people collected antiques, looking for the brightest and most interesting treasures, and assumed that she too became more interesting by association.

"This is… surprisingly good," Sally said slowly. "I just assumed that everyone built it up a ton, but… it's really good."

"I am SO proud of you," Victoria grinned at her and waved a loose hand. "About damn time."

Sally gulped hers down. "I'm already going to hell. I guess I might as well enjoy it." She poured herself another vodka and orange.

Good Lord, thought Grace. If Sally was going to hell, who wasn't?

Josh cheered, laughing. "Sally, if you're going to hell, what are the rest of us supposed to do?"

Grace giggled. Same old Josh. They still shared a mind.

Chapter 6

Saturday night

The sun had been gone for a long time but the last traces of light still lingered in the sky, throwing golden arcs that faded into the shadows on the ceiling.

Sam reached for a beer. In his post-Sally period he'd consumed more alcohol than he'd ever desired to, and his tolerance was high enough that he barely felt the effects of his first vodka and orange. He never thought that he'd like the taste of beer, but he'd warmed up to it over the past few months. It almost tasted good now.

They sat in silence, sipping their drinks. The traces of light disappeared but no one bothered to turn on the light. The tiny glimmer of the porch light shone through the window, softly illuminating their faces.

"So what do we do now?" asked Alex, sipping a beer slowly. He took off his Yankees hat, the pink glow of his face visible even in the fading light.

"We talk, I guess. Seems like we still have a lot to catch up on," said Josh, refilling his cup. Sally held hers out to him and he laughed. "For a first-timer, you're a natural."

"I'm southern, darlin'," she drawled, exaggerating her sweet accent. "I was born to drink." It was weird seeing her drink, thought Sam. It was weirder watching her place a hand on Josh's shoulder, naturally. It was weirdest seeing him not brush it away. Finally he finished pouring and she settled back against the couch. He felt like Josh was watching her more closely now. He drank faster, willing everything to make sense.

"So how are everyone's families?" asked Josh conversationally. "Sally, we'll let you start and set the bar high, as usual." Victoria smirked. "I didn't mean it in a mean way!" he insisted.

Sally sipped her drink, getting used to the taste. "Same as usual, I guess. My dad is coaching Jenny's fall ball team. Carly's starting ballet. My mom's hosting her big fundraiser dinner next weekend. She's been planning it all summer. Gramma and Grampa are flying out for it. We're all helping."

"God, your family is perfect."

Sally shook her head. "We're far from that, Vic."

"She kind of has a point," Josh cocked his head, counting her family members on his fingers. "We have Mr. Chandler, the awesomely cool dude who can barbecue like nobody's business. We have Mrs. Chandler, the southern belle and envy of every mom in the neighborhood. And we have three pretty girls. Yeah, pretty sure your family's perfect, Sally."

She shook her head, smiling sadly.

"Well if yours isn't, Erik's is." Victoria pointed her chin at him. "His family has *three* hot moms. And his super hot dad. And him. He's not a pretty girl," she said, unnecessarily, "but he's *Erik Armstrong the third* so I guess that makes him pretty." Alex coughed.

"You think my family's perfect?" Erik laughed. "You have no idea."

Victoria spread her arms and gestured around with her cup-holding hand. "Look at this place. This cabin is bigger than my apartment building and it's not even one-fourth the size of your *house*. Your mansion, I mean."

Erik tossed another empty cup to the floor. "I never asked for that."

"You never asked for a rich dad. Some people have worse problems."

"My dad is a legend. I'm expected to be a legend. That's kind of a problem."

"Dude, what are you worried about? You're a shoe-in." Josh sounded annoyed.

"Why does everyone care about it so much? It's just baseball."

"Why don't you care about it more? You're getting a full ride to school while some of us drown in loans." Victoria polished off the rest of her drink and Grace was a little impressed that she sounded so steady after drinking straight vodka.

"It's not my fault you're poor." Sam's eyes widened and Sally looked angrily at Erik.

"Dude, lay off," Josh snapped. "We can't all have inheritances."

"Then quit talking about my family. Let's talk about your family, Victoria, see how you like that."

"Tammy? Let's see, you mean the woman who can't stop sleeping around and dating guys that are bad for her? She's a great role model." She took a very large sip.

Sally looked like she wanted to say something.

"Yeah, I got that vibe from her," said Erik meanly. "What about your dad? Why have we never seen him?"

"My parents are divorced," she said through clenched teeth. "You know that."

"Yeah, but why do you never mention him?" asked Sam curiously. "You never talk about your dad."

"Well, that's probably because we have a restraining order against him," she muttered.

Josh looked up. "What?"

"Yep. Tammy got it right before we moved to LC. I haven't seen him since I was eight."

They fell silent. The wind picked up outside and leaves dragged against the window.

"I'm sorry," said Sally quietly. "I never knew."

"Why would you?" she shrugged. "I never told you."

"That sucks, babe," Josh said lazily, draping an arm around her shoulders. She pushed it off.

"Yeah, it does suck. And none of you get how much it sucks because you all have dads that live with you and take care of you instead of scarring you for life."

Josh laughed hollowly. "Oh, my dad doesn't exactly take care of me."

Erik grunted. "At least your dad doesn't treat you like – like a fucking horse he wants to train to win races, or something."

"Yeah? Your dad gave you a future. My dad is doing everything he can to take mine away from me."

Sally looked concerned. "What do you mean?"

Josh took a deep breath, staring into his drink. "So you know how my dad is kind of a shitty human being, right?" Grace nodded slightly. The others were still.

"He bet my college money on our sophomore season. All of it. Everything my mom saved up for me, gone over a baseball game." He looked directly at Erik. "You guys have to worry about other shit, I get that. But you don't have to worry about paying for your own education, which is really fucking expensive."

Victoria patted him on the knee. "I can honestly say that I'm the only other one here who knows what that feels like."

He smiled halfheartedly. "It feels pretty shitty, doesn't it?"

"How much financial aid do you get?" asked Sally.

"About seventy-five percent, which is good but not great, when you consider the cost of living there. I work two jobs while my frat brothers get wasted every weekend. It's kind of exhausting."

"I'm sorry, Josh." Sally looked up at him and Victoria snorted.

"You don't get to be sorry. You don't know what it's like."

Sally glared at Victoria "No, I don't know what it's like. I realize that I'm lucky that I don't know what it's like. But I can still be sorry."

Victoria looked ready to snap and Josh was ready for it.

"Thanks, Sally. Let's change the subject." Josh turned quickly to Alex. "So, Alex. Are you excited to see your brother next week?"

Alex grinned broadly, fiddling with his Yankees hat. "I can't wait to see him. We're throwing a party for him and everything. My mom's been talking about doing this for months."

"Your parents fascinate me," said Victoria. "They treat you like silver and you still think they're gold."

"Victoria!" Sally snapped. "Rude!"

"It's true, though!" she said defensively. "He spends his whole life trying to make them happy."

Josh patted him on the back. "Alex, you're a great guy, but you have to stop trying to only make other people happy. You'll just make yourself miserable."

"I feel like I disappointed everyone this year." The words were out of his mouth and he wished he could take them back.

"How?"

"Of course you didn't!" Sally said indignantly. "You're wonderful."

"Well, with…" His hand drifted to his knee again. "I feel like I let everyone down. My new coach. My team. My parents. You guys. Erik, especially." He turned to his friend. "Remember how excited we were to play each other? It was going to be like Little League again. UCLA vs. USC."

Victoria snorted. "That's some Romeo-and-Juliet-quality shit right there."

Josh hushed her as Alex continued. "We'd be playing NCAA ball in the same city, living the dream, and then I had to go and hurt my knee."

"Yeah, but that wasn't your fault," Josh said. "You didn't *choose* to – what was it? Tear your cartilage?"

Alex nodded. "Yeah, I keep trying to tell myself that… but I think if I had taken it easy and listened to the doctors instead of… pushing myself more, I would have healed by now. I could be playing this season."

Josh patted him on the back. "I'm sure it's not your fault. You just work hard. That's your thing. That's what's going to make you successful."

"Hey, look at it this way – you get a jump on your major! Engineering at UCLA is supposed to be really hard. You'll get better grades this way." Victoria actually said it kindly.

He grinned. "That's true. I do love my classes. They're hard, but I love them."

Sam reached around Victoria and refilled his cup. "I don't understand why you all like school so much. It's just school."

Grace felt Sally's internal fuming beside her.

Victoria laughed. "Oh, Sam. You make me so happy. I like knowing that there's one normal person among us."

"You're the weird ones," he said, grinning widely. "I can't believe you'd want to leave Cottonwood. We live at the beach. It's perfect."

"We built castles in the air and sand," said Sally, smiling to herself.

"Yeah, I miss it sometimes." Josh sounded sad.

"Me, too," Grace assented. Alex nodded. Victoria shrugged.

"You know what I miss most?" Josh said suddenly. "Besides my mom, obviously?"

"Mick's Burritos," he and Grace said in unison.

"Dude, I want one." Erik rubbed his stomach that had apparently already metabolized the two thousand calories of pasta he'd consumed for dinner.

Josh lifted his cup to Grace's. "Exactly! Grace gets it! When we decided to move to New York we forgot that there is a *significant* lack of Mexican food on the east coast! Towards the end of April, when it finally started getting warm? Man, I was *dying*."

Sam laughed. "I can't imagine life without Mick's Burritos. I eat there like every day."

"Lucky!" Grace grinned at him.

"I still think they're overrated. There's this place in Berkeley –"

Josh held his hand up to silence her. "Vic, I get that you're cool and sophisticated now, but nothing is better than Mick's Burritos." The others nodded in agreement and she laughed.

"Fine, fine." She waved carelessly. "I just think you should find a new favorite restaurant, or just one that's not in freaking *Cottonwood*."

"Hey!" Sally made a face.

Josh wagged his finger at her. "No talking crap on Cottonwood, Vic. Not tonight."

"It'll always be home," said Sam.

"Yeah, but it's the *past*. Don't you want to move forward?"

The collective subconscious *yes* hung heavily in the air and they all took a drink at the same time without meaning to.

"Face it, guys. We grew up as much as we could there. It's time to move on."

They were quiet as they contemplated this sad reality. Maybe it was true.

Sally took another sip and felt her mouth bubble and burnish with cheap pleasure. Oh, wow. So that was why people drank. She'd never desired to feel a lack of control, but now… maybe one drunk night was just what she needed. Maybe she could just not be Sally for a night and be someone else, someone more exciting and stress-free who didn't have to worry about things like kidney beans and ruined lives.

She turned to Erik. She felt so bad for him. It must be hard having so much pressure on him from people besides himself. He looked nicer than usual.

She reached out to pat him on the arm, since it seemed like everyone needed to be reminded of her before she talked to them. She couldn't help but run her hand over his enormous bicep. Wow. How did boys even get arms like those? He could probably lift her up with one hand. And his shoulders. Wow. Why did such a magnificent pair of shoulders have to belong to such a mean human being?

"What?" He probably looked annoyed but she didn't care.

"Please tell your dad thank you for letting us have the cabin this weekend. It's beautiful." She gestured widely and her orange juice-vodka sloshed around in the half-empty cup.

"Thanks." He said flatly.

"Are you going to tell him thank you for me?" She sat on her knees, leaning angrily at him, annoyed that he had not answered her.

"If I remember."

"Your dad is cool," said Victoria enviously.

"Fuck that," said Erik darkly.

"Erik! Language!" Sally leaned forward angrily and Victoria laughed.

"Jesus, Sally!"

"Jesus has nothing to do with it!" She felt herself yelling and part of her was embarrassed and part of her was happy that she was finally ready to yell at Erik, who didn't deserve to have such nice shoulders.

"Aren't you so proud to follow in his footsteps?" she asked. She couldn't even tell if it sounded sarcastic anymore.

Victoria cackled. "Yes, aren't you just ecstatic to be at USC doing everything exactly like your dad did, not having to try at all?"

Sally laughed and her mouth kept going and she wanted it to be quiet but she couldn't. She was drunk, she realized. Dangerous, tongue-loosening drunk, but she didn't care.

"Sally, stop," said Alex quietly, just finishing his drink.

"No, I'm serious. Be happy for him. We all turn into our parents eventually. Erik's just getting there ahead of schedule."

Erik chugged the rest of his beer and tossed the bottle.

Victoria laughed and stood up, only slightly shakily. She waved her cup in the air, eyes dazzling. "Ladies and gentlemen, Erik is demonstrating one of the few constant rules in the drinking game of life. When someone mentions your parents and you are reminded of your failures and fuck-ups and all that Freudian shit, you take a drink." She chugged the rest of hers and flipped the cup onto the table. Grace cringed. Could no one else feel Erik swelling in anger and Sally looking sad and drunk and Josh emanating anger?

She was careless, Victoria. She broke people for her own entertainment and let them crumble around her, then retreated to her selfish bubble and let her friends put themselves back together.

"Jesus. Let's not talk about parents," Josh said, nodding his head meaningfully towards Grace, less subtly than he would sober.

Grace set down her cup and felt the year's fury boiling inside of her. "Are you f – fu – fucking kidding me?" She almost wanted to laugh at her own cursing. She wanted to cry at how pathetic it sounded. She never cursed.

"Don't, don't," Sally sounded like she was going to cry as she crawled in between them. "I'm sorry I started it, I'm sorry." She looked fearfully between them.

"Okay, fine, we'll talk about parents and pretend like Grace's mom didn't die and you all aren't being selfish shits." Josh wiped his mouth.

"We're at the corner of Too Soon and Not Yet, and sooner or later we'll have to cross the street," Victoria said darkly.

Josh waved his hand. "You want to talk about shitty dads, Erik? You want to know why I quit in high school?"

"At least your dad's alive." They froze. Sam never talked like that.

Victoria laughed. "Well, I guess he told you."

Grace had never seen Sam drink, but she didn't like drunk Sam. The laughter was gone from his eyes, replaced by something steely and mean that didn't seem like him. Maybe he was mad because Sally was leaning on Josh instead of him. Josh ignored Sam and barreled on.

"So I really hate my fucking dad and I hope I don't turn into him. Erik, you are welcome to become your dad if you want, just know that I won't follow you around like a fucking remora fish."

"I will!" said Alex. He'd meant it as a joke but his voice was jumbled and it sounded weird.

Erik turned to him, scowling. "Don't be a kiss-ass, Alex. People are always kissing my ass and it bugs the shit out of me."

Sally rolled around to face Alex. "Why do you let him treat you like that?"

Alex looked bewildered. "Like what?"

"You know what. He talks to you like... you have no opinion. Like you don't matter."

"He – he doesn't treat me like that. We're best friends."

Sally snorted. "Best friends? How many of his parties has he invited you to? How many of his friends has he introduced you to?"

"Yes, Sally. Because that's such a deep, significant scale by which to gauge friendship," snipped Victoria sarcastically.

"You know what I mean," Sally shot back. "Erik. Alex calls you his best friend. He puts so much trust in you and you don't give him anything. You don't reciprocate and it's killing him."

"It's none of your business," Erik snapped. "And for your information, I do tell him shit. Like about practices and games and stuff."

"Don't you get it?" Sally gestured towards Alex's knee. "He loves baseball. He works harder at it than anyone. Harder than you, even. He would kill to be where you are. He wanted nothing more than to play college baseball and now he can't, and you can, and you don't even appreciate it."

Erik opened his mouth. Erik shut his mouth.

"I guess I'm right," Sally said quietly.

"Of course you are." Victoria glared at Erik. "His life is so fucking easy. He gets a free ride to school. He'll get drafted right out of college. He'll sign some multimillion-dollar contract and build a mansion next to his daddy's. He doesn't have to try, or worry about paying for things, or even bother studying, because God knows his professors will pass him without him opening a single book."

Erik whirled around towards her. "You've always been jealous of me. You think my life is some kind of cake walk, but it's not. Do you know how fucking hard it is? Do you know what my dad puts me through?"

"Oh, I'm sure the workouts are really tough. It must be so hard to lift weights when you inherited gigantic muscles that do the work for you."

"Did it ever occur to you that maybe I'm better than you and you're just a dumb bitch?" Victoria lunged at him and it was only Sam's ensnaring arm that kept Erik from getting mauled.

"Victoria!" Josh yelled at her, shocked.

"Shut up, Josh." Erik smirked maddeningly and she shook in anger. "Everything is so, so easy for you. Everything's always been easy for you because everyone knows your dad. You have everything. Your name is everywhere. Everyone's willing to bend over backwards for Erik Fucking Armstrong the Third."

"Do you think I like it?" Erik yelled. "Seeing my family's name on every fucking thing I pass? Having everyone expect me to be as good as my dad, if not better?"

Victoria glared at him.

"Do you think it's easy having a famous grandpa? A superstar dad? It's the worst goddamned thing in the entire world. I hate it. I really fucking hate it. I hate him."

"You don't mean that," Sally murmured.

"Yeah, I do," said Erik angrily, and Grace was amazed to hear tears in his voice. "I'm in his shadow everywhere I go. High school. Home. USC. I can't even go to the beach without seeing his name on all the fucking lifeguard towers."

"Poor little rich boy," said Victoria mockingly. "God, that must be so hard, to have to walk around and have everyone worship you because you're related to two other dumbass rich jocks."

"Who are both assholes!" Erik shot back. "Both of them, but my dad especially. He's so fucking determined to make me exactly like him and I hate it. I wish he were dead."

The room swelled with silence at this pronouncement.

"You don't mean it," said Josh.

Alex shushed him, Alex, the one who was there in the kayak and watched him get yelled at during practices and never asked him about the bruises.

"No, I do. I really fucking do. The only reason I went through the workouts when I was little was so that I'd get strong enough to hit him back." He picked up an empty cup and squeezed it until it cracked and he threw it at the wall. "By the time I was strong enough I realized that he'd always hit harder. He'd always be bigger than me, even if I was taller, because he still had that power over me."

"He's probably proud of you, at least," Josh said pointedly.

"I'm always going to be a disappointment to him." Erik leaned forward and Grace counted the empty cups around him. Even his considerable bulk was no match for that much alcohol swimming in his bloodstream. He buried his head in his hands.

"It's so. Fucking. Hard. I hate my old man. I hate when he hits me. I hate when he acts like he's God's gift to the world. I hate when we have to go places with him and smile at another fucking sign with his name on it and take another fucking family photo in front of whatever new thing he paid for."

Victoria opened her mouth and Josh shushed her. Erik had never said so many words at once. He seemed to be building up to something important.

"And I have to walk around like the big macho athlete," he continued, mostly into his palms. "There's girls on me all the time, doing stuff all the time. I can't go to a party without some chick trying to take my pants off."

"Erik problems," Josh muttered, and Victoria giggled meanly.

He continued without hearing them. "And no one gets it. No one understands." He rocked back and forth, his huge baseball body at odds with his infantile position.

Did he mean what he thought he meant? Alex wondered, not daring to believe it. Hesitantly, he reached out and put his hand on Erik's much larger hand. He felt alarmed when he realized that Erik was crying and he felt awkward and wanted to pull his hand away but Erik was warm and he kept it there.

"Alex… is everything okay?" Grace asked softly. "You seem sad. You've seemed sad all weekend."

He traced his finger around the rim of his cup, thinking. "I guess it's just... I keep being reminded of last summer. Running and hiking and not being in pain. Getting so excited to play baseball at UCLA. Making my parents proud, for once." His hand drifted to his knee and he seemed to deflate. "I love my brother. I really do. He's my favorite person in the world. I'm so proud of him, but sometimes I wish... that he wasn't so talented, just because then my parents would love me more." He looked up fearfully. "Does that make me a bad person?"

"No, that makes you a normal person," Sally said firmly.

"Your parents are crazy. You're like the only smart athlete I know. They should be proud of you."

He grinned sadly. "Thanks, guys. But I'm pretty sure my dad will never be proud of me now, the way that I am."

"Welcome to the club," said Josh bitterly.

Victoria raised her cup. "A toast, to the shitty fathers who will always be disappointed in us." She looked around the group. "Except Sally, of course." They laughed and drank.

"Your dad doesn't seem that bad, Alex. I mean, compared to mine." Josh smiled grimly.

"Your brother doesn't play for the Yankees," Alex reminded him.

Josh laughed. "Valid point, but you're way smarter than your brother, right? So your dad should be happy about that."

"Yeah, but even then. A's can always be A-pluses. A double should have been a home run. It's all the same. It's exhausting."

"Your dad's Asian, that's expected. My dad's angry because he hasn't accomplished anything since he was eighteen and no one cares that his baseball team won CIF in high school. Like really no one. What self-respecting adult goes around talking about what they did in high school? He's fifty-two years old, for God's sake. He peaked thirty-four years ago. That's pathetic." Josh stared down into his cup. "I'm going to a better school than he did. I'm going to have a better job than he did, and I'm going to treat my family better than he ever did."

Grace felt a sudden urge to hug him.

"Your mom is lucky to have you," said Victoria unexpectedly, kindly.

He smiled at her and Grace was startled to see that he had tears in his eyes. "I'm always the reason for his freak-outs, so I thought that moving to the other side of the country might... I don't know. Help her somehow. Take away the catalyst."

"You can't blame yourself," said Sally. "That's not fair."

"Sometimes I feel so guilty for moving. I feel like I should stay here in case I need to protect her."

"I thought about transferring," Grace said quietly. They all turned towards her. "After – after December. I felt like I should be at home. For Max."

"You don't have to," said Victoria at once. "I know I don't know anything about having a little person to take care of, but you don't have to sacrifice Cornell for him. You go to a fucking Ivy League. Your mom wouldn't want you to give it up."

They sat quietly for a moment, listening to the crickets chirping on the porch.

"Grace, that's ... that's a big decision," said Sally carefully. "Have you thought a lot about it?"

Grace nodded. "I think about it every day."

Josh looked at her seriously. "Do you like it there?"

Of course he would be the first to ask the most important question. No one had asked her that before. Her family was the Cornell family. Everyone knew that. No one questioned how much she liked it, or even considered the possibility that she didn't. It was expected that she would fall into line behind her parents and grandparents and aunts and uncles and embrace the ra-ra-Big Red attitude that defined the rest of her family.

Did she like it? She thought, wondering how she hadn't thought about this before now. Before December, before all of the events that obviously clouded her perspective on everything... had she liked it before she was terrified of it? During those early months, did she feel any of the warmth for it that her family did?

"You know what?" she said thoughtfully. "I don't think I do."

"It's an Ivy League," said Victoria, as if that was supposed to compensate for the crushing loneliness she felt when she was there.

"I know that. And on paper, it's perfect. It's a great school, it's the family school. There are so many amazing, smart, nice people there. But it's so, so cold. And I don't like any of the majors. I don't know what I want to do so I have to get perfect grades in everything…. It's exhausting." She leaned against the couch, deflated by honesty.

"You know, you don't have to get perfect grades to be happy," Sam piped up.

"Yes, you can live at home and go to community college and have no ambition at all, and you'll be perfectly happy," snipped Sally. She stared out of the group, eyes flashing, mouth grim.

Sam stuck out his jaw. "Seriously?"

"You don't understand the pressure. You never have."

"What I don't understand is why you guys only care about school. It's all you think about. It consumes you. And you let it. Sometimes I think you like being unhappy," he said directly to Sally.

She whirled on him. "Do you think I enjoy being stressed out? I don't. I really, really don't. I wish I could be a normal person and have time to hang out with my friends instead of studying all the time. I don't watch TV. I don't have time to do anything but school because that's what's going to get me a job and pay for my house and raise my – and take care of me."

"Yeah, I get that. What I don't get is how competitive you all are." He nodded towards Victoria and Alex. "I bet one of you will lose it. You need perspective."

"*Perspective?*" Sally looked livid. "*We* have perspective. *We* moved away. *We're* looking towards the future. You just don't understand. You've never had any ambition. You don't make plans for the future. You just do whatever you want and don't worry about the consequences and leave the messes for other people to clean up." She looked ready to cry. Or hit something.

He'd been saving this for a smoother delivery but the words tumbled out before he knew they were coming. "I got a job offer from Pixar!" he yelled. "How's that for ambition?"

She halted mid-diatribe. "What?"

"I entered a contest. They like my animation. They offered me a spot."

"In… Emeryville?" asked Victoria. She glanced at Sally, who was staring at her lap, biting her lip. She knew that she was thinking the same thing. Emeryville. He would be thirty miles away from Stanford instead of four hundred.

"Congrats, dude!" said Josh jovially, crawling forward to offer him a high five. "When do you move?"

"I haven't accepted it yet."

Josh stopped with his hand in the air. "What? Why not?"

"Are they going to pay you?" asked Victoria.

"Yeah," he said uncomfortably. "I would start at forty grand a year."

Josh whistled. "Forty grand a year at nineteen. That's a pretty sweet deal, bro."

"What about your degree?" asked Grace.

"I can transfer to a CC up there and take night classes or something. And they have extra employee training programs, so I can get more credentials and animation practice."

"Dude! Take it!" Josh said. Grace nodded encouragingly.

"I might," said Sam. "Depending on how some people would feel about me moving to the Bay Area." He looked at Sally meaningfully. They all watched her. Her cheeks reddened.

Finally she sat up. "Congratulations, Sam. That's really – that's really good for you," she said flatly.

"Toast!" yelled Josh, and they all drank, except for Sally, who leaned back against the couch, looking defeated. Grace wanted to hug her.

Josh surveyed their empty cups. "We need more alcohol."

"I'll go with you!" said Sally, needing to do something, anything to get out of there. She held the couch for support and followed Josh down the hallway into the dark kitchen. His hands scrambled loosely through the grocery bags and she wondered how much he'd had to drink. She wondered how much she'd had to drink. It felt like a lot. She still couldn't decide if she liked it or not.

She stumbled and he caught her. "Thanks," she said, giggling, trying to free herself.

It was very dark in the kitchen and they were all alone, hidden behind the kitchen wall, far enough away that their friends could not hear their whispers. His arms felt nice and he smelled good and she wondered if she was allowed to think those things.

"Sally." He pulled her face to his and she felt a swoop of something. His hands held her firmly and she wondered what their friends were doing in the other room and part of her didn't want him to hold her like that and part of her wanted him to pull her closer and the rest of her was confused.

"Yes?" she chirped. He smiled and she was happy that she made him smile.

"You're pretty."

She felt herself grinning sloppily and tried to pull herself away but ended up just holding his arm for what surely was an inappropriate amount of time.

"Well thank you. You're not so bad yourself." He was still cradling her face in his warm hands. His hands felt bigger too, and less shaky than hers. He was better at being drunk than she was.

"Sally, I want to kiss you."

She giggled without meaning to. "No, you don't."

"You're sad. I hate seeing you sad. I know I can make you happy. You deserve it."

Without hesitation or permission he pulled her face to his and she kissed the second boy of her life.

Panic welled up inside of her and she didn't know what to do and she tried to push him away but then she realized that she was enjoying it and she felt guilty and Sam was in the other room and Grace was there too and his arms were so strong and he finally let her go and she ran away.

Sam watched Sally's face as she re-entered the living room and saw her cheeks burning. She avoided eye contact and settled back into her original spot, away from where Josh sat coolly with the two new bottles.

"Holy shit, Josh." He snapped. "What did you do to her?"

Sally's eyes flicked over to him, wide and startled.

"Calm down, bro," Josh waved an arm lazily. "You guys are broken up, right? Let her try something new. Maybe she'd be happier if she were with someone. She looks miserable. You're the only guy she's ever been with."

Victoria's eyes widened and she almost grinned as her eyes darted between them, like she was watching a tennis match.

He really, really wanted to hit Josh but he also wanted to be the better guy but he really, really wanted to hit Josh.

"Are you fucking kidding me? And you're the only one that knew we had sex last summer!" The words toppled out of his mouth and he wished he could pick them up and put them back in. Everything was out of his control now, wasn't it?

Grace gasped and Victoria laughed. "Poor Grace. Finally realized that your perfect little hero isn't so perfect after all? That's the worst part of growing up, isn't it – realizing that your heroes are human?"

Alex barked a tipsy laugh. "You got that right."

"No," said Grace, collecting herself. "That's the second-worst part of growing up." She took a sip of her drink and seemed to drift to a darker place. "The worst part is realizing that there's nothing you can do to help them."

Even Erik was paying attention now. Victoria perched on the edge of the couch, watching intently.

"What the fuck, Sam?" Sally looked ready to cry. Grace cringed at how wrong the word sounded in her voice. "Thanks for announcing it to the world." She dropped her head in her hands and her shoulders heaved gently.

"Are you ashamed of me or something?

"No, God no." She finally looked up, horrified. Her eyes begged him to understand. "I just… I'm mad at myself for being so stupid. No one else has ever made me feel like you do… like you'll love me just as I am. You told me I was… perfect. You said that so many times that it made me afraid to change, to do something that might contradict that perception of me… and then I changed and ruined everything good in my life and scared away all the people that were nice to me." She buried her head again.

The silence was so awkward and blared at his eardrums and he wanted to say so many things and couldn't decide which one to start with.

"I wish we could just go back to how things were before. I wish we could go back to last year."

Sally buried her head back into her hands. "Go back to last year?" she laughed hollowly. "I was a completely different person then."

"You're the same person," he said. His voice cracked. "We're still the same people."

"God, Sam." She looked exhausted. "We changed. People change. We're different."

"No." He wanted to say this. He'd thought it so many times and had dreamed of saying it to her in person and wished it could be under different circumstances. "We're the same people. We're – we're soul mates. And I know that because I never believed in soul mates until I met mine."

Sally starting crying and folded her hands across her stomach. Poor Sally, thought Grace. She wasn't perfect after all. She was just like her, a jumbled mass of regret and insecurities. She watched Josh put an arm around her and Sally tried to pull away, crying into the couch. Poor Sally. Poor Josh. She watched them worriedly.

"Oh, calm the fuck down, Grace. He's a guy. Sally's hot. Get over it."

Grace whirled on Victoria. "You've been a bitch to me all weekend. What's your problem?"

"My problem? My problem is how you treat Josh, how you've been treating him since we left for school. You act like he's yours. He doesn't belong to you. He's a person."

"I know that," said Grace, her face hot.

"Really? Because you sure as hell don't act like it."

"Don't talk to her like that!" Sally sputtered.

"No, keep going, Victoria," said Grace angrily.

"He tried to reach out to you. He tried to be there for you and you ignored him. You guys are like – *family*, and you ignored him."

Grace was furious to feel tears in her eyes. "You know I'm right," Victoria said.

"Stop it!" Sally yelled. Alex watched, wide-eyed. Erik still sat slumped against the couch, eyes flickering between them as if he were watching a mildly interesting TV show.

Victoria leaned back against the couch. "Excuse me for not being the only one to treat you like a fucking vase. You're not going to break. You're already broken. Your mom died, and that sucks. But I'm not going to treat you any differently because of it."

Josh looked ready to slap her, but Grace held up her hand. "No, she's right. You've all been treating me like... like I'm a mental patient. And every time you – you stop yourselves from using the word 'mom,' or you act like I'm really weak or something – you just remind me. And you make me feel worse." Josh closed his mouth. "And you!" She turned to face him. "You're different. You haven't acted like yourself since you joined a frat."

He snorted. "What? Am I not allowed to get involved in things that you're not a part of? Am I not allowed to make new friends? We're not five anymore, Grace. I made new friends and that doesn't make me bad, that makes me normal. And I didn't forget about you. Pretty sure you're the one that ignored me the whole year. You never picked up the phone so I stopped calling. Simple."

It felt like a slap in the face, but she knew that she deserved it. She leaned her forehead against her knees, curling into herself. God, she was a mess. "You're right. Victoria's right."

"I know I am," said Josh softly, and he sounded like her best friend again. "I *have* changed, Grace. But I'm still your friend. And I did call you. You know I did. You're the one that stopped acting like yourself."

Sam laughed emptily. "Don't you know? Girls change, Josh. They change more in a month, in a week, than we do in a year. They really can – they don't even realize it. They go on believing that they're perfect because everyone still tells them that, including us, because we're too dumb to know any better."

Erik smiled grimly. "I'm not dumb enough to know better. I don't think they're perfect."

"Shut up, Erik," Victoria snapped.

Sally scooted slightly away from Josh, still contorted like a pretzel. He watched her concernedly. Alex leaned against the couch, looking exhausted, his hand on his knee. Victoria sprawled over the cushions, her hair spilling onto Sam's shoulders. "God, we're all messes," she muttered. They were quiet.

Josh sipped his drink thoughtfully, breaking the silence. "Grace?"

She looked up dizzily. "Yeah?" Drinking was weird. Feeling tipsy was weirder.

"What did you mean earlier? About realizing that you can't help someone?"

Her head spun a little and she looked away from her friends. The words were buried so deep, but the alcohol and the dark and the closeness could dig them up. Right? Could she tell them? Would she feel better? She hadn't told anyone. She didn't want to burden them.

They didn't want her to be sad. They were her friends.

They deserved to know.

"I never told you guys how my mom died," she said quietly, still not looking at them. Victoria spun to face her. Sally stopped crying. Even Erik sat up, alert.

"When... when I found her...." God, this was hard.

Could she say it? Could she drag the words out?

She'd already started down this road. There was no turning back.

She took a deep breath. "When I found her... there was a bottle of pills next to her." Sam coughed on his drink. "And... a note." Sally covered her mouth, looking ready to cry again. Victoria's eyes widened.

"I'm sorry," said Alex quietly.

Josh immediately scooted over, wrapping his arms around her. She remembered how he'd held her in the exact same way on that day. It seemed like ages ago.

Her head swam and she closed her eyes, but that didn't make it any better. She still felt dizzy, just ... lighter. Free. Anchorless. Not drowning. The same lightness she'd felt in the lake. Like everything was out of her control, but in a good way... like she didn't have to be in charge of all the secrets and the bad heavy things and she could just... float.

"Are you okay?" he asked her, just as he'd asked her on the sad nights when he picked her up from her house and rescued her from screaming parents. He was the only one that could possibly understand any of this.

She thought about it, swirling the remnants of her drink, watching the orange pulp stick to the sides of the cup. "I think so. Yeah. I think I am. I'm glad – I'm glad I told you."

Could she have avoided the months of isolation? She wondered. If she had told them in the beginning, would she have felt so lonely and awful for nine months? If she had handed the pills and the note over to the paramedics would everything be different?

"Why didn't you tell us that before?" asked Victoria. "God, I spent so much time researching, wondering... and I was going to call you to ask about the autopsy, but Sally got pissed at me."

Sally turned to her, puffy-eyed and aghast. "Of course I was mad at you! That would have been – tactless! And horrible! Her mom died and you wanted to treat it like a science experiment." Erik chuckled darkly.

"I wanted answers for Grace! Dammit Sally, I wanted to help give her closure! And find the reason, of course."

"You're unbelievable." Sally glared at her. "You think you're so – untouchable. Just because you're pre-med doesn't mean you're a doctor *now*. I'm so sick of you acting like – like you're better than all of us!"

"Are you fucking kidding me?" Victoria sat up, accidentally kicking Josh in the head.

"Hey!" She ignored him.

"You act like you're better than everyone. God, do you think that just because you're –you go to Stanford and your life is like a fairy tale you're a princess? Because you're not."

"'Scuse me?" Sally looked livid. Her face, already reddening, burned red with anger. The accent that had melted away over the years rose fiercely to the surface. "I don't think that."

"Oh, really?" asked Victoria angrily. "Because you sure as hell act like it. Face it, Sally. You live a charmed, rich girl life, and you act innocent and think that you're better than everyone. And you constantly remind us of it." Grace was shocked to see tears welling up in Victoria's eyes. Victoria, who never cried, ever.

"I don't think that now, and I never have." Sally crossed her arms, knocking over her drink. "And I sure as hell don't live a charmed life." Sam realized he was holding his breath. He watched them silently, waiting, hoping that Victoria would drag it out of her.

"You – have – everything," Victoria snarled, tears streaming down her face. "You have everything and you're Little Miss Perfect, and you treat people like shit. Sam loves you. We all know it. He still loves you after you've obviously ignored him and treated *him* like shit. Why don't you just appreciate what you have?"

"I'm not perfect," Sally said icily. "Please stop saying that." He hated seeing her like this but he wanted to know.

Victoria scoffed. "Oh, boo-hoo. Yes you fucking are. Your perfect parents and your perfect house and your perfect life. Your perfect boyfriend that you forgot about the minute you escaped from our crappy little town."

"I'm not perfect."

"You say that but you know it's true. Get rid of your false modesty, Sally. It's not adorable anymore."

"I'm not perfect," Sally whispered, closing her eyes, arms wrapped around her knees like she was trying to keep herself from falling apart. "I'm not perfect." He heard the words catch in her throat, the swelling before the flood.

"I had an abortion," she whispered.

His heart dropped in his chest. Grace gasped and covered her mouth. Alex spilled his drink and beer puddled on the carpet and no one did anything. Sam realized that Josh was staring at him accusingly.

"You – you what?" asked Victoria, stunned.

"You heard me." Sally said to her knees.

He felt five pairs of silent eyes on him.

"You were pregnant?" he breathed.

She nodded, pulling her legs further into herself.

"Was it… mine?" his voice croaked on the last word.

She sat up angrily. "Of course it was yours, Sam. God, how many guys do you think I've slept with?" She looked horrified. "What do you think I am?"

She finally broke down and her tiny frame racked with great, heaving sobs. Grace scooted over to her and Sally leaned against her friend and cried and Sam felt like he should do something but couldn't move.

Victoria's head snapped up and her eyes narrowed. "What do you mean by that?"

Sally kept sobbing, Grace's arm wrapped around her.

"Sally." She glared at the sobbing mess on the floor. "What do you mean, 'what do you think I am'?"

"Jesus, Vic," muttered Josh. "Let it go."

"Are you implying that if you sleep with more than one guy you're some kind of whore?" she asked viciously, spitting out the last word. "Is that what you think? That you can go ahead and sleep with one guy, but if there's more than one you're going straight to hell?"

Sally sobbed and Sam wanted Victoria to shut up but still sat frozen.

"Leave her alone," insisted Grace.

Victoria leaned forward, claws out. She was mouthing numbers to herself. "You stopped talking to everyone in October. That's when it happened, right? So you two" – she nodded at Sam – "decided to take each other's virginity during the sacrosanct Last Summer, right before Princess Sally left for Stanford. Isn't that sweet? Isn't that–" she stopped suddenly and fell on the carpet, rolling over laughing.

"What's wrong with you?" asked Josh angrily. "Can't you leave her alone?"

"Sally – perfect Sally –" she writhed on the floor, clutching her stomach, cackling. Erik laughed automatically but a glare from Josh shut him up.

"Shut up!" Grace yelled, still cradling sobbing Sally.

Finally she quit laughing and rolled herself back onto her stomach, facing them. Mascara streaked across her face. "You guys, this is what gets me. This really gets me." She held her hand up, swaying slightly. "Sally lost her virginity before I did." This set off another round of reeling on the floor and her laughter bounced around emptily.

Grace frowned. "But you always – you always have a string of guys. All through high school. You've been dating college guys since freshman year. You always bragged about blow jobs and stuff."

"Yeah, *and stuff*. Not sex. I was saving that for someone that deserved me," she said tersely. The hysteria slid off her almost instantly and she looked exhausted.

"Well, congratulations. Was he worth it?" asked Josh.

She closed her eyes.

"Well?" he prompted.

"I don't remember," she said, and more tears spilled out of her, dragging the mascara even further.

Confused silence. Then realization.

"What do you mean?" asked Grace tentatively.

Victoria glared at her. "What do you think I mean? I was drugged."

Sally pulled herself from her paroxysms of pain and dragged her puffy face from Grace's shoulder. "Oh my God," she said thickly. "Do you mean–?"

Victoria seemed to deflate in front of them. She nodded.

Josh stood up and sat down next to her. He put his arms around her and she clung to him uneasily, like someone who wasn't used to needing someone. She sank into his chest and he put his chin on top of her head.

"I don't remember it," she said softly. "I guess that's a good thing."

Josh looked like he was about to cry. "Did you go to the police and everything?" He stroked her hair and she leaned into him.

"No." She closed her eyes. "I didn't know their names."

He stopped stroking, horrified. "'Their'?"

She nodded again. "Three."

Sally burst into tears again and she and Grace scooted towards Victoria, both sobbing. The girls clutched each other and wailed. The boys looked like they had no idea what to do.

"They should be in jail," said Josh. Tears dripped down his face. "They shouldn't be allowed to walk around."

Victoria choked out a watery laugh. "Oh, I did better than that."

They turned towards her.

"I learned their names. I found out who they were. And I did the only thing I could to ruin their fucking lives the way they ruined mine."

"What do you mean?" Alex asked, confused.

She smiled grimly, tears still streaming down her face. "Oh, nothing. I just found a steroids guy on Craigslist, waited until they were hammered at their quarterly, and injected my – the guys who did it, then left an anonymous tip with the NCAA that our track team was using steroids. They sent out an inspector the next day. They tested positive and got kicked off."

"You bought *steroids*?" asked Alex, incredulous.

"From *Craigslist*?" Grace couldn't believe it.

"Holy shit!" Erik laughed.

Josh looked like he couldn't decide if he was more impressed or angry. "That's fucking brilliant," he finally said, grinning.

"You could have gotten arrested!" Grace squeaked.

Sam started a slow clap. "Well done, Vic. Well done." He broke into applause and the others joined in, laughing.

"Only you could pull that off!" yelled Josh. "Take a bow!" She stood up shakily and swept into a shaky low bow, hair whipping the couch.

"Thank you, thank you. I'm glad you can appreciate the effort I put into my greatest act of vengeance."

Their laughter died away as they remembered the reason for her story.

"Are you okay now?" asked Sally quietly. "Did you get counseling or anything?"

"Of course not." Victoria scoffed. "You're the first ones I told."

"I'm really sorry." Grace said softly. She held her hand out and was surprised to feel Victoria hold it firmly.

"It's not your fault. I shouldn't have been so trusting, I guess. I just wish... I could stop thinking about it all the time, but it's always there, hanging over my head." She felt tears welling in her own eyes.

"You will get past this," Josh said firmly. "No one has to be defined by the worst thing that ever happened to them."

She smiled through her tears and stared down at her thighs, remembering the bruises that had covered them. "No, I don't."

"You will always be defined by your drive. You're Victoria. You always come out on top."

"You'll be fine," Sam said, smiling at her.

Sally sat up suddenly. "Remember senior year when we had to write a sentence for the yearbook about our goals?" They all nodded. "Do you remember what Victoria wrote?"

Alex shook his head. Grace bit her lip, thinking.

"Everyone else wrote things like 'marry Ryan Gosling' and 'move to Italy,' but Victoria wrote 'conquer the world.'" Sally smiled at her. "And if anyone is going to conquer the world, it'll be you."

They all murmured assent, smiling kindly up at her, and Victoria felt the tears break the barricade and drip down her face.

"I feel... better." It was all she had to say. Grace held her hand and Josh held her other hand and her friends were around her and it was all she needed. Everything would be okay.

Sunday morning

Sally

Ow.

Her head hurt. The rest of her hurt. A bruise bloomed on her knee.

She cracked an eye open and immediately shut it. So bright.

Slowly, she opened both eyes, blinking against the brightness. Her eyes felt puffy and swollen. No wonder her back hurt – she was huddled on the hard carpet, her friends sprawled out around her.

Last night came flooding back and everything hurt worse. She told them. She told them everything.

She wanted to feel something right now, but she just.... couldn't. It was too early to think. She glanced at her watch. 6:30. Yep. Definitely too early to think, much less run.

For the first time in eleven months, she did not get up for her morning run, and she was okay with it.

Josh

He jolted himself awake, into the bright confusion of the living room. His friends were all still asleep and he had no reason to be up early – oh. That's why.

He got up as quietly as possible, stepping carefully over Grace's arm and Sam's head. His bare feet padded past the kitchen and he closed the bathroom door. Peeing the morning after drinking was the only good part about the morning after drinking.

As he peed he tried not to think about how much his head hurt. He forgot to drink water before going to bed – rookie mistake. Damn. He had to drive today.

Fragments of last night danced in his head and he felt a new throb as each confession unveiled itself again. Hazily he recalled cornering Sally in the kitchen… oh God. He kissed a childhood friend. He did more than just break the bro code – he violated a sacrosanct pillar of friendship. Multiple pillars, actually. Sally and Sam and Grace. He had a lot of rebuilding to do.

He washed his hands and returned to the kitchen, mid-morning rays of light darting across the empty grocery bags as if to illuminate the carnage.

It was already 10:30 and they were supposed to leave at 11… no bacon today.

Victoria

Fuck, her head hurt.

She rolled over and almost fell off the couch, catching herself just in time. She swore and lifted herself up, staggering slightly. Ugh. Mornings. Always the same sense of disorientation and confusion and trying to familiarize herself with her surroundings and find her pants.

Last night came flooding back to her and she wanted to throw up. Ugh. Emotions.

She followed the smell of coffee to the kitchen, where Josh was getting out the cereal and bowls. His hair stuck up at odd angles and she felt a rush of affection. He grinned at her – the old grin, same as before – and handed her a mug. He still wanted to be her friend, despite … despite everything.

"Good morning, Vic. Do you feel like I do?"

"Terrible but fabulous? Yes." She collapsed on her stool from yesterday, squinting against the bright window.

He laughed and shook his head. "You amaze me." His smile lapsed into a comfortable silence and she was thankful for it. He sipped his coffee and she leaned her head on the blessedly cool countertop.

"Last night…" he said tentatively. The two words in the English language with the most subtext and the heaviest insinuations.

She groaned. "So much to take in."

"I know. I knew we had a lot of catching up to do this weekend, but I didn't expect *that*."

"Seriously."

"Vic, I'm glad you came this weekend. I missed you."

"I missed you too."

"I wish we didn't have to head back to school so soon. I wish we had a little more time to – to hang out, and do normal things."

"Like drink copious amounts of alcohol and have huge emotional meltdowns and make dramatic confessions?"

He laughed and the wrinkle in his forehead loosened a little. "*Normal* things that *normal* people do. Like go to the beach and eat burritos."

She propped herself up on her elbows and looked down to the living room at their little circle of friends, their little heptagon of people that had woven themselves effortlessly into each other's lives. She'd always prided herself on her independence, but she needed the people who were here. All the people that helped shape who she was – all here. Within this cabin lay a tangled mess of who they were and who they used to be: the most masochistic of students, the happiest of lovers, the most loyal of friends, the simplest of dreamers.

"Oh, Josh. We'll never be normal."

He coughed a laugh. "You got that right."

"I wish I could go back to fall."

He looked at her seriously. She liked having friends that took her seriously.

"To change what happened?"

"I wasn't even thinking that… I just wish I could tell myself that it's okay to tell your friends the unflattering things…that they'll still love you."

He set down his mug and wrapped her in a quick bear hug. "Of course we do, Vic. Never doubt that."

"I won't have to." She pulled away and took a long draught of coffee. "I *will* have to remember to hydrate a little better next time."

"Yeah, we're all going to feel like crap today." He noticed her squinting and he closed the blinds, blocking some of the awful sunlight from drilling into her skull.

"Thanks, now I don't feel like I'm being stabbed in the eyes."

He laughed and glanced at the clock. "We need to get going soon. Wanna go wake up the kids?"

"Yes, dear." So surreal. She grinned and realized that this felt exactly like a morning-after, except now she was waking up with people she actually cared about.

Alex

Victoria's voice was so loud and his head hurt and he couldn't remember something important.

Last night. Oh. Oh oh oh. Everything. The big thing. Erik. Erik mad at his dad. Erik holding his hand in the dark. Did it mean - ? Maybe.

He followed his friends into the kitchen, not daring to make eye contact with Erik.

He hoped it did.

Grace

Josh poured her cereal and she smiled. They felt normal again. Maybe even better than normal. She'd been honest with him. He knew everything. He was still her... her Josh.

Sally brushed against her and she wondered what would happen to her and Sam. She couldn't believe it – any of it. It was all just... terrible. But, she realized as she ate her Cheerios and watched her friends – her beautiful, troubled, complex friends – maybe it was actually a good thing. After the school year started she worried that they would never be the same, that they'd all grown too much to maintain the comfortable niches of their friendship. She worried that they'd outgrown each other. After Christmas she decided it was inevitable.

But now... they were still friends. After a year that had changed all of them, they were still friends. Everything was different, except for the one thing that mattered.

They'd gone to hell and back, and there would be plenty more hell-and-backs... but she would not experience them alone. Her friends would make sure of that.

Sam

He helped Josh wash the last of the breakfast dishes and clean up the kitchen. The girls were upstairs packing the sleeping bags that they'd only slept in once.

He glanced at the clock. They were supposed to leave in five minutes. Only five minutes remained of this weird weekend, then there was just the drive home, and after that? Who knew how much time they had left?

The girls descended, arms full. Even Victoria helped carry stuff.

He walked around the cabin, slowly picking up his few scattered belongings, trying to prolong their stay. He opened the balcony door as if to look for something outside and just stood there, watching the lake. He fingered his necklace, still missing the ocean, but more appreciative of the lake than he'd been yesterday. He hadn't gotten to see it from the balcony during daylight, and the water looked bluer from this distance. God, it was pretty. Not as pretty as the ocean, of course, but still pretty.

He turned to look back at Sally, who was organizing their stuff into carry-able piles. She smiled at something that Grace said.

Not as pretty as Sally, of course.

Sally

She checked every socket for forgotten phone chargers, scoured upstairs for loose articles of clothing, swept the kitchen, carefully wrapped their wet towels and bathing suits in plastic bags so that they wouldn't smell in the car, and wrote a thank-you note for Erik's family. She found a magnet (Dodgers logo, of course) and hung it on the fridge.

They carried their bags to the cars and managed everything in two trips. Erik locked the door and they all made their way down the stairs for the last time this weekend. She turned to look at the cabin and hoped that she would see it again.

"C'mon, guys!" Josh climbed into the driver's seat of his truck and they all reluctantly followed suit. She didn't want to think about when they would be together again, so she didn't. She thought about how happy she was to be with them now, right now, just in this moment. All of them. Especially Sam.

Before Erik could climb in she slid into the passenger's seat. Sam smiled at her as he steered them down the driveway, pulling out onto the pine-lined diagonal. She held his hand and they began their long drive home.

Acknowledgements

I read somewhere that people are like geodes – if you want to see what they're made of, you have to break them. I never really knew what that meant until I was broken.

A few days after my high school friends and I got back from our own second consecutive camping trip, I wondered if other people our age had done the same thing. Were there other groups of friends who were coming to the same painful realization – that we weren't the same people we thought we were when we were best friends?

I struggled with the question for a few days before trying to answer it the only way I knew how: fiction. What started out as a short story grew longer and longer. I wanted to know more about these kids. I wondered if they had any answers for me. They were all fictional but they felt real. Now I think of them as Horcruxes of the collective unconscious of twenty-first century college students, kids whose expectations for their futures are now drastically different from what we originally envisioned.

When I started writing this at 18, I assumed it would be a cheery little tale about high school friends and home towns. I didn't anticipate its inevitable evolution. It grew as I grew, and over the course of four years I realized that I was writing about the journey that my UCLA peers and I were on together. We had to grow up more than we expected. We experienced pain and fun in equal measures. It was a hell of a roller coaster, and by the end we were kind of adults.

My four years didn't exactly go as planned. I expected that my home life would stay exactly the same and would be there waiting for me, blessedly unchanged, when I returned from my adventures. But things changed, and people I loved died, and things that were supposed to stay whole forever fell apart in front of me. I felt like I was caught in the washing machine of a wave much larger than anything I had ever even attempted to ride. Writing and friends kept me from drowning.

I honestly would not have pursued publishing this if it weren't for my friends' encouragement and insistence that people would connect with it. I'll never be totally satisfied with anything I write, but if at least one person who reads this identifies with a character or recognizes something they've been struggling with, all the effort will have been worth it.

Thank you to my camping comrades: Adam Stromlund, Adam Gutierrez-Luft, Alex Geffrey, Christina Guo, Ethan Singer, Kelsey Fitzgibbons, Krislyn Chan, Johnson Lay, Matt Morimoto, Paulina Chu, and Winnie Wang. You guys have been there since the beginning. Thank you for being a part of such a formative experience. I love all of you and can't wait to see what life has in store for you – you deserve great things.

Cheers to the God-sent roommates who tolerated the 2 a.m. Earl-Grey-and-writing sessions: Ben Nguyen, Jen Donn, Lauren Wong, Maureen DeChico, Nicole Malek, Ran Jing, and Tricia Mar. You've all seen me cry (and not wear pants) more than anyone. I am so thankful for you and no amount of baked goods will ever fully convey my gratitude.

Huge hugs and thank-yous to the friends and family who gave me countless pep talks after witnessing the blood, sweat, and tears of the past few years: Allie Schmelter, Amy Clarke, Andrew Nish, Anthony Cube, Aparna Bhat, Brittany Oliva, Brooke Mansfield, Charlotte Rose, Chelsie Dietz, Chris Rini, Christina Guo, Diana Johnson Nish, Edson Marquez, Erin Neipris, Estellaleigh Franenberg, Esther Lee, Jewel Pererya, Johanna Mort, John Guzman, Joyce Chang, Kailey Giordano, Karen Cunningham, Kristen Russo, Melanie Leiva, Michel Chu, Natalee Ellars, Rebecca Bucher, Richard Sambasivam, Riley Hunt, Rochelle Parker, Samuel Kim, Stacey Capoot, Tara Graff, Teresa Valenzuela, Tricia Mar, Tyler Overvold, Valentina Rabinovich, and Yasar Mohebi. You're the best people a girl could ask for to have in her life and I'm truly grateful for you.

I can't even begin to thank the brave souls who read the first few terrible drafts and gave the most constructive feedback I could ever hope for. Alex Geffrey, Amy Sherrard, Arielle Eckstut, Charlotte Rose, Christina Guo, Emma Zent, Helen Chun, Katie Smith, Molly Montgomery, Nicole Malek, and Winnie Wang, you guys demonstrated an incredible amount of faith and it means the world to me. Nick Greitzer, I am continually awed by your kindness and patience. You deserve a gold star for life.

Thank you to everyone who cheered me on and supported this little endeavor every step of the way: Oxfam, UCLA Alumni Affairs, the UCLA English department, Creators Publishing (especially Catherine DiGiacomo!), and most of all my family. Mom, Grandma, and Kels, you guys are my anchor and I love you more than anything.

Go Bruins!